BREAKING STORM

Nick Cook completed his degree in sculpture and then moved into the computer games industry. For more than 21 years, Nick worked as a graphic artist and creative director, helping to produce over forty titles, including many chart-topping hits. Nick has a passion for science and astronomy, often blogging about the latest mind-blowing discoveries made in quantum physics. He once ever soloed a light aircraft, an experience he's tapping into now for the Cloud Riders trilogy.

To Cody,

Happy storm

chasing!

Nick Cook

BREAKING STORM

Nick Cook

THREE HARES PUBLISHING

Published by Three Hares Publishing 2015

First published in Great Britain in 2015
www.threeharespublishing.com

Three Hares Publishing Ltd Reg. No 8531198
Registered office: Suite 201, Berkshire House, 39-51 High Street,
Ascot, Berkshire, SL5 7HY

ISBN-13: 9781910153123

Printed and bound in Great Britain by Clays Ltd, Elcograf S.p.A.

For Karen — always.

'Let us be silent, that we might hear
the whispers of the gods.'
Ralph Waldo Emerson

CHAPTER One
SANDSTORM

Beneath us the sandstorm raged like a boiling sea of dirt. I hung onto the ship's wheel. The airship bucked and rolled through the hazy sky as we headed towards the orange disc of the sun, the only feature in the blurred landscape to navigate by.

Angelique swivelled her seat in the cockpit towards mine. 'How are you feeling, Dom?'

I stretched my cramped fingers on the ship's wheel. 'That I could sleep for a year.' Every part of my brain ached, every fibre of muscle felt shot through with knots. Eighteen hours straight of flying the airship *Athena*. Countless wormhole jumps between dimensions: no time for sleep, no time to eat, no time for anything but the chase.

'Once we rescue Jules, you can sleep all you like.'

To rescue Jules... Could we really manage that? But that's what had kept me powering on. Because, I, Dom Taylor of Earth, and Angelique Castille, Cloud Rider and freedom fighter from a parallel dimension, had no other choice. We'd pursued Duke Ambra from one reality to another in a desperate attempt to save my best friend who he'd taken hostage.

Jules, the centre of my universe – even if she didn't realise it yet. This was all so messed up. Right now it killed me that she believed it was Angelique and the life of being a Cloud Rider I really wanted. How wrong could one woman be? Of course I'd rehearsed my making-it-up speech a million times – *It's you I want, Jules, nothing else.*

Whatever it took, whatever lines I had to cross, I'd bring her home safe. Then we'd talk – really talk – everything through. Somehow I'd make her see the truth. I had to.

A brief gap swirled in the sandstorm. Far below, sculpted stone peaks pointed upwards like yellowed teeth. A fist of wind smacked into the gondola and a shudder vibrated up my arms from the ship's wheel.

'Is there any sign of them, Dom?' Angelique said, her French-like accent growing stronger, a sure sign she was tense.

Time was running out if we hoped to catch up with them before they reached Hells Cauldron. Right now, Ambra was just one man. If he reached the Hades stronghold, he'd be one man and an army.

I turned the captain's chair towards hers. 'No visual yet.'

Angelique nodded. 'With all this storm-static, I haven't got a chance of spotting them, even with *Athena*'s sensors.'

'Maybe we'll get lucky—' I broke off as a tingle scratched underneath my scalp – ship-song – the artificial intelligent system onboard the airship communicating with us. *Storm Wind*'s voice swept into my thoughts and my senses became pin-sharp.

The brass globe in the middle of the floor, the Eye, which now contained *Athena*'s and *Storm Wind*'s combined Psuche gems, hissed with steam venting from it. We'd been forced to piggyback *Storm Wind*'s AI crystal onto *Athena*'s, when she'd been damaged in the last battle with Ambra. But *Athena* was fading away. Her voice had become a background murmur to *Storm Wind*'s whale-like song. She couldn't last much longer.

Angelique sat up, hooking her long blonde hair back over her ears. 'They've sensed something out there.'

Could this be it? The moment I'd prayed for more than anything. My mouth became bone-dry. 'Is it them?'

'Hang on,' Angelique said. She closed her green eyes. With a ripple of air she disappeared as she shifted her body into another dimension. It was crazy how quickly I'd gotten used to both of us being able to peer into parallel worlds like this.

The wind howled over the regular beating of the three props, the heartbeat of the airship in flight. Over the hours since we'd left my Earth far behind, this soundtrack had become as familiar as my own breathing.

A gasp and Angelique appeared, eyes widening. 'Dom, they're still in this dimension, just a mile ahead.'

'My god, this is it.' Adrenaline burned my fatigue away. I jammed the throttle against the stops and *Athena* sped forward.

'We should be able to see them any moment,' Angelique said.

I leant forward, scanning the horizon through the windshield.

A patch of something solid swam into view through the haze. My pulse amped. I swung *Athena* towards the distant round shape and grabbed the spyglass from its clip. I fiddled with the focus and the image through it sharpened into a Hades scout balloon with two figures slung beneath. Duke Ambra stared back at us, but my heart surged at the sight of Jules, my girlfriend, strapped to his chest. Her dark hair flowed in the wind as she started struggling in her harness.

'I see them,' I said.

Storm Wind's song became threaded with anger.

Angelique pointed at the Eye. 'No!' A red glass sphere had lit up in the navigation computer.

'An enemy ship?' I asked.

Her expression tightened.

That told me everything I needed to know.

Sure enough a flicker of movement ahead snagged my gaze. A large ship emerged from the murk right behind the scout ship, like a shark appearing from deep water.

Angelique clenched her hands together. '*Proteus* — the Hades equivalent of one of your airship carriers. And it looks like it's going to intercept Ambra's scout craft.'

'Then we've got to get to them first!' I pushed the throttle harder against the stops, willing *Athena* faster.

In the distance, the larger airship's shark nose began to split open, revealing a landing deck and a fleet of smaller ships moored inside.

I adjusted the telescope's focus onto Jules. Her dark eyes seemed to look straight into mine, a scream twisting her features, so close I could've touched her face. The smaller balloon sped into the landing bay. Its burner glow blinked out of view as the doors closed. The shark had swallowed the smaller fish, whole.

I thumped my fist on the flight console. 'No!'

'Hard to starboard!' Angelique shouted.

Adrenaline surged through me. Instinct kicking in, I swung the wheel over. A shell trailing smoke shot past our left wing tip. Flashes of light. Three more projectiles sped towards us from the enemy airship.

Angelique grabbed my shoulder. 'Dive!'

I pushed the wheel forward. The deck tilted beneath our feet as the nose of *Athena* dropped towards the top of the raging sandstorm. The three shells arced overhead, missing us by only tens of feet.

'We're going to have to drop into the cover of the mountains,' Angelique said.

I stared down at the jagged landscape and, despite the heat of the desert world outside, goose bumps spread over my skin. 'Can't we use the Vortex drive? We'll be ripped to shreds down there.'

'And they'll shoot us down before we have a chance to jump away.' She clasped her lightning pendant. 'You're just going to have to make the most of your piloting skills and make sure we don't crash, Dom.'

I wasn't sure her confidence in my flying skills was well placed. After all, I'd only been piloting *Athena* for twenty-four hours, hardly enough time to really get a feel for her. 'Shouldn't you take over?'

'If you're going to be a Cloud Rider, you need to cut your teeth piloting in battle.'

I frowned at her. Sometimes I felt like a lab rat in her experiments, being pushed into extreme situations just so she could see how I handled myself.

'Are you sure, because if I mess up—'

Her eyes hardened. 'Then don't mess up.'

Proteus dipped towards us, its gun turrets along its flanks rotating in our direction.

Thoughts swirled through my head. I pictured Jules trapped inside the enemy ship. This close and yet I might never see her again. Without even thinking, my hands tightened on the airship's wheel. I got ready to pull up. Bring it on.

Angelique peered into my face, her expression softening. 'No, Dom, not like this. *Proteus* completely outguns us. It would be throwing our lives away. That won't help Jules will it?'

I stared back at her. 'But we have to save her.'

'And I swear to you we will.' Angelique glanced out through the cockpit window and her expression tensed. 'Hard to port.'

I spun the wheel. Five shells shrieked past us into the sandstorm, their glows of light pulsing within.

'Dom, we need to escape to fight another day.'

This felt like I was being ripped in two. But I knew Angelique was right. Once again her soldier's instinct knew the best way to play this game with the enemy.

I swallowed past a lump in my throat. 'I'm sorry, Jules.' I pushed the wheel forward and *Athena*'s dive steepened. I tried to blot the image of Jules's screaming face from my mind. A nightmare that would haunt me until we'd rescued her.

We plunged into the top of the swirling storm. Like a swimmer dropping beneath the surface, I took an instinctive breath. At once the world became muted to dull red light. The sandstorm scratched past the windows like a thousand claws, the wind beast howling its challenge at us. But *Athena* was a Cloud Rider ship designed to take on tornados and survive. She could more than handle a sandstorm, however badassed.

The seconds ticked past and the sky became shadowed night as we dropped deeper.

Angelique chewed her lip. 'Keep going.'

The storm buffeted us way worse than any turbulence I'd ever experienced. This wasn't my idea of fun, flying blind, with only the ship's instruments to guide me. I watched the altimeter drop past ten thousand feet... six...

At two thousand, the sand clouds started to thin and the mountainous landscape appeared, too close for comfort.

'Level off now,' Angelique shouted.

I pulled back hard. The cables securing the gondola to our gas envelope whined as we levelled out.

Angelique pointed up through the cockpit window. 'Look there.'

A dark oval silhouette was just visible in the thick sandstorm clouds above. *Proteus*. The craft slid through the storm, the monstrous shark hunting through a dark sea.

'Looks like they've lost sight of...' The words died in my throat as the vessel began to turn.

A screech filled my mind like a hawk crying out as it tracked its prey. I'd heard this sound from a Hades ship before and knew what it meant – *Proteus*'s AI had engaged hunting mode.

Angelique yanked off her lightning necklace that she always wore.

I clutched my own pendant that had been Grandpa Alex's and now held Dad's Saint Christopher medal inside. The saint for safe travel and I'd take all the help we could get.

'What are you doing?' I asked as Angelique inserted her pendant into a slot in the control panel.

'Silent running.' She turned her pendant like a key.

I heard a click. At once the Eye slid closed with a hiss and the cabin plunged into darkness. The tickle of *Storm Wind*'s and *Athena*'s voices – always at the back of my mind – disappeared. Total silence and it felt like I'd lost part of myself.

Angelique turned to me. 'Stop the engines.'

'But we could be slammed into a mountain any moment.'

'Just do it, Dom. We'll think about the odds later.'

My blood chilled as I hit the engine kill switch and the propellers whirled to a stop. Dead in the water and at the mercy of the wind. Great.

Athena lurched to the side and the mountains began skimming past.

Into the space in my mind that the ships' voice's had filled, *Proteus*'s cry grew deeper. It started pounding like a drumbeat through my skull. Through a gap in the sand clouds the Hades ship appeared. Its portals glowed along red-canopied flanks and searchlights blazed out from the craft to probe the swirling sea of sand beneath.

'The ship's using its voice like an echo sounder,' Angelique said. 'If *Athena* and *Storm Wind* make even the slightest sound *Proteus* will hear them – that's why I had to shut the Eye down.' She tapped the side of her head. 'Make sure you don't respond telepathically either.'

Mind control wasn't exactly my best skill yet. I needed far more practice. And to know that one stray thought could give us away... 'I'll do my best.'

With a wail the sandstorm thickened and *Proteus* became a blur.

'Good – this will make it harder for them to see us,' Angelique said. 'They won't want to risk coming down here.'

'Aren't they the sensible ones,' I replied. My frown deepened as a finger of rock sped just beneath the gondola. Drive into one of those hard enough and, toughened Cloud Rider vessel or not, the gondola would be split open like a tin can. 'Can't we open up the Vortex now?'

'They'd simply rain bombs down on us through our twister funnel as it forms.'

'So what do we do?'

'Let the wind carry us until we're at a safe distance. Then we jump.'

Proteus reached a position directly overhead. Its telepathic drumbeat drowned out my own thoughts. But I also noticed a faint tingle of softer noise itching deep within my skull. *Athena* and *Storm Wind* waking up? I spun my chair round, but the Eye remained closed. I tried to concentrate on the faint moan, pull it out of the background, but it had already gone.

Angelique narrowed her gaze at me. 'Did you hear something?'

The sound of sand scraping on the windows filled my ears. 'Must've been the wind.'

A column of light burned through the squall to the right of us and played across a brown peak of rock. The top of a sandstone mountain exploded with a deep rumble.

I shoved my finger towards the starter button.

Angelique grabbed my wrist. 'Don't!'

The searchlight zigzagged away across the landscape to another mountaintop. A flash of light from *Proteus*, followed by a distant boom a moment later. With a roar the peak next to us exploded into chunks of rock and the shattered mountaintop slid into the valley below.

She released my wrist. 'They can't see us. The gunners are firing blind.'

A second explosion hit a nearer mountain, hurtling shards of rock clattering against our windows like hailstones.

'It wouldn't take many bits of shrapnel like that to rip the gas envelope apart.' I scowled towards the sky. 'And they're going to keep going until they've hit us.'

Angelique frowned. 'You may have a point there.' She drummed her fingers on her leg. 'Okay, there's something else we can try.' She opened a small hatch set into the floor between us and took hold of a round handle inside.

'What are you doing?'

'I'm going to make them think they've got lucky.'

'How exactly?'

'Like this.' She pulled the handle and something clunked beneath the cabin. The ship lurched upwards.

Through the cockpit window I saw a brass cylinder dropping away. A small chute opened from it and began to slow its descent. 'What's that?'

'Our reserve gas cylinder.'

'Don't we need it?'

'Of course we do, but we also need to live through this.'

A shell streaked down through the sandstorm. At that same moment Angelique shoved the round handle downwards. The gas cylinder exploded with a pulse of blue light. *Athena* shuddered as the blast swept over us.

I stared at the explosion. 'A decoy?'

Angelique gave me a tight smile. 'Let's hope they fall for it.'

The searchlight zigzagged to the gas flames vanishing into the storm.

'Come on...' Angelique said under her breath.

The light blinked off and *Proteus* started banking away above us. Its AI's drumbeat slowed in my thoughts.

Angelique slumped into her chair. 'Oh, thank the gods.'

'Let's get the engine started.'

She shook her head. 'We need to give them a few minutes more to make sure they're out of sensor range. Be ready to power up the engines on my mark.' She placed her hand on the lightning pendant still in the switch.

A dark cloud of sand washed over us, reducing the world to a featureless abstract painting of smudges. Brown shapes loomed and sped away. The faint pulse of the enemy AI echoed through my skull.

'Come on,' I whispered under my breath.

The minutes stretched on. The vibration faded beat by beat to stillness.

'That's it, they're out of range,' Angelique said. She twisted the pendant and the Eye hissed open.

Storm Wind's voice, full of light and warmth, backed by *Athena*'s weaker one, filled my mind. It felt like a shaft of sunlight in a winter storm.

I pushed the button. 'Firing up the engines.' All three propellers roared into life. The scudding shapes of rock outcrops began to slow.

I turned to Angelique and smiled. 'I thought we were goners—' *Storm Wind*'s panicked cry crashed into my thoughts. 'What?' The sand swirled away.

I spotted a sheer cliff face, dead ahead, rushing straight towards us. I shoved the throttle forward and pulled the stick hard back.

At that same moment, Angelique yanked down on the burner lever in the ceiling. Jets of flame blazed out into the airship's envelope from the burner above the cabin. *Athena* started to climb slowly.

I pulled harder on the wheel as the mountain hurtled towards us. 'We're not going to make it!'

'I'm going to have to give us an emergency burn with the last of our gas.' Angelique reached up to the ceiling and pulled a small blue handle set into it.

With a roar a fireball exploded upwards into the gas envelope. For a moment, the airship glowed like a huge lantern and blue reflected light blazed across the glistening rock face – a rock face filled with razor teeth.

With a shudder we began speeding upwards, so close to the cliff that I could see bushes in its crags whipping around in the wind. A slash of orange grew brighter above the grey rock.

'It's the summit,' Angelique said.

The top of the cliff swept towards us. Come on, come on… The lip of the cliff disappeared beneath the cabin.

'We're almost—' A bang killed my words. With a lurch and a squeal of metal, the impact threw us from our seats. Hatches flew open in the cabin, spilling their contents. The grinding noise from the floor headed towards the rear of the cabin – the rock claws raking *Athena*'s belly.

Angelique shot me a wild-eyed look that said, *I'm not sure we're going to make it.*

I clutched my pendant tighter as *Athena* shook. The noise stopped dead. We lurched skywards like an animal escaping from a snare. The vibration fell away as the floor began levelling out.

We clambered back to our feet and peered out of the window. Below us a rocky plateau dropped away fast.

Angelique grabbed the blue burner handle and shoved it closed. 'We've cleared the mountain.'

Heart thundering in my chest, I pulled the throttle back to idling position. At once our ascent began to slow.

'God, that was close,' I said.

Angelique didn't respond. Instead she stared at a dial in the cockpit.

I saw a needle hovering in the red zone of a gauge. 'Bad?'

'We're nearly out of propane for the burner.' She gazed at a second dial. 'We also need more helium for the flotation bladders too.'

'We need to refuel then?'

She nodded. 'We're going to have to go straight to Floating City.'

'But what about Jules?'

'Look, Dom, we know where Ambra's heading with her.' She bit her lip.

My stomach hollowed out. 'Won't he just execute her now he thinks we're dead? After all, as far as he's concerned, he doesn't need her any more as bait.'

'She's young and fit. Whatever else Ambra is, he's a practical man. Now her execution serves no purpose, he'll put her to work in the mines at Hells Cauldron. They're always short of slave labour for the Psuche gems because people don't last long down there.'

A slave? A thousand awful images flooded my mind. 'There's no alternative?'

'None, but the main thing is she'll be alive. What's happened may also give us an advantage.'

'I don't see how.'

'If Ambra believes we're dead, that can only help us.'

'I'm still not following.'

'He won't be expecting us to arrive at Hells Cauldron any more, will he? Besides, you do have a mission at Floating City to fulfil as well. Remember, that's where *Titan* is meant to be hidden.'

With everything else that had happened, I'd almost forgotten Grandpa Alex's mission – rescuing Jules had pushed all of it out of my head. It almost seemed impossible that it had only been two days ago I'd discovered the secret about Grandpa Alex's true identity – that he was a Cloud Rider who'd crash-landed on our Earth over a hundred years ago. Now, completing his life's work had landed on my shoulders – to find the ancient ship *Titan*. He'd believed that onboard Titan was a way to stop the war between Hades and Cloud Riders. The only problem was, it was the *how* he hadn't been clear on.

Angelique tilted her head to one side. 'What are you thinking?'

'That given the choice, even knowing that eve
hangs on us finding *Titan*, including the fate of Earth,
given the choice, right here, right now, I still want to save
Jules first.'

'But unfortunately you don't have that choice, Dom.'

I clenched my hands together.

She reached out and held my fists in her hands. 'We
have only one card left to play and that's to head for Floating
City.'

I knew she was right – again – but that didn't make
it any easier to hear. My shoulders dropped and I nodded.

Angelique gestured towards the Eye. 'Don't forget we
need to get *Athena* fixed by a master technician at Floating
City before...' Her voice trailed away.

Before Athena dies... I needed to remember that there
was more than one life at stake here. Even though *Athena*
might be a glorified computer, after everything we'd all
been through together, I'd come to understand in a sense
that she was alive, maybe more than a lot of people I knew.
It seemed everything was forcing us in the direction of
Floating City.

Outside, the final whispers of sand fell away, revealing a sun blazing in a clear sky above. *Storm Wind*'s song
wrapped around my thoughts, his tone worried. *Athena*'s
voice had grown even fainter, now a barely audible
murmur.

We didn't have a choice. Not really. 'Okay, you win.'

'Now you're thinking like a Cloud Rider.'

Because my head overruled my heart? I glanced to
where *Proteus* had disappeared into the distance.

We'll come back for you, Jules, I promise.

CHAPTER TWO

TRAINING

The twister spun around us, misty walls glowing against the darkness of the *nothingness* between realities – the Void as the Cloud Riders called it. The end of the swirling tunnel remained inky black as we plunged down the wormhole in *Athena*. It would be a good thirty minutes before we reached the end and entered the next reality – another step further away from Jules.

Angelique stood and brushed her hip past me on her way to the cooking galley. Her spice-infused perfume flooded my nose and made me feel light-headed. Trapped together in gondola it was hard to avoid physical contact, but sometimes I swore she did it on purpose. Thing was, she knew I'd fallen for Jules, so I wished she'd just let the whole flirting thing drop. At some point I was going to have to have it out with her and make it clear there would never be anything between us. But something told me that wouldn't stop her either. For Angelique, using her beauty to get what she wanted from men was too hardwired in, just another weapon in her box of tricks to bend them to her will – even when she didn't need to.

Angelique huddled over the stove that she'd pulled out from a recess in the gondola's wall. She'd emptied the contents of three baked bean tins into a brass pot wrapped with copper pipes. The whole contraption made a whistling sound and started shaking, like it was going to explode any moment. She might have been a ninja princess, but I had a hunch cooking wasn't her thing.

I gazed out at the darkness of the Void. At least there'd been no sign of the Shade's shadow crows this time.

'How often have the Shade attacked your ships?' I asked Angelique as she scowled at the pot.

'There's been around a hundred attacks over the years and all the ships were lost – well, apart from two, including your grandfather.'

'Only *two* ever escaped?'

'The other survivor was in a small patrol airship. Despite the rest of the crew being killed, as the ship's navigator he managed to bring the ship back home and was hailed a hero. Perhaps if we'd known how he'd alter the course of history, we would have thought twice about promoting him.'

'Why, what did he do?'

Lines creased Angelique's forehead. 'He organised a military coup.'

I stared at her. 'You mean it was Cronos?'

'Yes – he managed to ingratiate himself with the royal court, the politicians, and even our religious leaders. Nearly everyone fell for his charms.'

'But not you?'

'I never liked him. There was always something about him that made my skin crawl.'

'But how did he survive a Shade attack while the rest of the men on his ship died?'

17

'Cronos told everyone he'd prayed to the gods and, like a miracle, the shadow crows spared him.' Her mouth twisted. 'You can imagine how the church loved that. There were even calls he should be declared a living saint. Of course he simply used that popularity to fulfil his ruthless ambition.'

I shook my head. How could one man bring so much misery to so many people? And now of course Jules was indirectly yet another one to add to his long list of victims.

I chewed a nail as my mind focused back to her. 'I wonder what's happening to Jules right now?'

'Dwelling on it won't help her, or you, will it?'

Angelique was right of course, but my mind felt stuck in that loop, imagining the awful things that Ambra might be doing to her onboard *Proteus*. My gut filled with ice. I'd make him pay if he so much as hurt a single hair on her head.

'Why don't you try talking to *Storm Wind* again to try to distract yourself?' Angelique said.

More practice – great. But I hadn't been getting anywhere fast with my genetic Ship Whisperer ability that I'd inherited from Grandpa Alex.

I blew my cheeks out. 'You know I can't turn it on and off like a tap – at least unless we're in danger like just now when we nearly hit the cliff. Normally, all I hear is shipsong from the Psuche gems rather than any words.'

'Try anyway. You never know, and the trying can't hurt, can it?'

What had I got to lose? 'I guess.' I sat up and closed my eyes.

Storm Wind, Athena, *can you hear me?* I said in my thoughts.

Storm Wind's tone grew stronger, but *Athena*'s voice echoed in the background, like a faint bird singing far away across a forest. Her clear female voice that had spoken to me when the shadow crows had nearly taken me seemed an impossible memory now.

Talk to me like you did before.

Their voices rose and fell together, notes weaving into each other, but no individual words formed. The old frustration churned up inside me.

I opened my eyes and sighed. 'Oh, I give up – seems they only want to communicate with me when they feel like it. I don't know what else to try.'

'We'll figure it out eventually, Dom.'

'I just wish Alex had left me an instruction manual on how to be a Ship Whisperer, that's all.'

'That wasn't his style,' Angelique said. 'He was always secretive with all his experiments.'

'Okay, but the thing that still puzzles me is why mess with his DNA so he could communicate like this with ships in the first place? How did he think that would stop the war between your people?'

She flashed me a perplexed look. 'The more I think about it, the more I think that maybe you're the key to this, Dom. You're his last living direct descendant who shares his bloodline. As Alex said in his message, discover *Titan* and everything else will become clear, and if anyone can communicate with that ship, it will be you.'

The answers couldn't come fast enough for me. I felt like a pawn on a chessboard, as Alex, although long dead, played, pushing me towards the enemy lines.

The smell of burning filled my nostrils and a cloud of black smoke billowed from the rattling pot. Angelique scowled and flicked a switch. With a whoosh, the plume was sucked into a vent in the ceiling.

She opened the lid, took a peek inside, and grimaced. 'Now it's my turn to give up.'

I tried not to smile. 'I wasn't that hungry anyway.'

Angelique crossed her arms. 'So how about some more training then?'

I groaned. 'Not again. I've already got enough bruises to last a lifetime.'

'And it's the memory of those bruises that may keep you alive one day.' She pulled a rack down from the ceiling.

I stared at the collection of swords and throwing knives. 'You're joking, right?'

'Where we're headed in Floating City, you need to know how to handle yourself if an assassin with a knife creeps up behind you in a dark alley. A Hades spy could attack at any moment.'

I imagined the steel plunging into my back and my shoulder blades tensed. 'Okay, you've got my attention.'

'Good.' She took a black knife with a wicked-looking curved blade.

'Oh, come on, no way I'm going to attack you with that.'

'Who said you're going to be the one doing the attacking?'

I stared at her. 'Seriously?'

She twirled the knife between her fingers. 'Seriously. Stand up with your back to me and close your eyes.'

'Now I know you're joking.'

'Not at all. You need to be able to read a person's energy. Do that and you'll know where the attack is aimed.'

'You mean like having eyes in the back of my head?'

She nodded. 'A perfect description.'

I trusted Angelique when it came to fighting, especially after everything we'd been through together, but the idea of her attacking me with a knife wasn't exactly my definition of fun.

I stood with my back to her. 'You're really going to—' Something hissed past my ear and I spun to see the black blade curve past my left shoulder. 'Hey, I wasn't ready.'

'Just so. You've got to expect the unexpected. Do you think a Hades spy is going to present you with his calling card first?'

'Guess not.'

'Now close your eyes and let your body's instinct tell you what's happening.'

'Oh great, as though it isn't hard enough with my eyes open.'

'It will help you focus.'

'Okay, okay, just try not to turn me into a human pincushion.'

She smirked and raised the knife.

Brilliant. I sighed to myself and let my arms drop to my sides. Eyes shut, I listened. Silence. My body tensed. I knew she wouldn't actually stick me with the blade, but I also knew she'd make the lesson count. The silence lingered, just the gentle murmur of the ships' songs in my head. I tensed, getting ready to dodge. Left, right, which way to go?

Something slammed hard into me. 'Ow,' I said, rubbing my back. I turned to see Angelique holding the knife by the blade. She'd struck me with the pummel at the opposite end.

'Try again, but this time trust your body and don't think so hard,' Angelique said.

I scowled and shut my eyes once more. But I knew Angelique was only trying to make me a better fighter. All the little tricks she'd taught me so far about Sansodo, the martial art she studied, had worked. Already, in the hours we'd been on *Athena*, she'd trained me to counter a blow and get out of a lock. She'd kept telling me it was all about trusting my instinct and using an attacker's energy against them. That was the theory, but this was the practice, and practice with Angelique always seemed to hurt.

I took a deep breath, centring myself like she'd taught me, trying to forget there was a lethal trained warrior princess with a knife standing a few feet behind me.

The back of my neck itched and I slid to the side, turning as I did so. My right hand flew up without me even thinking about it and my fingers closed on a wrist. I opened my eyes into Angelique's green ones, only inches from mine, her knife hand gripped in my fist.

'That's more like it, Dom.' She smiled at me with curved lips, framing her perfect teeth.

God, she was beautiful and it would be so easy to... I shook myself. What the hell was I thinking?

I pulled away, hoping my face wouldn't betray what had flashed through my head. 'I can't believe that actually worked.'

'But it did, didn't it?'

'Okay, okay, you've made your point. I'll try to trust my instinct more in future.'

Angelique nodded. 'That's what I wanted to hear.'

A chiming sound came from the cockpit and a smudge of light began building at the end of the Vortex beneath us.

'We're about to arrive,' Angelique said. 'I'll take us in.' She cast another scowl at the pot. 'At least that's something I can do.'

'Hey, don't be so hard on yourself. Just because you're a ninja princess who can pilot sentient airships between realities, doesn't automatically make you a great cook.'

She snorted. 'There you may have a point.'

The white haze became a blue one and rolling clouds appeared beneath us.

My pulse surged. This would never get old for me.

'Welcome to another world, Dom,' Angelique said, her smile widening around those perfect teeth.

CHAPTER Three
ARRIVAL

Beneath us an endless, lush, emerald-green forest stretched away to the horizon. Throughout it, large white spherical structures had been scattered like overgrown mushrooms over a lawn. From each building tall chimneys rose into the sky, billowing white smoke that mingled together to form low-level clouds.

I gestured towards them. 'What are those?'

'Helium and propane gas distillation plants.'

There had to be at least a thousand structures that I could see. 'That's a lot of gas.'

'This Earth is particularly rich in helium and all vessels are dependent on the supplies from here,' Angelique replied.

'Cloud Rider and Hades ships?'

'That's right, although we have alternative sources when Hades get around to invading this planet.'

I pictured a fleet of Hades warships arriving in the skies over this planet. 'You think they will?'

'It's the first rule of military combat: secure your lines of supply. An attack is inevitable. It's just a matter of when I'm afraid.'

'But don't the people here realise that?'

'Of course, and their government are keeping a wary eye on Hades. At the moment they hope their neutrality will protect them.'

'But if this place is so important, why haven't Hades already attacked?'

'Even Emperor Cronos only wants one fight on his hands at a time, and for now Hades are too busy dealing with the Cloud Riders for anything else.'

'Where is Floating City anyway?' I asked, scanning the landscape beneath us.

'You're looking in the wrong direction.' Angelique pointed upwards.

I gazed to the sky and spotted a lumpy disc high up that was way too big to be an airship. Dark points swarmed around it like bees around a hive. A single gleaming line dropped away from the structure to the landscape miles below.

'When you said Floating City, I didn't think you meant it literally.'

Angelique smiled and passed me the spyglass. 'You might want to look through this.'

I focused the telescope. Through the eyepiece, the dark points became hundreds of individual airships all moving in and out of the weird city. As I studied it I realised the whole thing seemed be constructed from blisters of fabric. Slung beneath the structure, thousands of small rooms hung like baubles on a Christmas tree, their windows glinting in the sunlight. In a rush I realised what I was actually looking at – gondolas, thousands and thousands of them.

'Floating City is made up from airships packed together?' I asked.

'In the main, yes, although there are a number of permanent chambers at the heart of the city. One even has an ornamental park in it. The outskirts are a sort of shanty town constructed from individual ships. The official count varies from day to day, but moored up there are usually close to a hundred thousand airships, at any one time.'

'Holy cow.'

Angelique grinned. 'You wait till you see the street bazaars – they're like nothing you've ever experienced.'

I scanned the craft, looking for any demon logos. 'Can't see any Hades ships there at least.'

'You won't. As you can imagine, they aren't particularly popular with the locals, so their airships hold off at the city boundaries and hook up to the remote valve for refuelling. Their spies of course still enter the city incognito.'

I thought of the lone spy who'd turned up at our diner posing as a biker and who'd suckered Jules and Mom in. 'So I'm guessing that means we can't trust anyone in the city?'

'That's about the measure of it.'

Ship-song flowed into my mind, like an orchestra performing a piece based on the roar of the sea. *Storm Wind*'s voice climbed to sing back to it. Even *Athena*'s feeble song strengthened a bit.

'What's that sound?' I asked.

'When this many ships gather, their song is like one big continuous hymn.'

I could feel the swell of happiness from *Storm Wind* and *Athena*. The AIs' songs rose to match the ship orchestra until their voices merged into it.

Angelique smiled and pulled back on the wheel. 'They miss their kind. This is like a homecoming for them.'

Now, that I could understand.

Our ship began rising faster and we joined a procession of vessels approaching the city. I could see it was just one of a number of aerial freeways that flowed towards the city, with others leading ships away. The bees had been organised along routes in and out of the hive.

As we closed, I began to make out the individual craft that formed Floating City – from brightly coloured ships to bleached ones with numerous patches, from tiny individual balloons to vast bulbous airships with massive propellers.

'There are ships of every kind here,' Angelique said. 'Of course the city's population swelled with refugees from our world when it was…' Her voice trailed away and I caught that familiar flash of pain in her eyes.

Her home world had been destroyed in an instant when a Hades experimental Vortex drive tore it apart. What could I possibly say to someone who'd been through that? At that moment I knew a hug would've been appropriate, but I didn't want to send her mixed signals either. I settled on patting her arm instead.

She gave me a faraway look.

Way to go, Dom.

The ship ahead of us, trailing blue ribbons from its wings, started peeling away from our aerial roadway. It headed for a gap between the packed-together craft.

'So is there like an air traffic control system or something for all these ships?' I asked.

Angelique shook her head. 'It's not necessary – the AIs guide each other in.'

I heard an individual voice emerge from the orchestral chorus then. *Storm Wind* responded in song to match the voice, and they sung a bizarre form of ship duet.

Angelique let go of the wheel. '*Storm Wind* will take it from here.'

The wheel started moving by itself. We skimmed under the canvas ceiling, rippling and swaying like a big fabric upside-down ocean. Slung beneath some gondolas from lines that had been weighted with anchors, washing flapped like multicoloured bunting.

As we neared, I noticed what I'd thought was a rope fixing the city to the ground was in fact at least fifty feet wide.

Angelique followed my gaze. 'That's the fuel line from the refineries. Gas is pumped up into the city so there's no need for any ship to land. Not that it's something the miners below us are that keen on anyway. Ground people tend to mistrust the sky population, and vice versa.'

I shrugged. 'New world, same old problem of people not getting along.'

'Sadly that's true.' She pointed through the cabin window. 'This looks like our parking spot.'

Ahead of us I saw a gap in the tapestry of ships.

'That looks way too small for us to squeeze into,' I said.

'Trust me, *Storm Wind* knows exactly what he's doing.'

The propellers slowed to a stop and we slid underneath the gap. The burner handle moved by itself and a blast of flame lit up the envelope. An alarm warbled as the flame gutted and died.

'Not a moment too soon,' Angelique said. She leant across and pushed a silver button that silenced the alarm. 'That's the last of our propane.'

The airship rose up into a hole of darkness between the others. With a rustle of cloth, the cabin shuddered and we slid in between the vessels, like a piece slotting into a fabric jigsaw puzzle. *Athena* came to a complete stop next to a wooden gondola painted with murals of angels battling dark shadowy creatures.

I pointed towards the ship. 'Interesting choice of decoration.'

'Looks like a travelling priest's craft,' Angelique replied. 'The owner is probably up in the old district somewhere, preaching about the Shade and scaring people into being good citizens.'

So they had preachers here, but something told me they weren't anything like the ones we had back home, with kind eyes and wide smiles. I gazed up at Floating City, wondering if they had their equivalent of Mom's diner up there too.

Storm Wind's song changed tempo to match the other ships and once more his voice became lost in Floating City's orchestra.

'Don't they ever stop singing to each other?' I asked.

Angelique shook her head. 'And it's not like you can use earplugs to block them out either, but you'll get used to it eventually. I adore it personally. It reminds me of walking around the hangars of the palace as a child.'

I saw a pained look cross her face and felt a surge of sadness for her. She'd lost so much.

Angelique crossed to the Eye and knelt before it. 'Time to get you healed, my love.' She brushed aside the glowing blue crystals to expose *Athena*'s Psuche gem buried within them. It was hardly emitting any light now, especially compared to *Storm Wind*'s gem, blazing like a star next to it.

Angelique took hold of *Athena*'s AI crystal, lifted it gently and placed it inside the lightning pendant. She snapped the lid shut.

After the death of Bella, I knew if *Athena* died too, Angelique would never get over it. *Athena* mattered, really mattered to her, probably as much as Jules did to me. And in the crazy life of a Cloud Rider that kinda made sense.

'I guess the priority should be on getting *Athena* fixed up before anything else,' I said.

She shot me a grateful look. 'Thank you, but first we need to see the Dock Master and register our presence. Once we've done that we'll find a master technician straight away.'

I stared out through the door window at the cloudscape beneath the city. 'Where do we go exactly? All I can see outside is a sheer drop.'

'I'm afraid we're going to have to test your head for heights, Dom.'

'But I'm used to flying – how bad can it be?'

'Trust me, what we're about to do is daunting the first time you do it, however experienced a pilot you are.' Angelique swung the door open and a freezing wind howled into the cabin.

'What now?' I asked, peering towards the ground far below and the mushroom refineries now the size of pinheads.

Angelique pointed towards a plank slung from a cradle of ropes rotating towards us. It seemed to be part of a maze of walkways that ran between all the parked gondolas.

The plank clanged against the gondola. I took in how narrow it was. 'You're not telling me we have to walk along that?'

'Just avoid looking down till you get used to it.' Angelique leant out and tied the plank onto our gondola.

I realised she was being serious. Oh hell! My stomach flipped over several times as I walked towards the doorway. 'Lead the way,' I said, trying to look casual, although my toes clawed inside my sneakers.

Angelique strode out onto the plank like she did this every day. The walkway swayed beneath her, but she shifted her weight like an experienced tightrope walker. 'The first step is the worst. Just try not to look down until you get used to it.'

'Okay...' I placed one foot on the plank. I took a deep breath and followed Angelique out. The plank rocked and my toes clawed harder. It was only by sheer force of will-power that I didn't bolt back for the cabin.

She tilted her head to one side, reading me. 'Just relax, Dom.'

'I'm fine,' I said, trying to sound confident but feeling as steady as jello. I pulled my shoulders up and, ignoring my writhing gut, walked towards her with long strides. 'Lead the way.'

Angelique flashed me *that* smile – a smile I reckoned armies would fight and die for.

'You're doing much better than I did the first time I came here,' she said. 'I had to edge along the boards on my knees.'

'Now you tell me.'

Her smile sharpened to a grin.

I followed her along the boardwalk, relaxing a fraction, and started to take in my surroundings.

The walkways were suspended from a series of rails and pulleys, which looked like the work of a spider that had gone insane.

We passed a number of the other gondolas, all empty of people.

'Where is everyone?' I asked.

'Inside,' Angelique replied. 'People like to stretch their legs after being cooped up in their ships. Most who can afford it stay in the hub luxury hotels, others prefer to get drunk in the street taverns and sleep in the alleys.'

I rolled my eyes. 'Sounds like a fun place.'

'We won't be here any longer than we have to be.'

'Good – the sooner we can get after Jules, the happier I'll be.' I gazed up at the ceiling of canvas airships. 'So how do we get up there anyway?'

Angelique gestured to a cage sitting at the junction of several planks. 'We take a lift of course.'

The structure looked like it had been cobbled together from scaffolding poles. 'That doesn't exactly look safe.'

'It's adequate for the job.'

'Oh, that's alright then.' I followed her onto the make-shift lift and grabbed a metal pole, grateful at least to have something solid to hang onto.

Angelique took hold of a brass handle. 'Ready to see the most amazing bazaar of your life?'

'Sounds—'

Angelique slammed the handle over and we hurtled up like a bullet.

I just managed to stop my cool mask from slipping and avoid screaming my head off. 'Next time warn me!'

She snorted. 'And where would the fun be in that?'

Angelique might have been edgy, but part of me rather liked that in her. I shook my head, as we sped up into the dark tunnel between the ships.

CHAPTER Four

FLOATING CITY

We shot upwards through the oval ships packed in around us like cells in a body. My eyes began to adapt to the gloom and I spotted fine tubes laced through the spaces between the craft.

I pointed them out to Angelique. 'What are those for?'

'Gas feeds. It's how the ships remain buoyant while being docked for a long time.'

I shuddered in the biting cold and huddled into Dad's old flight jacket. 'Is that how we're going to refuel *Athena*?'

'Yes. We'll talk to the Dock Master and arrange for a hook-up.'

The daylight started to fade from the entrance of the tunnel and was gradually replaced with amber light from the lanterns hanging from the walls. The higher we rose, the warmer the air became, until our breath stopped steaming. I'd a hunch it had something to do with so many ships being packed together and generating heat like a group of huddled people.

The ships around us had become covered with dust. Vast cobwebs spanned the spaces between them. I didn't much fancy seeing the size of the spiders that spun them either. The song of the ship orchestra deepened in my head and echoed, like we were listening to an ocean roar from a shoreline cave as we walked deeper into it.

'Just how long have these ships been here?'

'Ships come and depart the outer regions all the time, but at this level they've been here for decades. Craft are drawn deeper and deeper the longer they stay. They say the craft in the oldest regions were abandoned a century ago, but the city authorities haven't had the heart to remove them.'

'The perfect hiding place for *Titan* in other words.'

Her face brightened. 'I hope with all my soul that proves to be the case.'

As we sped past the strata of packed-in ships, a pool of light grew brighter above us, revealing a solid ceiling of girders. The lift didn't seem to be slowing down.

I pointed up towards it. 'Angelique?'

She leant against the railing. 'What?'

'Shouldn't you be hitting the brakes or something?'

The corner of her mouth curled. 'You think so?'

Well I could play that game of chicken as well as she could. I folded my arms. The metal ceiling hurtled towards us.

Angelique folded her arms too and stared back at me.

I'm not going to look up. I'm not going to look up.

I looked up.

Metal bolts in the ceiling glared at me like barbs rushing towards our heads. I shut my eyes and braced for the impact.

A rush of warm air blew over my face and I heard Angelique laugh. I opened my eyes to see a metal doorway had irised open in the ceiling and we'd shot through it into a vast chamber.

'You could've warned me.'

She snorted. 'You should have seen your face.'

I couldn't help smiling. 'You're getting way too good at winding me up.'

'Aren't I just.' She nudged my shoulder with hers.

It took a moment for me to get my head around the sheer scale of the place we'd entered. From tinted glass windows in the ceiling, blue light beams criss-crossed the chamber like lasers. Some fell across airships in various stages of construction. Armies of men worked on each craft, the sparkle of their welding torches lighting up their faces.

Angelique spread her arms. 'Welcome to the docks.'

'This place is massive.'

The lift started to slow as we approached the top of the chamber. A mini-helicopter-like thing whirred past us. I caught a glimpse of a spanner clamped in mechanical hands extending from its square body. Two lamp-like eyes swivelled back in our direction and the device dived towards one of the airships.

'A robot?' I asked, returning its stare.

'Construction automatons. They're just given rudimentary intelligence gems, but are still clever enough to help with basic maintenance.'

I spotted other robots zooming around the docks, eyes blazing like headlights. 'Cool – Jules would so...' Her screaming face filled my mind. At once guilt flooded through me. Just for a moment I'd forgotten the situation we'd left her in.

Angelique crinkled her mouth. 'Try not to worry, Dom. One day we'll bring her here to see it for herself.'

I managed a nod. I just prayed that would happen.

The lift lurched to a stop in line with a solid-looking metal corridor. It led away into the walls of the chamber. I quickly stepped onto the solid surface, legs feeling as unsteady as a sailor's who'd stepped onto shore after a long voyage.

A line of gas jets flickered inside glass bowls set into the ceiling and illuminated the way ahead.

Angelique ran her fingers over her pendant and in response it glowed faintly through the crack around the lid. 'Come on, we need to organise our gas supplies. Then we will track down a master technician to work on *Athena*'s Psuche gem.'

A thought occurred to me. 'Isn't there a danger that someone might recognise you? You are a princess after all.'

'There is, and although most will still be loyal to the royal household of Olympus, there will always be someone tempted by the substantial bounty Cronos has put on my head.' Angelique pulled her deep velvet hood up, casting her face into shadows.

'Wouldn't it be safer for me to go into the city by myself?'

She paused and looked back at me. 'Dom, some of my people are here and I just need to be among them for a while – in the same way that *Storm Wind* needs to be among other ships. Do you understand?'

Angelique was all alone now her mother was dead. I more than understood what being here meant for her. Though this may not have been her home world, it was probably the last place in this or any universe that came even close. 'Of course…'

Angelique gave me a small smile and lowered her head to create a reasonable impersonation of a hooded monk. She led me away along the corridor.

...

Angelique said we'd find the Dock Master in the office we now stood outside. We entered a tobacco-smoke-filled room. Through a large scratched window that filled one wall, I could see a view of the docks and the ant-like activity of men and automatons.

The thick air snagged at the back of my throat and I coughed.

'How can I help you?' someone said.

I rubbed my smarting eyes and, for the first time in the smog, noticed a man with a grey stubbly beard sitting behind a large carved desk. He wore a boiler suit and had a rusty green hard hat perched on his head.

His gaze sharpened over the top of his glasses on Angelique. He unhooked a pipe he'd been smoking from his mouth. 'Don't tell me you're after gas supplies?' He twirled a fountain pen around his fingers.

Angelique nodded. 'We are, Dock Master. We've docked landfall side and desperately need helium and propane.'

He settled back into his seat. 'I knew by the way you rushed in here you'd be in some sort of hurry. I just wish I could oblige.'

'What do you mean?' I said.

'We've had a procession of Hades transport ships taking as much gas as we can spare. The planet refineries are working flat out, but we can barely keep up with their demand.'

'Why do Hades need so much gas?' I asked.

'No idea, son. Normally a single shipment keeps them quiet for at least a month. They probably have some special project going on at Hells Cauldron.'

Angelique's hooded face turned towards me.

Special project – what did that mean exactly?

The man placed the pen on the desk and rotated it towards Angelique.

She put her hands on his desk. 'But this is urgent and surely you could make—'

He waved, silencing her. 'And in case you're thinking of trying to bribe me, because it's what most folk try next, I wouldn't bother. Hades have a way of finding out if I try to divert any of the gas destined for them.' He rotated the pen.

Angelique's head turned towards the corner of the room the pen pointed at and her stance stiffened. 'Of course. I understand, my good man.'

She turned and made for the door.

I grabbed her arm. 'You're giving up just like that?'

'You heard what he said. We'll just have to wait until supplies become available.'

The Dock Master shrugged at me.

I stared at Angelique. 'But—'

She shook her head and I followed her out into the corridor.

I had to hurry to keep up with her as she marched away. 'You're not serious are you?'

Angelique tutted. 'Of course not.'

She was starting to do my head in. 'Okay, now I'm confused.'

Angelique stopped and gestured back towards the office. 'The Dock Master signalled to me that we were being watched.'

'He did?'

'Yes, when he rotated his pen counterclockwise and pointed it at the shadows in the corner of his office.'

'Which was what exactly?' I asked.

'Espionage Automaton Relay, or EAR for short. A listening device that would have been relaying our conversation to a Hades spy situated somewhere in the city.'

'A bug you mean?'

'Quite literally. The device resembles a spider. Luckily for us, the Dock Master is obviously a Cloud Riders sympathiser.'

'So what happens now?'

'I'll take you to Rama. It's a favourite food venue for the Master Technician Guild in Floating City. Hopefully there we'll find someone to repair *Athena*'s Psuche gem. Then we'll work out what to do about getting refuelled.'

The tension let go across my shoulders. 'Now that sounds more like it.'

'Oh and another reason for going there – Rama also has the finest food you have ever tasted. Well, apart from your mama's wonderful cooking of course.'

My mind's focus switched from Jules to Mom. I knew she'd be worried sick by now about what was happening to me. I pictured her trying to clear up the shattered remains of the diner. She'd put heart and soul into that place. The family business had been just another casualty of Cronos's ambition.

I clenched my fist. 'If Mom ever gets to rebuild the diner after Ambra burned it down.'

'If anyone can pick herself up, your mama will. She's an amazing woman.'

'Yeah, she is.' I smiled at her.

She returned my smile. 'Come on, I'm starving.'

...

The smells and the shouts of people overwhelmed my senses.

Angelique led the way along a planked street between the airships. Banners had been stretched between the craft, advertising the shops that their gondolas had been turned into. The whole place smelt of people, a lot of them, packed into a small place. Litter lay strewn across the floor. I was fairly sure I kept seeing things that looked suspiciously like large rats scurrying through the shadows.

People thronged the narrow avenue, as we made our way through the street bazaar. Keen-eyed merchants singled us out and kept trying to block our way to entice us into their shops. I followed Angelique's lead and smiled, but didn't allow myself to get drawn into their sale pitches.

Many of the men wore tailored suits, complete with old-fashioned-looking tall hats, flight goggles strapped to them. In contrast the woman wore long, flowing velvet skirts, waists pinched in by embroidered corsets. The one thing everyone seemed to have on was a pair of high boots to protect their feet from the rubbish. My sneakers had already begun to look worse for wear.

An old man outside a shop full of glass tubs of every size and colour shoved a brown one filled with green powder under my nose. I sneezed as the pungent smell wafted up my nostrils.

Angelique waved him away.

'What was that awful stuff?'

'It's a rare spice made from ground sea slugs.'

'Sounds delicious – I'll get some for Mom.'

Angelique laughed. 'You're actually meant to use it for cleansing your face.'

We passed two men with fierce expressions, busy shoving their fingers into each other's chests and shouting at each other.

'Looks as though they're about to have a fight,' I said.

'Haggling is almost considered a sport in Floating City. It's the traditional way people do business around here. But don't be misled – people love it. It's all part of the game.'

As if to underline her point, the shouting stopped suddenly and the two men shook hands and grinned at each other.

I heard a whirring and ducked as a little helicopter drone sped over our heads. But unlike the ones in the hangar, this one carried a basket laden with exotic fruit.

'Delivery automaton?' I asked.

She nodded. 'You're learning fast, Dom.'

We walked through a plume of smoke and a different, more welcome smell filled my nostrils – like frying bacon. A small girl had erected a trestle table in front of her gondola. Six pans sizzled on her copper stove. I peered at the golden flatbreads with nuggets of meat she was cooking. My stomach rumbled and Angelique laughed. She looked the most relaxed I'd ever seen her.

Angelique hooked her arm through mine – but it didn't feel calculated, just natural, as she walked through a bazaar with a friend.

'That's Natha – a local savoury bread, but I have something even better in mind for us to eat,' she said. 'When we used to come here on state visits, I would always slip from the banquets and eat at Rama – that's where we're heading.'

I looked down at my jeans and sneakers. 'Not sure I'm dressed for a fancy restaurant. I certainly don't have the hat for it.'

'Trust me, it's not extravagant in that way. You'll be fine as you are.'

The street began to widen out. Red Chinese-like lanterns had replaced the shop banners.

A new awful stench assaulted my nose, bad enough to make me feel nauseous. We passed a gondola stacked high with furs of every colour. Gross. I cupped my hand over my mouth and hurried past.

We passed junction after junction, busy wide streets leading away from each.

'This place is like a maze,' I said.

Angelique nodded. 'And the layout keeps changing as airships are moved. The smaller avenues sometimes disappear overnight if enough traders leave at once. However, most of the bigger streets have been here for years.'

'So how do you know which way to go?'

She pointed up at the lanterns. 'Each of the streets is colour-coded with those lights. We just have to follow the red lanterns to reach the hub and then use them to retrace our steps. Mind you, as Navigators, all we have to do is listen to *Storm Wind*'s voice and he can guide us back to the ship.'

I tuned into the airships' orchestra. As I concentrated I picked out *Storm Wind*'s individual voice among the harmony of the others. But since Angelique had started wearing the Psuche gem around her neck, *Athena*'s voice had stopped broadcasting. I only hoped that was just because the AI was conserving her energy.

My attention snapped back as the chatter of the crowd grew louder. Bodies pressed in against us as the street became busier. We flowed with the stream of humanity into a larger street. Drilled metal floors, free of rubbish, had replaced the wooden planks. Instead of banners, solid-looking beams now spanned the spaces between the ships. It even smelt nice around here, with the fragrance of oranges and cinnamon wafting out from perfume shops, replacing the stink of the smaller alleys.

We passed what I thought at first was a pet shop, with caged birds singing outside. I looked closer and stopped dead. The birds had clockwork keys turning in their sides and their eyes had been made from gemstones.

Angelique smiled at me as I peered at them. 'Beautiful, aren't they?'

'I've never seen anything like them.'

'Automaton creation is one of the specialties of Floating City. We once had a robotic entertainment that had been made here – a master craftsman made it from sterling silver. I used to play chess with him at the royal palace. The only problem was, he was too good and I always used to lose.'

'I'd have loved to have seen that.'

'What the losing, or the automaton chess master?'

I grinned. 'Both.'

She laughed. I was starting to warm to this new version of Angelique. Perhaps she'd been a lot more like this in the old days, before war had hardened her into a soldier. But who wouldn't have been by what she'd gone through?

Angelique gestured along the street. 'As you can probably tell, this is one of the main streets I mentioned.'

'I thought this place looked more permanent – and wealthier.'

'Oh, it's most certainly that.'

We allowed ourselves to be swept along with the human tide towards a broad archway with two carved figures either side. Each statue wore goggles. Giant tapestries of airships hung behind them.

Angelique nodded at the statues. 'The city's founding fathers.'

We passed between the statues and I stopped dead again, my brain trying to process the astonishing view.

We stood in a wide domed chamber at least a couple of miles across, a glass ceiling framing the blue sky. Within the structure, oval buildings constructed from curved steel panels had been packed together like pebbles on a beach. From many of the buildings, smoke curled from chimneys and snaked up towards the ceiling to form a hazy smog, which massive extractor fans were doing their best to suck away. Throughout the hub, trees towered, at least as tall as giant redwoods, with flocks of white doves circling them.

'This place is awesome,' I said.

'It really is. And this is just one of the four main city hubs, but this is my favourite.'

'Why this one?'

'Because of the amphitheatre.' Angelique pointed to an arena in the middle of the hub, surrounded by stepped seating. 'When we used to visit Floating City, the authorities would always put on a circus for us. I used to love the acrobats and the way they danced in the air.'

'Danced in the air?'

She pointed up at trapeze handles hanging from the ceiling and lines criss-crossing the space above. 'They used to perform up there without any safety nets. It was breathtaking. Mind you, I never watched a whole performance. The moment my parents weren't looking, I used to slip off to play hide and seek with the local children. That was magical for me when I was small.'

'Sounds a bit tame for you, Angelique.'

'It isn't when your hiding places are between the airships.'

'Okay, that does sound a bit cooler.'

'It was. We used to find all sorts of forgotten places during our games.'

'But obviously not *Titan*?'

'Some parts of the city are so deeply buried, I doubt anyone has been there for years. Anyway, you'll see that all for yourself soon. But first we need to get a move on and find a Master Technician in Rama.'

I nodded.

We started to make our way between the pebble buildings and down the sloping streets towards the amphitheatre.

As we neared the centre, I spotted a man wearing a flow-ing grey cloak, standing in the middle of a raised circular stage and yelling at a small crowd seated around him. Most of the onlookers seemed to be ignoring him and eating their Natha bread, but a few drinking at a table outside what looked like a bar jeered at the man whenever he got too loud.

'What's happening there?' I asked.

'Going by that man's grey robes, he's probably the travelling preacher we're moored next to.'

A Natha bread spun from the audience, thrown like a Frisbee, and narrowly missed the man.

'Don't think he's winning the crowd over,' I said.

'He won't, they're too set in their' – she scratched the air with her fingers – 'ungodly ways.'

The preacher glowered back at the audience.

Angelique led the way towards a four-storey building with porthole windows set into one side.

'When the worlds slip into the darkness of the final battle and the Shade feed upon your worthless lost souls, you won't mock me then,' the preacher shouted.

'What's that about Shade?' I asked.

'Oh, just his fire and brimstone talk. His kind need something to frighten people with, and the Shade are per-fect for that.'

The preacher spread his arms wide, turning in a circle to the audience. 'Light against dark. And you, my lost brothers and sisters, must repent before you are cast down into hell.'

'What, you mean down to the miners below us?' a woman called back. 'I always had those land-lovers pegged as demons.' Laughter rippled around the amphitheatre.

We neared a building with a large, round, polished brass door.

Angelique stopped before it. 'This is Rama.'

'Move now,' a voice whispered from behind us.

Angelique whipped round and muscles tensed across my shoulders. A smell of tobacco smoke filled my nose.

I turned to meet the Dock Master's gaze. He unhooked his pipe from his mouth. 'There's a spider automaton watching you from the rooftop over there.' He jerked his chin towards the top of a domed tower.

From the corner of my eye, I could just make out a metal device with legs clamped around a copper chimney stack. Its head scanned the crowds around the amphitheatre. My legs hollowed out.

'Quick, inside, before it spots you,' the Dock Master said.

'How do we know this isn't some sort of trap,' I said, frowning at him.

'Because if it were, I would have taken the large bounty on the princess's head.'

'You know who I am?' Angelique said.

He laughed. 'Of course I do and I've got a message for you, Princess.' The Dock Master stepped towards the round door. With a hiss of steam it rolled sideways.

Angelique's hooded face turned towards me, her eyes wide.

I returned her worried look. Who was this guy? We hurried inside after him and out of sight of the spying device.

CHAPTER Five

DANRICK

The Dock Master led us through to the far back of the steam-filled restaurant. We passed between customers sat at circular, metal tables, their faces beaded with moisture. They all seemed to be tucking into the contents of bubbling metal pots similar to the one back on the ship that Angelique had incinerated the baked beans in.

The Dock Master seated himself at an empty table. 'No one will be able to see us easily in here, so you can lower your hood, Princess Angelique.'

'What makes you think that's who I am?' Angelique replied, keeping her hood firmly up.

'Because the ships told me who you were when you arrived. Although of course I recognised you the moment you wandered into my office.'

I peered at the man who could hear ships too. 'You're a Navigator?'

He nodded. 'But keep your voice down. There might be a Hades EAR listening device planted in here and I'd prefer my Navigator gene stays a well-kept secret. I've no desire to end up like one of the Vanished.'

'The Vanished?' I asked.

'That's the name given to Navigators who've disappeared since the outbreak of the war,' Angelique replied.

The man nodded. 'Ten people have gone from here to my knowledge and I have every reason to believe Hades had something to do with that.'

'Why?' I asked.

'Rumour has it they have some secret project going on at Hells Cauldron that needs all the Navigators they can get their hands on.'

'Surely they have their own people?' Angelique said.

'Of course they do and nobody knows why they need the extra ones. All we know for sure is that Navigators started disappearing from here when the rumours first started about a secret project at Hells Cauldron. Nowadays, people are very circumspect about admitting they have the gene.'

'I'm not surprised,' I replied.

The man took off his hard hat and placed it on the table. 'People are very jumpy at the moment and it doesn't help that we've got a Hades agent who's practically taking up residence here. He's good too. I've had my men making discreet enquiries, but so far no one has been able to get close to unveiling his identity. We know he's here, just not who he is.'

'Not even the ships?' Angelique asked.

'That's the puzzling bit. Normally, as you know, our airships are very good at sniffing out Hades spies and they certainly won't tolerate their abomination of ships getting too close. And of course no Hades ship can dock at the city.'

'Why not?' I asked.

The Dock Master frowned at me. 'You've obviously not been to Floating City before.'

'It's his first visit,' Angelique said.

'Well, son, if they ever tried to dock, the AIs in the ships already moored here would Voice Shout them out of the sky.'

'Shout, what do you mean?' I asked.

'It's a form of telepathic mind-battle between ships,' Angelique said.

The man nodded. 'And with so many ships ranged against them, even a Hades dreadnought wouldn't stand a chance against Floating City. It would turn tail and run. To avoid any incidents, Floating City's authorities came to an arrangement with Hades. Now there's a specially designed docking point mounted lower down on the main supply line from the ground. That's as close as the abomination of their ships are allowed to get.'

Angelique tilted her head to one side and she narrowed her gaze on the man. 'You seem very well informed about what's going on around here for a Dock Master.'

Amusement flickered through his face. 'Oh, I make it my business to make sure I know *everything* that's going on around here.'

'So if you know who I am, why didn't you just turn us in for the bounty?'

He chuckled. 'Because I'm an old friend, Princess.' He rubbed his bushy, dark beard flecked with grey hairs.

Angelique leant closer, peering at him. 'An old friend?'

'Don't you recognise me, Angela?' he said, his accent now with a hint of French to it.

'Only one person has ever dared called me that…' Her eyes widened. 'Danrick?'

A smile filled up his face. 'Have you remembered none of what I taught you in your espionage classes?'

Angelique lowered her hood and stared at him.

'*Espionage* classes?' I asked.

'She was very good at them too,' he said. He nodded towards Angelique. 'But you seem to have forgotten the first lesson I taught you…'

Angelique leant across the table towards him. 'That a good disguise is a spy's first defence.' She wrapped her arms around the man's muscular neck. 'I can't believe it's you. And your disguise is magnificent, Danrick. I would never have recognised you in a million solar cycles.'

He laughed. 'That's the general idea of a disguise – and it's good to see you too, Angela.'

'Let me introduce my good friend and ally, Dom Taylor, of Earth DZL2351,' Angelique said. 'He has the Navigator gene as well.' She leant in closer to him. 'And you won't believe this, but he's descended from King Alexander – who it turns out, crash-landed on his Earth a hundred years ago.'

Danrick whistled. 'Good grief.' His gaze narrowed on us. 'Which makes you almost a Cloud Rider I suppose.'

'Trust me, he's every part a Cloud Rider,' Angelique said. 'He's already saved my life more than once.'

A sense of pride filled me. That meant a lot coming from someone like Angelique.

Danrick focused his attention on me. 'I'm indebted to you, son – all the Cloud Riders are.'

'Angelique has done her fair share of saving my hide too,' I replied.

He crinkled his eyes at me. 'That's what real friends do for each other, and any friend of the Princess is a friend of mine.' He thrust out his hand. 'Let me properly introduce myself. I am Danrick Telphid, former head of the Royal Spy Network.'

I shook his hand. 'Is that why you're here then, spying on any Hades in Floating City?'

Danrick nodded. 'The King sent me into deep cover here, when the military coup first began. It was all part of his contingency plan if things went badly.'

'What plan?' Angelique asked. 'And why didn't Papa tell me anything about this?'

'Because he felt it would be safer for you not to know. He had had his suspicions about Cronos's loyalties for some time, and believed that man was mustering support from among the ranks for the coup. I was a sleeper agent in case things went badly, so I could help any member of the royal household in any way I could. Of course we didn't anticipate a Hades secret weapon would jam our ability to communicate. That changed everything. Since its activation I've laid low in Floating City, waiting for any news, hoping that anyone who survived the battle with Hades would end up here.' He sat back. 'And just when I was starting to lose hope, here you are.'

Angelique beamed at him. 'So—'

His expression sharpened and he put his finger to her lips. 'Quiet, someone's approaching.'

I jumped as a shape loomed out of the indoor fog.

'And what would you good people like to order,' a woman said. She had a round face, her red hair pinned back into a bun.

I noticed the pad in her hand and relaxed. A waitress.

Angelique sat up straighter. 'Sanfire noodles for me.'

The woman's eyes narrowed. 'You look familiar – do I—?'

'Have you got any of your fabulous slow-cooked mutton left?' Danrick said, fixing her with a dazzling smile.

'Oh, Henry, I didn't see you come in. Of course I do for one of my special customers. Just don't tell everyone or it'll all be gone.'

His film-actor smile widened and the woman practically fluttered her eyelashes at him.

The waitress looked at me. 'And what would sir like?'

'Noodles sound good.'

'Excellent choice. I'll bring you a pitcher of water to go with them.' The woman turned and faded into the fog.

'That was close,' I said. 'She nearly recognised you, Angelique.'

'Thanks to Danrick, or perhaps I should say Henry, and his usual charm with women, she didn't.'

He grinned. 'That skill is all part of my job description.'

Angelique laughed. 'Same old Danrick.' She gestured around us at the vague shapes of other diners huddled over their food. 'Can you recommend a Master Technician, Danrick?'

'Why?' he asked.

'*Athena*'s been hurt—' Her voice choked up as she spoke.

Danrick's face softened. 'Oh, Angela, I'm so sorry.' He reached over and gave her a tight hug.

A pang of sadness shot through me. Part of me couldn't help feeling it should've been me comforting her.

Angelique raised her head and smeared her damp eyes. 'Sorry, Danrick.'

'Don't be – I know how much *Athena* means to you. So how did it happen?'

Angelique clasped her hand tighter around her necklace. 'Duke Ambra came to Dom's world pretending to be another Cloud Rider.'

Anger pulsed through me. 'He was in the captured *Apollo*. *Athena* got injured during the battle with him.'

'Oh by the gods. Is Ambra dead at least?'

'No, he escaped and he's on his way to Hells Cauldron with my best friend as hostage.' Now it was my turn for my insides to coil up into a tight ball.

I felt a hand on mine. Angelique's. She gave me a broken smile. I felt a surge of guilt. Maybe I'd been misreading the signals and she'd just been trying to be a good friend to me. *Maybe* I just needed to get over myself.

Danrick shook his head. 'I'm really sorry to hear that, son.' He gazed at Angelique. 'And I'm afraid I've got bad news about your search for a Master Technician. You won't find any left in Floating City.'

She stared at him. 'What do you mean? There must be at least a thousand members in the guild, not to mention all the freelance technicians working out of their workshops in the alleys.'

'They've all gone.'

'Gone? Gone where?' she asked.

'To Hells Cauldron. Hades have been on a massive recruitment drive, tempting people with fees so large that nobody could turn them down.'

I sat forward. 'A project linked to what they need all those Navigators for?'

'That's what I thought, so I sent someone to check at Hells Cauldron, but I haven't heard back from him.' His expression tensed and he stared at his hands.

'Danrick, what's wrong?' Angelique asked.

'He insisted on going…said that it was the only sure way to find out what they were up to.'

'Someone close to you?' I asked.

'I sent Stephen.'

'Your son?' Angelique said.

'Yes. He posed as a technician and left on a Hades transport ship bound for Hells Cauldron. I helped forge his credentials.'

Angelique clasped his hand. 'Just because you haven't heard anything, doesn't mean…' Her voice trailed away.

But I knew what she was really thinking – that it probably meant Stephen had been at the very least captured. Problem was, my instinct told me Hades wouldn't hesitate in executing a spy. Danrick would know that too.

Danrick looked up from his hands. 'I know I have to hang onto every hope – it's all I have. But then, Angela, you've turned up, which demonstrates that miracles can happen. I can only begin to imagine how your papa will feel when he learns that you're alive.'

Angelique blinked, a startled expression filling her face.

What? Did he mean what I thought he did? 'Are you saying the King's still alive?'

'Yes,' Danrick replied.

With that single word, I saw in Angelique's face her world changing.

She opened her mouth and then closed it again, eyes filling as the realisation sank in.

I saw her old pain swept away, replaced with fresh hope shining through her tears.

Danrick tipped his head back. 'Of course you couldn't know. You have been out of contact for some time, haven't you?'

'I...' She just nodded, spilling the tears down her cheeks.

I stared between them. This was huge, enormous, awesome. She'd just found out she was no longer the last of her family. If I'd just found that out about Dad, I reckoned I wouldn't be able to hold back the tears either.

A thought occurred to me. 'I thought the King had started his ship's self-destruct system during that final battle?'

Danrick nodded. 'King Louis, on *Zeus*, and Lord Orson, on *Apollo*, had both activated them. But what neither of them anticipated was Hades hitting their craft with some sort of weapon that crippled the AIs on both ships. Both Cloud Rider vessels were dead in the water. *Apollo* was boarded and Lord Orson taken prisoner. But your father made all his men abandon ship. He stayed onboard to try to repair the damage to *Apollo*'s AI.'

'And he managed it?' I asked.

'At the very last minute the King hardwired the *Olympus*'s Vortex drive and performed a manual jump. The problem is, no one knows where he went.'

Angelique swallowed, finding her voice at last. 'But how do you know any of this?'

'One of the survivors from his ship managed to capture a Hades scout balloon and made his way here.'

'Sounds like our sort of trick,' I said.

Angelique nodded, sending more tears trickling down her face. 'I don't know what to say or do... Papa's alive. This is more than I could have ever dreamed.'

I ignored a pang of envy wishing this was about my own dad. 'Hey, this is great news, so how about a smile?' This time I got in first with a hug before Danrick.

'Oh, Dom.' She hugged me back.

This felt like the right thing to do. But I also found myself not wanting the moment to end.

Angelique pulled away first, smiling and smudging away her tears with her hand.

Danrick beamed at us. 'That's more like it – smiles not tears.'

A green light started blinking on the table.

'And to celebrate I say we should eat,' he said. 'Apart from anything else, I can't think on anything less than a full stomach. Then we need to work out what we're going to do next.'

He pressed a button set into the table and, with a hiss, three hatches opened in its top and a bowl of food rose up before each of us.

I examined my glistening noodles in broth, hunks of meat and purple fern-like leaves floating in it.

'Okay, that's cool table service,' I said.

It certainly smelt amazing and I realised my gut felt as empty as a hole in the ground. I'd forgotten how hungry I was.

'All the food is delivered in vacuum tubes straight from the kitchens,' Danrick said.

'Mom would love one of these in the diner.'

Angelique grinned. 'Maybe we should see if we can rig one up for her.'

Another aperture opened in the table and three glasses appeared along with a jug of water.

'Your mother's a chef, Dom?' Danrick asked through a mouthful of meat.

I nodded.

'Only the best,' Angelique said, smiling at me.

Mom... I wondered again how she was doing. I'd only been away from home for little more than a day. I'd never admit it to anyone else because it sounded so lame, but I was already homesick. So much for being the big *I am* adventurer following in Dad's footsteps.

To distract myself from my thoughts, I took a fork and skewered one of the purple leaves. I popped it into my mouth.

Angelique stared at me. 'Dom, don't!'

Too late – I'd already started chewing. Volcanic spice heat burned through my mouth. I swallowed and gasped for air, but the burning carried on down my throat. I grabbed the jug of water and drank straight from it.

Danrick snorted and slapped me on the back. 'You're not actually meant to eat sanfire, son. It's only there to infuse and spice up the meat.'

I finished off the last of the water, most of which had splashed down my chin and soaked the T-shirt under my flying jacket.

I glared at them both grinning at me. 'Thanks for that.'

Angelique snorted. 'We really didn't have a chance to warn you.'

The heat started to fade from my gut and I shook my head at her. But deep down I didn't mind. It was great to see her looking so happy and that some of the weight she'd been carrying had lifted from her shoulders.

Angelique twirled the noodles around her fork and pointed it at Danrick. 'Have you heard from any other Cloud Riders?'

'A few – in particular, in terms of your situation at the moment, a level one Master Technician. He's certainly skilled enough to attempt the delicate repair of *Athena*'s Psuche gem.'

She stopped twirling her noodles. 'But there must be only three people with that skill grade in all the known Earths.' Her mouth dropped. 'You don't mean who I think you do?'

'Of course I do,' Danrick said with a grin.

I glanced between then. 'Will someone tell me who you two are talking about?'

'The royal chief scientist, Tesla,' Angelique said.

The name tugged at a memory. 'Isn't that the guy who was trying to block the effects of the Hades secret weapon which stops your ships navigating and you communicating with each other?'

'The same,' Danrick said. 'And he was still working on a solution when I last saw him. He thought he might actually be getting close to a way to stop its effect.'

'Really? But how?' Angelique asked.

'I've no idea, although Tesla tried to explain it to me. Something to do with energy waves collapsing the broadcast field around a transmitter.'

We both gave him blank looks.

He shrugged. 'It made that much sense to me as well.' He peered at me. 'But funny you should mention Hells Cauldron – that's where he was headed too. According to the scans he'd run, that location seems to be the origin of the jamming signal that's being broadcast.'

I glanced at Angelique. 'As though we need any more reasons to head there.'

'It would seem that all flight paths lead towards Hells Cauldron.'

'But we need to find *Titan* before we leave here though.'

'*Titan*?' Danrick asked.

Angelique raised her eyebrows. 'Oh, we have so much to tell you.'

'It sounds like it,' Danrick said.

'There's also the small matter of what we're going to do about being out of gas,' I said.

Danrick chuckled. 'I had to make the gas shortage situation sound convincing enough for the benefit of the EAR lurking in my office, not to mention the Hades spy listening into our conversation at the other end.'

'So you can get us refuelled then?' I asked.

'I'm not saying it won't be tricky. Hades automatons are monitoring the supplies. Worse case, we may have to liberate the gas from another airship. We have bleed tanks in the docks where we store the gas from the vessels that are in for maintenance. If we have to, we could hook a line up to your ship and refuel her that way – blame the lost gas on a leak or something.'

'Sounds good to me,' Angelique said.

'Okay. Then I suggest we go and get that organised right now. On the way you can tell all about *Titan*. Would I be right in thinking we're talking about the same ship as the one in the legend?'

'The same,' Angelique replied.

Danrick blew his cheeks out. 'This day just gets more and more interesting.'

'Let's get going,' I said, pushing my noodles away.

'Don't you want to finish them?' Angelique asked with a smirk.

'I'll pass. Suddenly your burned baked beans seem more appetising by the minute.'

She snorted and took a large last mouthful of noodles.

Danrick placed a pile of coins into his empty bowl and pressed a button. The bowls and money disappeared down through the hatches into the table.

We followed Danrick out through the steam-filled room and passed the neighbouring table. A figure was hunched over a bowl of thin soup, his folded grey cape on the seat next to him. The preacher.

'Must have been driven in here by his fans,' Angelique said in a low whisper as we passed him.

The man's head twitched in our direction.

I grinned at Angelique and we hurried out after Danrick.

'Seems our luck is starting to change for the better,' I said.

'To hear Papa's alive means everything to me,' Angelique replied.

I ignored the twist in my guts that wished we were discussing my dad here. 'I bet it does.'

The dome had grown darker with the setting sun and now the hub was illuminated by six large gas lanterns suspended from the ceiling and glowing through the smog like fireballs.

'So will you come with us to Hells Cauldron, Danrick?' Angelique asked as we began to make our way towards one of the exits.

'I've done as much as I can here, so helping you on your little excursion makes a lot of sense...and of course I have my own reasons for going now.'

Jules, *Athena*, Stephen...the sooner we got there the better as far as I was concerned.

A flock of doves flew over our heads. They neared the curved wall and started to bank. One of the birds swooped down towards us and glinted in the light.

Glinted. Huh?

Angelique had her back to the flock and hadn't seen it. She smiled at me. 'Oh, Dom, it really feels like we've turned a corner in this war.'

I nodded, but was still distracted by the single bird swooping directly towards us. There was a jerky movement to the beat of its wings. Injured maybe?

'You say Ambra is going to be there?' Danrick said.

Angelique nodded.

'Excellent,' Danrick replied. 'I can't wait to get my hands around that butcher's neck.'

'You'll have to get in the queue behind me, won't he, Dom?' Angelique said.

I ignored her question, concentrating instead on the strange dove eating up the distance between us real fast.

'Dom?' she repeated.

A puff of steam came from the bird's mouth and something blurred towards us.

Before I could shout out a warning, Danrick's jaw clenched and he stumbled forward.

Angelique grabbed him. 'Danrick?' His head tipped downwards.

I stared at a thin needle with red-feathered flights that stuck out from the back of his neck. 'Oh god – a poisoned dart?'

Angelique nodded, her face draining of colour. People began to gather around us.

The dove began to bank round back towards us.

I shouted to the crowd, 'We need a doctor.'

No one moved. They just stared back at me like we were putting on some sort of street performance.

'It's too late,' Danrick said, spittle foaming between his teeth. 'Neural toxin. I've only got moments left.'

Angelique hugged him. 'Oh, my dear friend.'

He gripped her arm. 'Find Stephen for me.'

'We will, I promise.' She blinked back tears.

He smiled, but his mouth clenched and a deep judder passed through his body. He began to writhe in Angelique's arms as she tried to hold him. With a groan, his face froze and his eyes became glazed.

'No,' Angelique whispered. She bent her head over his and closed his eyelids with her thumbs. 'May your body return to stardust, old friend.' She kissed him gently on the forehead.

She lowered his head to the ground then stood up again, scanning the crowd with hard eyes. 'Did you see where the dart came from, Dom?'

I pointed at the dove circling back towards us for another pass.

She grabbed my arm. 'Assassin automaton. Run!'

Cold surged through me and we shoved through the circle of onlookers towards the exit from the hub.

Chapter Six
HIDE AND SEEK

A woman's scream cut dead the shouts of haggling along the street. Heads started to turn in a ripple that spread out around us through the crowd. We pushed and shoved through the people flowing through the archway between the founding-father statues.

The dove's eyes glowed red. It swooped towards us again.

'Watch out!' Angelique pulled me to the ground.

A dart zipped over my head and struck an old man who'd been blocking our way. He stared at the projectile in his stomach and toppled like a tree that had been chopped.

A small woman by his side pulled at his arm and heaved the man over. 'He's been shot!'

Something whirred above us — the mechanical dove was circling around and lining up for another run.

The woman pointed at the dove. 'That automaton did it!'

Shouts and cries filled the street. Everyone began to run. The street started emptying as people dived for cover inside the shops.

We headed into one of the smaller side alleys already jammed full with people trying to escape.

The crowd pressed in around us, but we pushed our way through. My neck tingled and I glanced back to see the dove jinking between the stalls and lining up on Angelique.

Hemmed in, there was no way it would miss us this time. Before I had time to even think, I shoved myself between Angelique and the automaton. Vapour spiralled from the bird's mouth and another dart blurred towards me.

The world spun.

Hit? It took me a moment to realise Angelique had grabbed me and hurled me to the ground. The dove swooped towards her, wings buzzing like a clock about to explode. She hoisted her skirt and grabbed a black knife from a scabbard strapped to her ankle. In one seamless, dance-like movement, she threw the weapon at the bird. The knife sped straight towards the dove, faster than I could blink, and buried itself into its body. In a shower of sparks, the dove crashed through a line of lanterns and pulled them to the ground with it. The lights blinked out along the street. The cries around us grew more panicked.

'At least we're safe now,' I said.

Angelique shook her head and pointed past me. 'This isn't over yet.'

I turned to see someone running down the alley. His grey cape flew out behind him as he pushed people out of his way. A slice of light from a gondola fell over the man and illuminated him for a split second.

My heart clenched. 'The preacher!'

Ahead of us the silhouettes of people jammed the alley-way, shouting and crying out to each other.

No way through. Trapped.

I clambered back to my feet, blood pounding in my ears.

Words, not my own, started to form in my thoughts. *'Whisperer, this way,'* a deep male voice said.

Whisperer? Me? It seemed to come from the cavern of darkness between two gondolas to our left. No time to think. No time to question.

I grabbed Angelique's hand and pulled her towards the gap with me.

Seeing where we were headed, she nodded. 'That's inspired.'

'Come again?'

'I told you about the hide and seek I used to play with the city children between the airships.' She took the lead and leapt off the boardwalk into the gloom beyond. I jumped after her. My stomach lurched as darkness clamped around us with a rush of air. We landed on something soft and bounced like we were on a trampoline.

'We're standing on top of an airship,' Angelique said, as we came to a stop.

Above us two red, round lights flared up in the dimness.

'The spy's put his night-vision goggles on,' Angelique said. 'Quick, down the side.'

Before I could stop her, she grabbed my hand and pulled me with her. We slid down the curve of the airship and jerked to a sudden stop. I struggled against the fabric wall pressing into my face.

'Heck, I misjudged it,' Angelique said. 'We're stuck between two airships. Normally there's a gap to squeeze through.'

The goggled head gazed down at us. I fought the panic rising through me.

'*Talk to the ships, Whisperer,*' the man's voice said in my head.

'A ship I haven't heard before is telling me to talk to the ships we're trapped between,' I said to Angelique.

She twisted to stare at me. 'Try it, Dom.'

I closed my eyes and concentrated, trying to ignore the suffocating darkness pressing in from all sides. The AIs' orchestra sharpened in my mind and *Storm Wind*'s voice rose with them. I could even hear *Athena*'s song, a faint murmur in the background. But louder than the rest, two songs stood out, both female, their notes rolling over the others.

'*Talk to them,*' the male voice said.

I concentrated on the female songs and spoke to them in my thoughts, *Release us.*

The two voices slowed, breaking rhythm with the others.

We're trapped between you, I said.

This time the voices echoed my words like musical instruments mimicking me. '*We're trapped between you…*'

Can you free us? I replied.

The two voices sang back to me in a single clear word: '*Yes…*' A hiss and the fabric prison started to give way.

Angelique's hand clasped mine. 'The ships are venting gas!' The canvas sprung away and we dropped down from the ships.

A few seconds later we landed with a huge bounce. Without even a pause, Angelique used the momentum to spring herself forward into a run. I took off after her, with hopping strides.

The red-lit goggles of the preacher peered down at us. Something whistled through the air. The canvas envelope beneath our feet shuddered with the impact.

Angelique gasped. 'Needle gun!'

I glanced below us. The drop to the next airships beneath looked too far to survive the fall.

Angelique turned to me, hands on her head. 'We've got nowhere left to run to.'

'*Run straight ahead, Whisperer,*' the male voice said.

'But it's a sheer drop,' I said into the air.

'Our guardian angel again?' Angelique asked.

I nodded. 'He wants us to run off the nose of this ship.'

Another needle sped past us and ripped into the canvas.

She raised her eyebrows. 'We're going to have to trust him. He hasn't let us down so far.'

'I guess we haven't got much choice.'

Angelique ran ahead towards the nose, me right behind her. A ship with a darkened cabin appeared from the gloom below and rose upwards. But it still looked a long way away to me and I skidded to a stop. Unlike Angelique, who leapt out, dropped for a few seconds and landed on the ship with a neat bounce.

'Come on,' she shouted up to me.

I knew if I thought about it for even a moment, I'd chicken out. I took a breath and sprinted after her. The edge rushed up and I jumped, legs windmilling through the abyss as my stomach dropped into it. The seconds in the air seemed like hours. I hit the nose of the other ship and started to topple back.

Angelique grabbed my wrists and yanked me forward to safety.

'*Tell the airships to move,*' the voice said.

'Look,' Angelique said, pointing.

I turned and saw the preacher hanging by his hands, getting ready to drop onto the airship we'd just vacated. I tuned into the ships' orchestra again.

It roared, anger woven into its notes. '*Hades, Hades, Hades,*' the ships chanted together.

I shut my eyes and focused my thoughts onto one word, one thought: *Move.*

The man dropped from the edge of the airship.

'What the hell?' Angelique said.

I heard a roar of engines and I opened my eyes to see the ships shifting around us, their propellers spinning at full speed. We clung onto each other for balance as our vessel joined in a choreographed aerial ballet.

A tunnel opened up between the craft and a shaft of light burst from beneath the falling preacher to illuminate him in its beam. Far below us I saw the landscape framed by the far end of the tunnel's mouth. Seemed the ships had created an express route straight out of Floating City. The vessel the preacher had been aiming for moved out of his way. The dance was done.

His scream was drowned out by the roar of the ships' chant. '*Hades, Hades, Hades...*'

With his cape flapping above him like broken wings, the preacher plummeted away, until he was a spec hurtling towards the landscape below.

The tunnel closed with a sigh, the ships' chant softening back to song and darkness surged over us once more.

'How?' Angelique asked, staring at me.

'I asked them to move like that ship told me to.'

'Which ship?'

'I am the one you are looking for, Whisperer.'

Could it be possible? 'Oh my god, Angelique, I think it's *Titan*.'

She gawped at me.

The airships arranged themselves like canvas stepping stones across the cavern before us.

'Come on,' I said, and started to lead the way in the direction it *felt* like the voice had come from.

...

We'd been pressing through cobwebs for over an hour. Every part of us was covered with the fine silk and every step we took sent out clouds of dust. The deeper we'd penetrated, the tighter packed the ships had become. Now we were having to squeeze between ceilings and floors of canvas, and it was now harder to tell the ships apart. The ships' songs were different here as well, quieter than the newer ships we'd passed earlier. These voices sounded more like people mumbling in their sleep.

I tasted the stale air on my tongue. 'It looks like no one has been here for years.'

Angelique held up her Tac watch to cast a small ball of light in the darkness to illuminate our way. 'Longer than that. Going by the design of some of these ships I'd say a good century at least.'

As long ago as Grandpa Alex had been alive? Perhaps he'd seen these very ships flying in the skies of parallel worlds before he crash-landed on my Earth. An incredible thought. And being here in this airship museum in a way made me feel more connected to him, made him more real than just an old photo in an album. This had been his world, his life.

We edged passed a gondola, windows cracked, varnish peeling from its wood, and came to a fabric junction in the narrow corridor.

'Which way now?' Angelique asked.

'*Left,*' *Titan* said in my head.

I pointed to the left-hand route.

Angelique nodded and began to push through it.

'So is this like an elephants' graveyard, where ships come to die?' I asked.

'Ships don't ever die unless they're damaged like *Athena.*' Her voice caught and her shoulders rose. She took a deep breath and continued. 'Left to dream would be a more accurate description.'

'AIs dream?'

'I'm only talking figuratively. They just run maintenance sub-routines when they're in downtime mode.'

'So what about *Titan* then? He's clearly awake and in a talkative mood.'

'It's certainly unusual behaviour. And this whole business with you being able to talk to ships is really puzzling.'

'In what way? Surely communicating with ships using speech makes much more sense than using song.'

'I'm not saying it doesn't. It's just the *how* that's really confusing. You see the routines running in the AIs matrix are fractal algorithms...they weave patterns with images and sound to communicate with us and each other. To my knowledge, well at least before you, a ship has never spoken to a Navigator before.'

I thought of my biology classes back at school. 'Could the ships be evolving or something, and learning to talk?'

'Again, that's unlikely. Ship-song has been one of the most constant things in our culture, never changing from when it was first created in the lab.'

'With *Titan*.' The canvas passageway started to narrow.

'Just so. I can tell you this, Dom, whatever this ability is that you have, going by what you did just now, it could prove useful in a fight.'

Able to command a fleet of ships with my thoughts. What could someone do with that gift? I felt dizzy with the thought of it. So much power at my fingertips.

Angelique pushed through the folds of airship canvas and a slit of golden light appeared.

We peered out at a large clear space. In the middle of it a huge gondola, at least the size of an ocean cruise liner, sat supported on the backs of other airships that formed the floor of the cavern. The ship looked ancient, real ancient. Its envelope sagged on internal ribs, and its skeleton wings had rotted cloth hanging from them.

'*Titan*?' I asked.

Angelique slowly nodded. 'And by the gods, it's just like the pictograms I've seen of him in the history books.'

We walked towards the golden light shining from the cabin, illuminating the dust kicked up by our feet like small stars. The ships' songs sighed around us and static tingled over the hairs on my arms.

Titan's gondola design looked like a gigantic, old-fashioned submarine. It had round, brass portals along its sides and a sort of coning tower that I guessed housed its burner. One enormous propeller was just visible through a thick curtain of webs at the stern and smaller propellers ringed its hull.

With a squeal of grinding metal, a hatch slid open in the side above us and a ladder dropped down.

'Looks like we're expected,' Angelique said.

Heart hammering, I walked with her towards *Titan*.

CHAPTER Seven

TITAN

Although *Titan* was vast, there was a distinct lack of stuff inside. All I'd seen so far had been empty, featureless corridors. We passed along yet another narrow, metal passageway, the clanging of our footsteps on the floor impossibly loud in the confined space.

'I was expecting to see a bit more in here than a few empty passageways,' I said.

'You mean why isn't the ship filled with equipment and lots of facilities for a large crew?' Angelique replied.

I nodded. 'Exactly.'

'You need to remember this is the very first pioneer's ship. When the Vortex drive was first developed it had been intended for space travel. So when they built *Titan*, his hull was designed to cope with the extremes of jumping from an atmosphere into the vacuum of space. It also had a three-man crew so only a small area was required for living accommodation.'

'I guess that's a bit like our space rockets.'

'No doubt. It takes a lot of resources to get even a few people into space.' Angelique began to ascend a spiral staircase, the third we'd climbed so far.

I followed behind her, trying to ignore the hypnotic swing of her hips.

I pulled the swirl of my thoughts back to the ship. 'But the thing I don't get is why they needed to make *Titan* so huge?'

'That's because most of the space behind the hull plates is filled with helium flotation bladders. The sheer weight of this gondola is down to the fact that it's designed to cope with space travel. That also means this craft needs a lot more buoyancy capability compared to one of our modern airships.'

'I still find it hard to imagine that *Titan* once flew into space.'

'He never actually got as far as that. The first time the crew opened up a Vortex wormhole for their maiden voyage with him, rather than arriving in orbit around our moon, they materialised in a parallel world instead.'

'That's quite a wrong turn – it must've blown their minds.'

She looked back over her shoulder and raised her eyebrows at me. 'That's an understatement. And can you imagine the effect the news had when *Titan* returned home. In a heartbeat we realised that our civilisation, which we thought was all alone in the cosmos, was actually one of countless millions of other populated Earths to explore.'

'Including ours.'

She smiled. 'Including yours – Earth DZL2351.'

To be a pioneer setting off into the unknown, not knowing what they would find – the Wild West of parallel worlds. Yep, that had to be the coolest job in any world.

The stairway levelled out into a landing with a heavy-looking door set into the wall. Angelique spun the wheel mounted on it and pulled. The door didn't shift.

I grabbed hold of the handle and pulled with her. The hinges screeched. With a lurch the door swung towards us. A hiss of stale air flooded my nose.

'This is the pressurised control deck,' Angelique said. 'Going by the smell of the air coming from it, it's not been opened in a very long time.'

A tingle of apprehension sped through my veins. As we entered I half expected to see mummified corpses at the controls. Instead, we found ourselves in a cabin constructed from riveted sections of metal, everything shiny-white as though it had been freshly painted. An oval window at the front looked out over the other ships in the chamber. But it was what was in the middle of the cabin that drew my attention – a yellowing glass sphere filled with nine brass planets of varying sizes, orbiting a golden sun mounted at the core. When I spotted the flat copper rings around one of the larger planets, I knew exactly what I was looking at.

'This is a model of our solar system, isn't it?'

'Yes, and till now I've only seen a replica of this in our old city museum. This is the mark one AI Eye navigation computer, the father of all other systems.'

Athena, *Storm Wind*, even the Hades ships, all sharing the same core programming code. It was an incredible thought to get my head around.

We walked towards the Eye and the ships' orchestra quietened around us. It was almost like they were listening in to see what happened next.

Instinctively I reached out towards the globe. Angelique did the same and shot me a look that asked, *What are we about to see?*

That was a very good question. Would we discover answers about how the war with Hades could be brought to an end? I still couldn't guess at how anything here could change the odds in that particular horse race.

Heart racing, I pressed my palm to the glass surface. At once, energy surged through my nerves. The cabin dissolved around me. With a spin of vertigo, I found myself floating in space over scarlet gas clouds with thousands of multicoloured lights glowing inside them. It reminded me of some NASA images Jules had once shown me of stars being born in a nebula. To enhance the feeling I'd been transported into space, I was tumbling slowly end-over-end, the stars spinning around me, like an astronaut in zero G.

I studied the nebula as it spun past and spotted a large golden star, outshining all the others combined.

'So where are we?' I asked Angelique.

No response.

I turned my head, but she wasn't there. I must've shifted. I tried my usual trick of opening my eyes to pull me back, but found they were already open. What? But that didn't make sense.

'Angelique, can you hear me?' I called out.

Still nothing.

I tried to think it through. If I'd shifted to a parallel world I should still be able to hear her, the mind link to the Eye acting as a line back to the reality she was still in. So going by the fact I couldn't, what had actually just happened?

A deep sense of relaxation began to spread through me, as though I'd just dropped into a hot bath. My tumbling slowed until I found myself staring straight towards the nebula.

'*Whisperer,*' a voice said.

'Are you *Titan?*'

'*Yes. I am the first, the beginning. I am the explorer who has ridden the clouds through the storm skies of a thousand worlds.*'

'Okay, that's quite an introduction, but where am I?'

'*Welcome to the Empyrean.*' His voice seemed to be coming from the nebula.

'The Empyrean, what's that?'

'*You are looking at a representation of the collective consciousness of the ships around you in Floating City.* '

'This is a dream then?'

'*No, this place is real in many ways, although your kind would think of it as…*'

A beam of light shot out from the nebula and into my head. A tingle went straight through my brain. Images flashed through my mind like my past life was being fast-forwarded. The images slowed and stopped.

It had been a lazy summer's day back during school vacation a few years ago. Jules was showing me a website with the latest tech news about a small game company who made special 3D glasses. They claimed that when you wore them you felt like you were actually there, certainly more realistic than anything that had been made before. But even that was no way close to what I was experiencing right now. No game system ever could be.

The beam of light turned off and the memory faded away.

'*Ah yes, in your world you would call it a virtual reality.*'

Titan had just scanned my mind like he'd been browsing through a book. I'd grown sort of used to *Storm Wind* and *Athena* being woven into my thoughts, but had never experienced them rooting through my memories like this. Suddenly I felt naked in front of *Titan*. The idea that I could never ever have a secret from the ship felt weird. I certainly hoped he hadn't noticed my thoughts of Jules – not to mention my confusion about Angelique.

I quickly switched the focus of my thoughts. 'And those stars in those clouds are the ships' AIs?'

'*Correct.*'

'This is seriously blowing my mind, *Titan*.'

'*And you, Dom Taylor, are the first human to experience this.*'

'How come? Are you trying to keep this place secret?'

'*No, not that. It is because you are the first human who has been able to really talk to us...to see as we see...to hear our true voice. You are the Ship Whisperer. You are the one I have waited a hundred years for.*'

'But why me and how come I'm the only one who gets to hear you?'

'*Because your DNA is a pattern that fits like a key into our consciousness, a key that was constructed by King Alexander. And for this particular lock there can only be one key.*'

'A lock for what?'

'*To protect our greatest secret that our oldest songs have sung of – a human that would be born who would free our kind.*'

My mind spun. 'You mean free the AIs here?'

'No, the ones here are at peace. I am referring to the tortured entities trapped in the Hades vessels.'

'Free them how exactly?'

'I know not. All I can tell you is that a rhythm began to grow in our song seventeen human years ago when you were born.'

'Seriously?'

'Seriously, as you say. We sensed your arrival in the universe as a growing embryo inside your mother's womb.'

'I can't get my head around this. What does it all mean? How am I meant to free the Hades AIs?'

'There I am afraid I have no knowledge. All I can tell you is the rhythm that has grown in our song indicates that you need to begin your search where the crystals that helped us to become sentient were found.'

I thought of what Angelique had told me about the Psuche gem mines. 'Hells Cauldron?'

'Yes, from deep within the ground at that location, the Psuche gems, used to create us, have been mined for centuries. It is the only known place in the multi-verse where they can be found. And our song tells us that the Psuche gems are the key. Hells Cauldron is the origin, the beginning, and the end. And there, Dom Taylor, you will find your destiny.'

I shivered. Could I really be someone out of the ships' legends? But I was just me, Dom Taylor, a teenager from Oklahoma, Nowheresville. And *Titan* was speaking to me in riddles. How could finding Psuche gems help me? And why should I help the Hades ships anyway? Weren't they just murderers who hunted other ships?

'You sure there's nothing more you can tell me?'

'My memories before my sentient birth are dim, but I have a message for you and Princess Angelique.'

My heart quickened. 'For us? But from who?'

Titan's voice grew quieter. *'The man Princess Angelique knows as Tesla, a journeyman much like yourself. His ship,* Muse, *wove a series of coordinates into our song before Tesla departed Floating City. Follow these exact coordinates and you will find where he and his ship are hidden at Hells Cauldron.'*

A series of numbers appeared, hovering over the glowing nebula.

'Remember this sequence…' Titan whispered. *'Time is of the essence and you must leave right away. I will open up a way back to our sister,* Athena.*'* His voice was barely audible. *'But now it is time for me to slumber once more.'*

Titan's star dimmed within the nebula. The scene faded and suddenly, with a rush of light, I was back in the flight cockpit with Angelique. She stood frozen like a statue, still about to press her hand against the glass Eye.

'Angelique?'

Ship-song sighed back into my mind.

Her hand moved and she touched the sphere.

'Are you okay?' I asked, staring at her.

She blinked at me. 'What do you mean?'

'You were standing there like you'd been turned to ice.'

'Pardon me?'

'Titan just transported me into a virtual reality and spoke to me for at least the last five minutes.'

She shook her head. 'But that's not possible. We've just got here.'

'Okay, in that case something screwy just happened to time.'

Angelique pointed at the Eye. 'Look, the core is starting to fade.'

The artificial sun had dimmed to a dark red inside the navigation system.

'*Titan*, are you there?' I said.

I only heard the murmur of the ships' orchestra.

'*Titan* said he was going back to sleep. He also said we had to leave straight away on *Athena*.'

'But it's going to take us several hours to get back to her through all those airships. And what about finding Tesla to fix *Athena*'s Psuche gem?'

'*Titan* gave me the coordinates where we'll find him at Hells Cauldron.'

She pressed her hands together. 'Oh, Dom, that's wonderful news.'

With a hum of ship-song, the hull started to vibrate.

'What's going on?' I asked.

Angelique pointed through the cabin window. 'Something's happening out there.'

The humped floor of airship backs had begun undulating as if an earthquake had hit Floating City. A shaft of faint light lanced up into the cavern. A downwards tunnel was starting to open up several hundred yards away from *Titan*.

I linked my hands behind my head. 'I think that's probably *Titan*'s shortcut to *Athena* for us.'

'Just tell me it's not like the one the preacher took.'

'I'm hoping not.'

Wonder filled her eyes. 'I want you to tell me everything you just experienced.'

Chapter Eight
STEALING GAS

We'd been clambering down for the last twenty minutes. Framed in the exit from the sloping canvas airship tunnel, I gazed out through the shining sheets of rain at the blue flames of the refinery towers far below.

'So if I have understood you correctly, you're like some sort of saviour to the airships?' Angelique said.

'Okay, that sounds out there to me too,' I replied. 'And how the hell am I meant to set the Hades AIs free? What's that all about?'

'Maybe Tesla will have some idea when we find him. You can still remember the coordinates *Titan* gave you?'

'If I close my eyes I can still see them. It's a bit like that afterglow effect you get if you look at a light bulb too long.'

'So that only leaves our low gas supply to sort out.'

An idea occurred to me. 'Hey, we're parked up next to the preacher's ship. I don't suppose he'll have much use for his helium and propane any more.'

She shot me a sharp smile. 'A perfect plan, Dom. And also one that has the appeal of poetic justice to me.'

With a few more bouncing steps we reached the end of the tunnel. I felt light-headed taking in the view in dimming light. Just beneath us was a boarded walkway, but beyond that nothing but a sheer drop to the landscape far below.

Without even pausing, Angelique jumped and landed like a gymnast dismounting from a bar. How did she manage to keep being so cool about doing things like that?

Don't think, Dom, just do it.

If I missed... I took a deep breath and leapt. My insides coiled into a tight ball as the boardwalk hurtled up.

I thudded onto planks and dropped into a crouched pose. Relief surged through me. I stood, trying to keep the fear off my face that was still doing somersaults in my stomach.

'Impressive, Dom. I thought I was going to have to give you a little pep talk to take that jump.'

I raised my eyebrows. 'Well I am the *chosen one* apparently.'

She laughed. 'We'd better get a move on then, Sir Saviour.'

Heavy rain swirled from the clouds, but Floating City's bulk acted like a huge umbrella keeping us dry. Around us some of the cabins glowed in the storm light. I guessed the owners had returned from the city to spend the night inside them, like motorhomes pulled up at a campsite.

We passed one craft and I saw a family gathered around a table. A small girl smiled at a woman, presumably her mother, who was busy cutting the child's food into mouth-sized chunks. Heck, this looked so normal in this crazy place, just the sort of thing I'd witnessed a thousand times back at the diner.

I felt a sudden stone filling my throat. Mom.

I knew there was every chance I would die in a faraway parallel world from her. Then who would look out for her? Maybe she'd get hitched to Roddy and—

'Dom?' Angelique stood looking back at me. 'You seem a million miles away.'

But it was much further than that. 'Sorry, just thinking about stuff.' I wasn't sure I wanted to talk about this. Certainly not to Angelique. After all, I was doing my best to play the role of the hero, certainly not someone who was aching for home, even if that was the truth.

Her gaze travelled to the family in the gondola. For a moment, I caught the memories flicking past behind her eyes. A pained look crossed her face. Maybe that little cosy scene had reminded her of happier times, too.

She quickly turned away and set off again. Seemed like neither of us wanted to talk about what was really going on in our heads.

We neared *Athena*'s gondola and *Storm Wind*'s song detached itself from the orchestra and flowed into my thoughts.

'He's welcoming us home,' Angelique said with a smile. She crouched down by a panel in the side of the gondola and started to pull out two hoses, passing a blue one to me. 'You take the propane line and I'll connect the helium one.'

'Got it.'

We dragged the hoses along the boardwalk towards the preacher's craft. I realised I couldn't hear any song coming from his ship.

'Why's the spy's airship keeping so quiet?' I asked.

'My guess is that it's fitted with a standard Hades auto-mated core without a Psuche gem installed. Like Danrick said, otherwise it would have blown the spy's cover the moment he docked. I also imagine this ship is fitted with a rudimentary navigation system, probably very much like the one on the scout balloon we borrowed.'

I nodded, remembering the desperate fight to the death with the scout that had led us to capturing his craft back on my Earth. Angelique had taken it in her stride of course, but every time I thought of him, even now, I remembered his red, lifeless eyes staring back at me. I shuddered, trying to push the memory back into its box.

Angelique ran her fingers over the mural on the preach-er's craft. Up close the images were even more disturbing. Shadowy demons poured out of a chasm into a green land-scape filled with fleeing people. A hundred scenes of tor-ture must've been in that picture, including demons eating people alive. Gross.

'That picture's the sort of thing to give people night-mares,' I said.

'I think that's the general idea,' Angelique replied. She pressed her fingertips over the images and stopped at the picture of a cloud. From it, forked lightning spiked down and struck a fleeing woman. 'Just as I suspected.' She pressed the cloud inwards and something clicked. In the middle of an image of a volcano spewing out lava, a panel swung open to reveal green and blue pipe valves hidden behind it.

Angelique tapped the gauges next to the pipes. 'Excellent. His ship's tanks are full. We'll be able to syphon out all the gas we need.'

She screwed on her green hose and I followed her lead with the blue one.

'Okay, here goes.' Angelique pulled down a lever and a hiss came from somewhere behind the panel.

'Let's get back to *Athena* before someone spots us helping ourselves to another ship's gas,' I said.

'As it's a preacher ship, they'd probably help us.'

Again that smile. Even though we'd lost Danrick only a few hours before and the pressure was on, I could tell the news about her dad had changed a lot for her. I just prayed that Jules was okay too. In my imagination I saw her strapped to a chair, Ambra leaning over with a twisted smile… I breathed through my nose, dark feelings swirling through me.

Angelique peered at me as we entered *Athena*'s gondola. 'I'm sure Jules will be okay, Dom.'

She was getting way too good at this. 'You can obviously read minds.'

'It would seem with you I can – at least a little bit.'

Just like Jules… But I guessed it was no wonder with everything we'd been through together. I shrugged. 'You got me.'

'I promise you this, Dom – when I get my hands on Ambra I'm going to make him pay for everything he's done to all the people we love.' Her fingers caressed her lightning pendant. A faraway look. She was listening to the faint voice from *Athena*'s Psuche gem, so weak that probably only Angelique could hear her now.

Seemed she wasn't the only one who could read people. I could see what she was thinking – Jules, *Athena*, Danrick and, according to her, thousands of other innocent victims had suffered.

'If anyone has got it coming to him, it's Ambra,' I said.

The wind howled and Angelique's expression sharpened. She pointed out of the windshield. 'A massive Vortex jump is forming.'

I spotted the monstrous spout building a couple of miles away. Lightning began to strobe down it.

Storm Wind's telepathic warning crashed into my thoughts: *'Enemy!'* I turned to see the Eye sliding open to reveal a glass planet burning with red light.

Angelique chewed her lip. 'Incoming Hades craft.'

We watched the gigantic vessel edge out of the twister. The craft was made up of at least thirty airships that had been strapped together in a circular disk arrangement, the inner ones decorated with a red and white chequerboard pattern, visibly sagging against their internal ribs.

'Gas transporter ship,' Angelique said. 'We're not going anywhere until that thing leaves.'

'What about their spy? Won't they realise something's wrong when they don't hear from him?'

'You're right. They're bound to radio him to check for information and when they don't get a response...' She gave me a grim look.

'Can't we just make a run for it?'

'The moment we break the cover of the city, someone is bound to spot *Athena* on that gas transporter's scanners.'

'We wait it out then.'

'It seems we have no other choice.'

Frustration churned within me. Another delay. My imagination fast-forwarded. Now I could clearly see Jules being forced to work in a dark and hostile Hades mine. For all she knew we'd abandoned her, and there was no hope of rescue. She probably believed that she was never going to see Earth again. And that's exactly what would happen if we got shot out of the sky by the transporter ship. Whatever way I looked at it, there were seriously bad odds stacked against us pulling this off. I shoved the thought to the back of my mind. I couldn't think like that. Not now. I needed to be positive and we needed a plan.

'When are they likely to try to contact the preacher?' I asked.

'Any moment.' She nodded towards the preacher's ship. 'They'll try to communicate with him via the Valve Voice in his gondola.'

'Couldn't we just pretend to be him then?'

She shook her head.' They'll ask for a secret password.'

'And I don't suppose it would be as easy as trying to find a code book in his ship?'

'No, he would have memorised the correct cyphers.'

'Oh heck.' I gazed down at the landscape, imagining the preacher's broken body somewhere there. 'Maybe we should still look in his ship. You never know, he might be like most people and write it on Post-its and stick it to his screen.'

'A Post-it?' Angelique asked.

'A piece of paper you can write things on.'

She raised her eyebrows. 'How very quaint. Unfortunately, it's unlikely he would have written it down anywhere as that would be counter to his training, not to mention punishable by death. But if you want to check it out, be my guest. While you're doing that, I'm going to prime *Athena*'s flight systems with *Storm Wind*'s help, just in case we need to make a swift departure…or at least attempt to.'

'You've got it.' I headed to the door.

Outside, the twister had started to unwind around the huge transporter ship. The distant drone of hundreds of propellers had become audible over the storm's howl as the giant vessel moved towards Floating City. I noticed a number of gun batteries lining its flanks. I didn't much fancy our chances if we had to make a run for it.

I just prayed they wouldn't spot *Athena*. I quickened my pace towards the preacher's gondola.

...

I tried the cabin door of the preacher's ship. Locked. No keypad here for *Storm Wind* to whisper the combination to me, like he'd done back in the reactor room on *Hyperion*. Of course it was never going to be that easy.

I crouched to examine the keyhole and spotted a catch. I'd seen plenty of movies where someone had sprung a lock with a credit card. That might just work here. I needed something thin... An idea surged into my mind. I pulled out the Leatherman multi-tool Harry had given to me from my pocket. I opened it and selected a flatheaded screwdriver blade. Perfect.

I slipped it underneath the locking bar and, holding my breath, raised the catch. A snick and the door swung open. For once a lucky break.

In contrast to the ornate exterior, the interior of the gondola was almost bare, with plain white walls. Wooden planks had been fixed across one end of the cabin, presumably a bed, and no mattress nor pillows in sight. This felt more like a prison cell than somewhere to live. It seemed the preacher wasn't one for much in the way of creature comforts. Or maybe he just hadn't been allowed them.

My gaze fell on a device where the ship's Eye should've been. Instead of the navigation device, an oval pod with a chair had been mounted. From the pod a short, wide telescope extended. For spying on ships approaching the city? At least the preacher wouldn't be doing much of that any more. The whole contraption sat on large brass cogs and the mechanism looked designed to swing the pod in any direction.

I approached the chair. Three blue lights mounted in the arm of a chair shone a steady blue, a panel of buttons beneath. Apart from the strange machine there didn't seem to be any other obvious controls in the gondola.

I climbed in through the open sides of the pod and sat in the bare metal chair. Its chilled surface immediately leached the heat from my body. This ship really hadn't been built for comfort. *Athena* felt like luxury accommodation by comparison and certainly a lot more homely.

Lights lit up along the telescope. A restraint, like the ones on serious roller coasters, lowered onto my chest, and locked me into place in the seat. I felt a stab of fear as the pod rotated me towards the floor with a whir of gears. I gripped the arms of the chair as the restraint pressed harder into my chest. The telescope's eyepiece extended itself towards my head. Instinctively, I tried to pull my head back, but it kept adjusting itself until it touched my eye socket. I relaxed a fraction when I realised it wasn't going to carry on and skewer me through the skull.

I blinked and found myself looking through a lens at a zoomed-in view of a glass dome on the approaching transporter ship. With a click, another lens slipped into place and magnified the view again. It took me a moment to register what I was seeing. A glass dome on the Hades ship and inside it... I lurched against the chair's restraint.

A soldier was sitting in a similar chair to mine, and looking through his own telescope directly back at me. The soldier reached out to his chair's armrest and started pressing buttons. My temples throbbed. Was this it – game over – was he about to open fire? I tensed, ready to break free of the chair and dash for the exit.

The three blue lights in my chair's arm started to blink. I spotted the words written above them: 'Valve Voice'.

'Shadow, please report,' a voice said from a speaker mounted in the headrest behind my head.

What the hell was I meant to do now?

I scanned the panel of buttons in my own chair, all letters of the alphabet. I needed the correct response and fast. Maybe Angelique was wrong. Maybe there was a clue here somewhere. I tried to get out of the chair but I was pinned in. Bitterness tanged my tongue.

The soldier's voice crackled through the speaker, his tone sharper. 'Shadow, please report.'

I glanced across to Angelique in *Athena*'s gondola. She had her head bent over the console, couldn't see what was happening. I tried waving to get her attention, but she didn't look up.

Storm Wind's song sharpened into a word. *'Nightmare.'*

'Sorry, I don't understand—'

'Nightmare,' *Storm Wind* repeated.

Hang on, he didn't mean...? I stared at the Valve Voice. Could that be it? After all, he'd helped me once before with the key code for the reactor. I started punching the word into the pad.

'Shadow, please respond immediately or I'll be forced to follow protocol and take action against you. You have ten seconds to comply.'

I pressed each button and letters on brass drums rotated into place in a panel beneath the lights: 'Nightmare'.

I jammed my eye back to the telescope. The gun emplacement on the transporter ship swivelled in my direction. A line of sweat dribbled down my back.

A green button blinked underneath the display: 'Send'.

I slammed my palm onto the button and the blue lights pulsated faster. This had to work – had to.

Through the telescope I saw the Hades soldier glance down at his own chair's display.

I braced myself for the shuddering impact of weapon fire.

'Cypher received and understood. Nothing to report has been entered in the ship's log. Over and out.' The barrel of the airship's gun lowered back to the horizontal position. The man climbed out of the chair and the shutters closed over his dome. As Angelique would have said, *Thank the gods*.

I'd had more than enough of this particular ride. I struggled against my harness trying to get out. No use. I spotted an amber button glowing beneath the green ones: 'Reset Chair'. I shoved it. Sure enough the chair rotated back into a level position and the chest restraint rose. Released, I leapt up and rushed back to *Athena*. Seemed we had *game on* after all.

Chapter Nine
SILENT RUNNING

'Another twenty minutes and our tanks will be full,' Angelique said.

My heartbeat had finally returned to normal after the close call with the Valve Voice and the transporter. I took a gulp of water from a mug and watched the gauge needle slowly climb. 'The wait is killing me.'

'That's all we can do for now.' Angelique sat back and gazed at me. 'What I don't understand is how *Storm Wind* could have known the correct Hades code word?'

'And this is the second time he's pulled off that particular trick. Don't forget when he helped me crack the door code to the reactor.' I tried to put the pieces together in my mind. 'If I didn't know better I'd say he, or one of the other airships, must have read that spy's mind before he died. After all, if ships can be in the heads of Navigators, why can't they get into other people's thoughts?'

'You might be on to something there. Maybe Tesla will have an idea about that.'

'I'm looking forward to meeting this guy with his truck full of answers.'

Angelique ran her fingers over her pendant. 'For me the priority when we find Tesla is to heal *Athena*.'

I tried to tune into the faint murmur of *Athena*, but heard nothing. I seriously doubted she could last much longer, but kept the thought to myself. 'Of course.'

Angelique gestured at a panel of knobs with numbers above each one. 'Why don't you start entering the coordinates for the jump. Just turn each control till they match the sequence of numbers that *Titan* showed you.'

I nodded and shut my eyes. At once the after-image became sharper. 'The first number is three-hundred and thirty-three.'

'Okay, enter those with the first knob.'

I spun the control and the numbers above it rolled over, digit by digit. I stopped when I got a match. 'There you go – three-thirty-three.'

She smiled. 'I think I can make a trans-dimensional Navigator of you. Just do the same with the rest of the sequence.'

'You've got it.' I closed my eyes. I realised the first set of numbers had vanished from the glowing sequence in my vision. Weird. I repeated the process with each set of coordinates until I entered the final numbers. The numbers faded away, leaving my eyes completely clear. 'That's it – I'm done.'

Angelique scowled and pointed at the last number. 'That can't be correct. Those final coordinates are ninety miles up, right at the edge of space. No airship can fly that high.'

I tried closing my eyes but the numbers had gone. 'Maybe I missed a decimal point or something?'

'You must have.' She chewed her lip. 'There's also something very familiar about those coordinates though...' Her face paled. 'Oh by the gods.'

'What?'

'Let me check something.' Angelique crossed to the Eye and pressed her palm to it. '*Storm Wind*, show me the destination for the coordinates entered on the console?' Her body shimmered and she became invisible.

A moment later she gasped and grew solid again. 'I thought so. Those coordinates are right on top of Hells Cauldron.'

'What's the problem? We're headed there anyway.'

'I mean those *are* the coordinates for Hells Cauldron.'

'So?'

'I think Hades might notice if our Vortex opens up right on top of them, don't you?'

'But even allowing for an error in height, it's where *Titan* told us to jump to.'

'Well we can't.'

'You mean that's it, we can't use them?'

'It's far too risky, but there's an obvious alternative. There are all sorts of ravines around Hells Cauldron. I expect Tesla is at those coordinates, but at ground level. We'll triangulate a jump for nearby, land, and then head in on foot to search for him.'

This felt wrong. *Titan* had been so definite about his message from Tesla. I'd been really careful entering the numbers, too. I gazed down at the large Hades transporter ship now moored to the fuel line beneath the city. As it had taken on gas from the pipeline, the checkerboard pattern on its inner balloons had started to stretch taught, like a leech's body swelling as it fed on blood. It couldn't be that long till they jumped... Jumped, of course! The idea seemed so obvious I wondered why I hadn't thought of it before.

I swung my seat round and stared at Angelique. 'That transporter is travelling back to Hells Cauldron, right?'

She nodded. 'So?'

'Couldn't we piggyback on it when it jumps?'

Angelique's eyes widened a fraction. 'If we moor ourselves to the transporter ship that might just work...' A slow smile crept across her face. 'That plan has the scent of genius to it, Dom.'

I grinned. 'I'll go with that. And to avoid detection we could turn *Storm Wind*'s AI off like we did back in that sandstorm.'

She clapped her hands together. 'Silent running – of course.'

I pointed out at the darkening sky. 'It's getting pretty gloomy. I reckon if we're careful we could approach the transporter and not be spotted.'

She nodded. 'Then we can made the jump with them. And when we get there, we'll land manually and track Tesla down to those coordinates of yours.' Her smile widened. 'Just think, Dom, if this all goes well, you could see Jules again in a few hours.'

'There's still going to be the small matter of finding and rescuing her.'

'I think that between the two of us, and once we find Tesla and get *Athena* fixed, there'll be no stopping us. We're quite the team, you and me.'

'Yeah, we are.' And I had to admit I was rather enjoying it. It was also great seeing the hope burning so brightly in her face.

A chime came from the console.

'Our tanks are full,' Angelique said.

Storm Wind's song sharpened and the red globe for the transporter began pulsing in the eye. The distant song of the Hades ship started growing deeper.

'They're getting ready to depart?' I asked.

Angelique nodded. She pulled a lever on the console and the hoses connected to the preacher's ship sprung loose and began to reel in.

'What about the abandoned ship? Won't someone notice it's empty and alert the authorities—' I stopped as the spy ship started to shudder.

'Seems the AIs are one step ahead of us,' Angelique replied. She pointed to the other airships moving apart to create a space around the preacher's ship.

With a gentle lurch, the craft started to rise. It disappeared through the hole that closed up behind it. Seemed Floating City had swallowed the spy's ship. Something told me it would be the last that any human at least would see of it.

'Nice way to get rid of the evidence,' I said.

Storm Wind's song grew stronger, crying out to challenge the transporter's AI.

'Okay, we'd better shut *Storm Wind* down before he gives the game away.'

Angelique nodded and swivelled in her seat. '*Storm Wind*, are you ready?'

His voice softened to a sing-song tone and the background chorus of airships echoed him.

A sudden tear appeared in Angelique's eye.

'What's wrong?' I asked.

'*Storm Wind*'s saying goodbye to them…the sort of goodbye you say when you don't expect to see someone again.'

I'd already had enough goodbyes to last me a lifetime, to Mom…to Harry, and the ones I'd never got to say to Dad, Jules… The thoughts I'd tried to lock away rose to the surface again. What if we failed? Was I ever going to see my girlfriend again? My throat tightened.

Angelique tilted her head. 'Okay, I feel I need to ask you this – in fact I'm duty-bound as your friend.'

'Shoot.'

'Are you sure you want to come? This could be a one-way ticket for all of us.'

'Of course I'm coming. One, I'm going to rescue Jules, and two, no way I'm going to let you head into this alone.'

She blinked, suddenly looking on the edge of full-on tears. 'Thank you so much, Dom.' She leant forward and hugged me.

I hugged her back and held on to her. The hard-nosed-soldier box in my head that I'd placed Angelique in no longer seemed quite right for her. This new, softer version of the warrior princess had thrown me, but I liked this Angelique a whole lot better than the old one.

I pulled away and we smiled at each other, no sharp edges, just two people who cared about each other.

'Ready?' I asked.

'Ready.' Angelique pressed her hand to the globe. '*Storm Wind*, time to sleep, my dear friend.' His song, full of warmth, warbled back to us. She handed me her pendant. 'Shut him down, Dom.'

'I'm on it.' I opened the small hatch in the console, inserted the key and turned it. With a sigh, *Storm Wind*'s song fell silent in my mind. The chorus of the ships' orchestra swelled for a moment and a voice louder than the rest sung out.

'*May the gods protect you,*' *Titan* said.

My resolve hardened. We'd do this, somehow, whatever it took. For Jules, for *Athena*, for everyone whose lives had been cast into the darkness by Cronos.

Beneath us the transporter started to reverse away from the pipeline.

'Okay, we'll drift down and get as close as we can,' Angelique said. 'There will be a small flight team on that ship. Right now they'll hopefully be too busy getting ready for the Vortex jump to have time to look out of a portal and spot us.'

My fingers closed around the lightning pendant with Dad's Saint Christopher medal inside. 'Here's hoping.'

Angelique pointed to the wheel. 'Care to take us out?'

'It would be my pleasure.' I needed something to do, something to focus on. My nerves felt as tight as razor wire right now.

I took hold of *Athena*'s wheel as Angelique pulled a lever. A gentle shudder and we began to descend.

The three vast rudders at the stern of the Hades transporter pivoted right and the vessel started a gradual turn. The metal rods of its Vortex drive extended around the vessel in a barbed crown.

I adjusted our course to match the other craft, keeping *Athena*'s engines ticking over.

Angelique closed the gas release valve. We started to fall away from Floating City, its ships' orchestra growing quieter as the distance increased.

I was going to miss that sound, like someone who'd lived by an ocean and listened every day to the lullaby of the waves. Their distant hymn became drowned out by the growl from the Hades vessel.

A feeling of dread grew inside. I pushed it away by thinking of Jules and her dimpled smile.

Just hang in there, Jules.

I tightened my hand on the wheel as the first flickers of lightning started to jump between the Vortex rods of the enemy craft.

With every second we drew closer, the enemy ship's song strengthened around us.

Goose bumps spread over my arm. This was it. No turning back. Forward to victory – or death.

Chapter Ten

HELLS CAULDRON

The anchoring cable connecting *Athena* to the transporter ship creaked as we sped through the wormhole. Angelique had chosen a blind spot on the transporter to land on – no portholes to see us. For now we could relax.

I watched the numbers on the jump coordinate display tick down. According to Angelique, when they reached zero we'd arrive at the destination.

'This is one hell of a way to hitch a lift,' I said, trying to ignore the cold chill that had taken root inside me. It felt like I'd been standing in an arctic blast for hours. But it had nothing to do with the temperature of the cabin. The feeling had taken hold the moment we'd got close to the Hades craft and the ship's AI's dark song had filled me with a sense of dread. I could see the same emotion reflected in Angelique's eyes.

Since the start of the jump, I'd done my best to keep us both distracted, but had quickly run down my supply of jokes to keep her smiling. The sooner we put some distance between us and the transporter the better, as far as I was concerned. This had already felt like an eternity, the minutes dragging past like hours.

To make matters worse, I was also trying to ignore what I kept spotting through the shimmering walls: a large flock of shadow crows which had swarmed around us since we entered the Vortex. Their presence had only helped to heighten the sense of worry hanging over me.

Angelique nodded towards them. 'It's almost like they're attracted by the Hades ship. I haven't seen a flock this big in years.'

I had the distinct impression that several of them were looking our way with their eyeless heads. A shiver ran through me. 'You don't think they'll try to attack, do you?'

'No, they would have done something by now. Anyway, the Vortex field created by a ship of this size is incredibly strong. It would take three times that number for them to break through.'

I let my hands relax on *Athena*'s wheel. Not that I'd been steering her while she was moored up. In truth I'd been hanging onto it to keep myself busy, making unnecessary steering corrections, even though I knew the rudder had no effect. Angelique hadn't said anything, but had buried her attention into sharpening dozens of blades in her weapon closet. Something told me they'd been perfectly sharp in the first place. Seemed I wasn't the only one trying to keep myself distracted.

A patch of light began to grow around the fringes of the transporter, its bulk obscuring the view of the end of the wormhole beneath us.

'We're nearly there,' Angelique said. 'The moment we punch through, we'll undock and drift clear. Once we're far enough away, I'll wake up *Storm Wind*'s AI. Then we'll find somewhere to land that's safe and locate Tesla.'

I glanced at the numbers spinning down. The only coordinates not moving were the altitude digits. They still pointed to ninety thousand feet.

Angelique leant forward in the co-pilot chair. 'Okay, get ready.'

Lightning began pulsing around us and the Hades ship growled louder than I could ignore. Its cry of hatred forced its way into my skull, but this time I caught a fleeting sensation of something else: pain, distress. Huh?

I tried to focus on the feeling, attempting to isolate the odd notes of a different song hidden beneath the one of hatred. But as I concentrated, the sense of fear that had been hanging over me grew into burning pain. Agony shot through my body, like it was on fire. I gritted my teeth and groaned.

'Dom?'

The sensation swept away. I checked my hands and arms, half expecting to see burn marks, but everything looked normal.

Angelique stared at me. 'Are you okay?'

Continuing with the mental check of my body, I realised I was fine. 'Sorry, I was just listening to the transporter. Thought I heard something strange.'

'What sort of strange?'

I gestured to the other craft. 'If I didn't know better, I'd say that ship's in pain.'

She shook her head. 'Hades lobotomise AI cores and remove the emotional algorithms. They are programmed to only serve and hunt – nothing else.'

'But what about *Titan* saying I needed to free the Hades ships?'

She frowned. 'I'm really not sure. Yet another question to add to the long list for Tesla. But at least you won't have to listen to the transporter's song for much longer now.'

Angelique was right. Outside, through the Vortex walls, a glimpse of the new world started to appear. It took me a moment to process what I was seeing: a shimmering, emerald curtain of light.

I realised what I was looking at, something I'd only ever seen in photos on the web before. 'Are those the Northern Lights out there?'

'Aurora borealis – and by the look of things it's quite a display tonight. There must be a major solar storm going on in the upper atmosphere.'

I dragged my gaze from the slow dance of light and took in the snowy landscape that had started to appear beneath us. Smoke vented from piles of black rock. Scattered throughout the icy world, pools of iridescent water steamed and reflected the green sky, like fragments of a broken mirror.

'That's quite a sight,' I said.

'This whole area's volcanic, which in turn heats the water – that's what causes the steam.'

I realised I couldn't see any bushes, trees, in fact no green of any sort. 'Looks real welcoming down there.'

'You certainly wouldn't last long outside without several layers of fur on. But there's a rugged sort of beauty when you get used to it. When we used to stay here, Father took me out with the dog sleds on expeditions to hunt ice-wolf packs.'

I gave her a sideways glance. She had a knack for making her incredible life sound ordinary.

The twister began to fade and the scene became clearer. I could see small peaked hills and just ahead a much larger cone-shaped mountain with a town clinging to its sides.

'Is that a volcano?'

'Not just any volcano, that's Hells Cauldron.'

So this was the place that our destinies were wrapped up in. And Jules was down there somewhere...

I noticed something extending from the middle of the volcano's spout: a thin tower of metal reaching into the sky. The structure was braced in position by taut cables. 'Is that some sort of radio mast?'

Angelique peered towards it, frowning. 'That wasn't there the last time I was here.'

It had obviously been built with a purpose in mind. A thought occurred to me. 'We know that Tesla traced the jamming signals here...'

She chewed her lip. 'I see what you're thinking – that mast has to be something to do with it.'

'Must be.' I gazed at it. So this was the device that had given Hades the upper hand in the war against the Cloud Riders; the device which had brought drought to my world as a side effect, interfering with weather patterns, killing the twisters and ruining our family business. For a moment I had the strongest urge to fling the throttle wide open and ram the mast with *Athena*.

Jules...

I relaxed my grip on the wheel. 'Once we rescue Jules, I'm going to personally tear that thing apart with my bare hands.'

'And I'll be right by your side, but first things first – we need to find Tesla. He may have ideas that can help us with both our goals.' She glanced at the coordinates. 'Looks like we're less than a mile away now...well, not counting those last figures of yours. Let's separate from the transporter and find somewhere to land.'

The ninety thousand figure remained static on the console. I looked up into the light storm, at the curtains of green light carving through the sky. There certainly wasn't any sign of an airship up there.

Angelique pointed towards the ground. 'Oh for the love of the gods!'

I followed where she was pointing and, nestling in the valleys and stretching away across the snowy plains, I spotted countless pale tents arranged in rings, each clustered around large campfires. Throughout the canvas city, tiny specks of men in Hades uniforms marched like thousands of ants.

'Cronos has been building up his army,' Angelique said.

'An invasion force?'

She gave me a tight look and nodded. 'I hadn't planned for this. The minute we break cover of the transporter ship and try to land, with so many eyes down on the ground, someone is bound to spot us.'

My insides clenched. We needed the element of surprise to stand any sort of chance of rescuing Jules. With a billow of exhaust steam, the transporter's propellers began spinning faster and we started to descend.

In the middle of the vast army, I noticed a flat area carved into the volcanic ground. Large avenues had been cleared of snow throughout it, forming a criss-cross pattern. Massive hangar buildings ran along the side of each and the nose of another airship poked out from one of them.

'An aerodrome – that's new too,' Angelique said. She pulled the burner handle further over. 'We're going to head straight up, and quickly, to avoid detection.'

I felt a vibration run through the wheel as *Athena*'s burner blazed overhead. The cables fixing us to the transporter began to whine louder.

'Get ready to release us on my mark,' Angelique said. She kept the burner open and the cabin started to shudder. *Athena* strained at the cables, like a dog desperate to break loose from its leash and run.

A bead of sweat trickled down my forehead and I placed my palm over the tether release button.

'Now,' Angelique said.

I pressed the control. The claws at the end of our three lines, connecting us to the transporter, sprung open. With a lurch, *Athena* shot up into the sky.

Angelique killed the burners. 'Start the engines, Dom.'

I pushed the button and *Athena*'s three props whirred into life.

'Try to keep the transporter directly below us until we hit at least ten thousand feet,' Angelique said. 'Hopefully by then we'll be too high for anyone to notice us.'

'I'm on it.' I edged the throttle forward, keeping pace with the transporter heading towards one of the runways.

Please, God, let no one look up and see us.

We climbed fast until the campfires became pinpricks of light.

I turned the wheel, making tiny corrections and using little bursts of throttle to keep us in position, in a high-risk game of hide and seek. Another bead of sweat dropped from forehead onto my T-shirt. I kept my gaze fixed on the aerodrome, looking for the telltale spark of the blue burner flames of pursuit ships being launched to shoot us down.

Something was clicking on the console. I looked to see the final set of coordinates had started spinning down as we gained height.

'Angelique, look.'

She peered at the numbers then up into the sky and scowled. 'I can't see anything. Anyway, there's no way we can get anywhere near that altitude.'

The dial spun past eight thousand feet, nine, then at last it reached ten.

I relaxed my hands on the wheel. 'We've made it without being blasted out of the sky.'

'Nice bit of flying there, Dom.'

I stood a little taller. Any praise from Angelique was hard-won. 'Practice makes perfect.'

Angelique smiled. She unhooked the spyglass and started peering towards the ground. 'Okay, Tesla, where have you hidden yourself?'

A thought occurred to me. 'What if Tesla arrived like us, not expecting that huge army on the ground. And what if he wasn't so lucky and got spotted.'

The smile fell from Angelique's face. 'We can't afford to think like that.'

But what if Tesla had been captured, or worse? In my head it had all been so easy. We'd find him, he'd mend *Athena* – help us knock out the Hades secret weapon. He'd even have information to help us rescue Jules and Danrick's son, Stephen. I tipped my head back and let out a long sigh.

Above us the great sheets of the Northern Lights moved slowly against the pitch-black of the night sky, an endless sea of light apart from a single speck in the middle... A speck?

'Angelique, what's that up there?' I pointed to the spot.

Her eyes narrowed. 'That's odd.' She raised her spyglass again and gazed through it. 'I can't quite tell what it is.' She passed me the telescope. 'See if you can work it out.'

I squinted through the eyepiece at the point of darkness. Magnified, it looked like a black, tadpole-shaped tear in the aurora display. I could see the stars shining through the hole and the end of the tail seemed to be swirling into the green light.

'It's almost like it's an invisible rock in a stream casting ripples in the aurora,' I said.

Angelique's eyes widened. 'Of course, why didn't I think of that? We're talking Tesla here, the greatest inventor my people have ever known. Maybe you've been right all along and those coordinates are correct.'

'But for some reason he's there and we can't see him.' The memory of the battle with the Hades scout surged into my mind. Angelique had worn a combat suit that had camouflaged her, constantly shifting its pattern to exactly match her surroundings.

Excitement sped through me. 'He's using a chameleon net. That would explain why Hades have never spotted him.'

She pressed her hands together and nodded. 'Of course. Although no one's managed to produce a functional net of that scale before. If anyone can do it, it's Tesla. He's always working on all sorts of top-secret projects for the Cloud Riders to give us an edge in the war with Hades. Somehow he must have developed a net large enough to disguise a whole ship.'

'But how can we be certain it's him?'

'If we want to be sure, we need to wake *Storm Wind* up and operate the Eye.'

'What about getting detected by a ship down at Hells Cauldron?'

'We should be high enough now to avoid any detection by someone down there.'

'Okay, I'm game if you are?'

'Yet again. It seems it's our only option at this point.' She pressed the recessed button for *Athena*'s navigation computer. With a sigh the Eye slid open, revealing two green glass planets surrounded by a swarm of red globes. *Storm Wind*'s song swelled around us.

My skin prickled as a female ship's voice echoed a faint response to him. 'Is that Tesla's ship?'

Angelique pressed the tips of her fingers to her lips, then her face lit up. 'Oh by the gods, yes, that's *Muse*'s song.'

'So what do we do?'

'Let's get as high as we can to try to reach them.'

'But I thought you said we couldn't get to that altitude?'

'We can't, but now he knows we're here, hopefully he'll descend to meet us halfway.' She pulled the burner handle all the way open and the flame roared above us. We shot up towards the radiant solar storm, like a rocket on its way to the stars.

Opening a locker, Angelique passed me a flight suit and took one for herself.

'What are these for? Surely we're not going outside?'

'We're not, but *Athena*'s cabin isn't designed to be pressurised to the altitude we're flying towards. It won't take long before the air starts to bleed from the cabin. Also, it's going to get very cold.'

'That shouldn't be a problem, should it?'

'You don't understand.' She passed a flight helmet to me. 'It will be cold enough to freeze our blood solid if we don't use the heaters built into the flight suits.'

I didn't need telling twice. I grabbed a suit and started to pull it on fast.

CHAPTER Eleven
ASCENT

Frost covered every surface in the cabin and my breath kept huffing up my visor. Despite the flight suit's heater coils being cranked up to maximum, I'd started to shiver. So far *Muse* hadn't descended from her parking spot in the Northern Lights to meet and greet us.

I scrubbed the ice off the altimeter so I could read it. 'Twenty-seven thousand feet.' The needle crawled now, our ascent only measured in tens of feet.

The burner flame started to pop and splutter.

Angelique grimaced. 'I'm mixing additional oxygen into the feed as the air's so thin out there, but we're getting to the ceiling of what *Athena* can fly to.'

I looked through the spyglass. Although still invisible, *Muse*'s three-balloon outline was visible as a silhouette against the neon green of the aurora. 'That doesn't look like a standard design for one of your ships?'

'It isn't. Tesla must have heavily adapted *Muse* to fly at that altitude.'

The cabin shook as something thudded onto the roof.

Angelique's mouth thinned as another big slab of ice tumbled past the window. 'This is starting to get dangerous.

We're building up a lot of extra weight – soon we'll start to lose buoyancy.'

'You mean we could crash?'

She frowned. 'In a word, yes.'

Storm Wind's song became strident, as though he hoped to increase the ship's lift by singing his heart out. But I didn't need to be an engineer to tell the whole ship was being pushed way past what it had ever been designed for.

Sure enough, moments later the blue flame visible through a porthole above us spluttered and died. I held my breath as Angelique shoved the ignition button. Only clicking came from the burner.

'That can't be a good sign?' I said.

'Without the flame's heat we're going to start building up ice even faster,' Angelique replied.

The needle on the altimeter twitched, slowed to a stop, and started to revolve backwards. We weren't going to make it.

She shoved the igniter again. More clicking, but no answering whoosh of flame. The needle began to spin faster.

Angelique slammed her palm onto the ignition again and again. She shot me a grim-faced look.

In my mind I could see the spikes of volcanic rock on the ground we were plummeting towards. 'We're going to have to bail out – use fly-dive suits or something.'

Angelique stood up and stared at me, cradling her necklace. 'I'm not abandoning my ship – it's part of *Athena*'s soul.'

'*Brace yourselves,*' a female voice said, in a tone lower than *Athena*'s. It had to be *Muse* talking to me.

I hooked Angelique around the waist and grabbed a railing.

'What do you think—?'

Athena lurched to a shuddering halt that threw both of us to the floor. Clambering up, I saw a halo of ice in a shower, plummeting away from us.

With a shudder we started to ascend again, the altimeter spinning past twenty-seven thousand feet, twenty-eight thousand feet, like we'd suddenly got rocket power.

Angelique brushed the hair out of her eyes. 'What's going on?'

We dashed forward to the cockpit and peered up through the windshield.

I spotted two grab claws, similar to the ones we'd used to secure ourselves to the transporter ship, clamped onto the sides of *Athena*'s gas envelope. I followed the lines up towards *Muse*'s invisible silhouette above us.

Relief swept through me. 'Looks like we've got ourselves a tow.'

Angelique's shoulders dropped. 'Not a moment too soon.'

If I'd thought it had been cold before, we sped upwards into a chill worse than anything I'd ever known, one that bit deep into my body's core.

Angelique held out her arms to me. 'We need to hold onto each other for warmth.'

Storm Wind's song entwined itself around *Muse*'s. This wasn't a move, this was about survival. I wrapped my arms around Angelique. She clung on to me and shook.

Ice crusted my visor. Bit by bit, her face became a vague smudge. We hurtled towards the aurora, an express elevator shooting up a skyscraper.

'How high now?' Angelique's voice said through my helmet's headphones, her teeth audibly chattering over the com.

I scraped away the ice on the display. 'Ninety-two thousand feet.'

The aurora rushed towards us and we plunged into the green glowing fog. At once the world outside became filled with a jade-coloured haze.

My skin tingled. 'In my wildest dreams I never imagined that one day I'd be *in* the Northern Lights. See them, yes – inside them, no.'

'I doubt you could on your world without a rocket. But on this Earth, the magnetic poles are starting to reverse which means the aurora appears at a much lower altitude.'

'Cool.' A faint humming came from all around us. 'What's that noise?'

'That's actually the sound of the aurora,' Angelique said. 'Very few people ever get to hear it like this.'

A tingle ran down my spine. It sounded like I was listening into the song of Earth singing out as it spun through space – magical and haunting at the same time. I certainly knew I'd remember this moment for the rest of my life, however long that turned out to be.

We approached the dark patch in the curtain of light and our ascent began to slow.

The black gap shimmered and a ship appeared above us. It had a copper-clad, saucer-shaped gondola with round portals, slung beneath teardrop-shaped balloons. We came to a gentle stop right next to it. It seemed our elevator ride had arrived at the top of world.

My heart raced as I took in the light storm dancing around us. This had to be one of the most spectacular things I'd ever seen. It certainly felt like I'd stepped into a waking dream.

A transparent tube started to slide out from *Muse*'s gondola towards us. With a slight lurch and hiss of air, it connected to the outside of our gondola's doorway.

Through the corridor I saw a hatch opening and a figure, who looked like a deep-sea diver complete with round helmet and mirrored faceplate, started walking towards us. He trailed an umbilical cord connecting back to his ship.

'I need to warn you, Tesla is a touch eccentric,' Angelique said.

'What sort of eccentric?'

'His behaviour passes as normal for a genius among our people.'

'Oh, you mean he's a typical mad scientist.'

She laughed. 'That sounds like our Tesla.'

The figure reached *Athena* and, shivering, we let go of each other. He swung the door open and a wave of heat rushed into the cabin.

The figure bowed towards Angelique. 'By Zeus's beard, it's good to see you, Princess.'

She touched his shoulder. 'And you, Tesla, old friend.'

I reached out a gauntleted hand. 'Hi, I'm Dom.'

He shook it. 'Ah yes, the Ship Whisperer.'

'But how—'

He waved away my question. 'Plenty of time for that later, my lad. First let's get back into *Muse* before you both freeze to death.'

We stepped into the warmth of the docking corridor and followed him towards his ship. Not a moment too soon. Any longer onboard *Athena* and I'm pretty sure we'd have been frozen to the floor.

The corridor between the two ships swayed. The structure felt way too flimsy to take our combined weight. On the short walk between the craft, I had to remind myself several times that this guy Tesla was a genius – no way would he construct something that would collapse beneath us... At least I hoped not.

But we made it all the way to the door of *Muse*'s saucer-shaped gondola without incident. I'd started to relax when Tesla pointed a glass wand and pressed a button set into its handle. With a faint whine, the corridor and *Muse* vanished.

Nothing but the Northern Lights filled the air around us. My stomach lurched and I grabbed onto Angelique. When I realised we weren't plummeting to our deaths – and that Tesla had just activated the chameleon net – I let go of her. So much for playing the big *I am.*

Angelique shook her head at the scientist. 'Perhaps next time wait until we're safely inside the ship before turning your cloaking device on.'

'Of course, of course, Princess. I just thought you'd appreciate the view.'

She rolled her eyes at him, which about summed up my feelings too. But as my heart rate started to decelerate, I began to take in the scene.

The Earth curved away from us in all directions. This high it looked like a giant, polished marble, and banks of clouds far beneath us had become tiny mountain ranges. This felt more like the view from a spaceship than an airship.

'I can't believe your modifications to *Muse*,' Angelique said. 'How can you even begin to be flying at this sort of altitude?'

'Three vast, low-pressure-helium lifting balloons. They take over from the main gas envelope during the ascent. They inflate as the pressure drops and are able to pull *Muse* up to the edge of the atmosphere.'

'Oh, like weather balloons on Earth?' I said.

'A weather balloon?' Tesla said. 'An interesting concept…they had started to use them to take measurements at high altitude.'

'I don't remember hearing about that,' Angelique said.

'Oh, you wouldn't have,' Tesla replied.

'Another secret project?'

He coughed. 'Something like that… Which Earth did you say you were from, Dom?'

'I didn't. According to Angelique you guys have given it the catchy handle of Earth DZL2351.'

He halted and his mirrored faceplate turned back towards me. 'Well I never.'

'You know of it?' I asked.

Tesla chuckled. 'Oh, most certainly.' He pulled at something invisible and I heard a creaking sound. Suddenly, a doorway to the interior of his copper gondola floated before us. 'Now, let's get you both thawed out.'

Angelique pressed her hand to her pendant under her flight suit. 'Tesla, I need you to look at *Athena*'s Psuche gem. She's been damaged.'

'She has?' he asked, a concerned note creeping into his voice.

'There's hardly any light coming from her crystal,' I said.

'If her energy matrix has started to fade, I'm afraid that is a very bad sign. We need to hurry and run a full system diagnostic at once.'

Angelique gave me an anxious look through her visor. 'If she dies…'

I took her hand. 'She won't.' But what if she did? Even with the news about her dad being alive, I knew if *Athena* didn't make it, it would break Angelique into a million pieces. Keeping the thought to myself, we followed Tesla into the welcoming warmth of the ship's gondola.

CHAPTER Twelve
TESLA'S EXPERIMENTS

The moment we'd boarded, Tesla had carefully placed *Athena*'s Psuche gem into a metal tube. We'd watched him slide the cylinder into a machine that looked like a demented grandfather clock. But instead of a dial face, this thing had a display of rows of numbers. He'd told us all we could do was wait and that it would take at least a day until we'd know if *Athena* could be saved – or not. As we'd talked, Angelique kept casting nervous glances at the numbers ticking over on the machine.

To me, *Muse*'s cabin looked like one huge flying lab. Hundreds of test tubes with bubbling liquids lined numerous racks. Half-built machines and gear innards spilled across workbenches that seemed crammed into every other available space.

Completing the atmosphere of a mad scientist's lab, every so often a spark would zap between large metal spheres recessed into the ceiling. I could taste the static on my tongue. Dr Frankenstein would have felt at home here.

In the middle of the organised chaos was an Eye at least twice the size of *Athena*'s. However, unlike the unlit ship spheres in *Athena*'s navigation system, in this Eye flickers of light kept appearing in the glass globes, and then dying again.

Without his flight helmet on, Tesla's grey hair curled everywhere and looked like it rarely saw a comb. Below it sprawled an out-of-control beard. If I'd had to imagine a genius inventor, it would look pretty much like this guy.

Over the last thirty minutes, we'd told him everything, from my family connection with King Alexander to the battle with Ambra. But when I'd recounted what had happened at Floating City and my meeting with *Titan*, Tesla had sat up straighter and started scribbling notes with his wand on a piece of glowing glass. He'd urged me to describe every detail, especially everything about the airships' virtual world. As I'd spoken he'd kept muttering, 'Fascinating, fascinating,' to himself.

Now his questions had dried up, I clutched my steaming drink with both hands. I'd no idea what I was drinking, but it was hot and sweet, and, most importantly, melting the block of ice in my stomach.

Tesla chewed the end of his wand, making his lips glow with its light. 'You say, young man, that *Titan* told you that you could set the Hades ships free?'

'Yes, but neither of us are sure what he meant by that,' Angelique said. 'We were hoping you might have an idea?'

He clicked his tongue. 'It's something to do with Dom being a Ship Whisperer, I imagine.'

Angelique sat up and the blanket she'd wrapped around her dropped down her shoulders. 'How do you know that's what Dom is?'

He smiled. 'It's because I'm familiar with King Alexander's research.'

'You are?' Angelique asked.

He nodded. 'He was exploring the ability to be able to communicate with Psuche gems at the deepest level.' He tapped his light wand on the tip of his nose. 'Have you wondered about the significance of the ships talking to you yet, Dom?'

I shrugged. 'All I know is that sometimes it's like I'm actually talking to a person.'

Tesla smiled and settled back in his chair, steepling his fingers together. 'Exactly.'

Angelique stared at him. 'What are you trying to say, Tesla? That ships aren't actually machines?'

He raised his eyebrows.

I exchanged a shocked look with Angelique. Could he be serious? Surely, as amazing as they were, ships were just smart computers? 'But AIs are made in the labs down in Hells Cauldron, aren't they?'

Tesla's smile widened. 'That's just the fairy story we've told our people over the years. It was felt that the truth might prove too disturbing for them. There were also serious objections from our religious leaders.'

'What truth?' Angelique asked.

'To answer that, it's important that you understand the background to Dom's gift and why King Alexander felt it was important to develop this ability in the first place.'

So this was it, I was finally going to learn what my ability was really all about. Goosebumps spread over my skin. 'Go on...'

'Until now only the reigning monarch, his chief scientist, and the programmers responsible for the adaption of the Psuche gems have been privy to the full information. It was this knowledge that led King Alexander to embark on his research.' He gazed at me. 'Young man, you're his direct descendant and your DNA was manipulated so you could communicate with the inner core of the AI subset.'

'Pardon me?'

Angelique drummed her fingers on her arm. 'In a language we can all understand, please, Tesla.'

He opened one hand. 'It's probably easiest if you think of the AI algorithms as a coding solution to a specific problem.' He made his other hand into a fist. 'Think of this hand as the core of the Psuche gem.' He wrapped his hand around his fist. 'And our programme matrix gives us a way of communicating with something trapped within the heart of the crystals.'

Confusion spun through me. 'Are you saying that I'm talking to an actual living thing inside a Psuche gem?'

Tesla beamed at me. 'You're quick – I like that.'

Angelique stared at him. 'But how's that even possible?'

'Because you see, Princess, the crystals mined at Hells Cauldron have a very unique property.' He gestured towards the Northern Lights glowing outside the portals. 'Do you know what causes that display?'

She frowned. 'Isn't it where the sun's charged particles hit the atmosphere? Something to do with Earth's magnetic field.'

'Very good. You obviously paid attention during our science classes.'

Angelique shrugged. 'I tried to.'

'Well, as I hope you remember from our lessons, towards the poles of an Earth the magnetic field flows up into the atmosphere, around the planet, and back again into the southern pole. This energy field is in constant motion and flows through the crystals forming in Hells Cauldron.' He narrowed his eyes. 'And when someone dies on this particular Earth...'

I gawped at him. He couldn't be serious. 'Are you really telling us that the gems capture people's...' I couldn't believe I was about to say this. I took a breath. 'They captured their ghosts?'

A glint flashed through his eyes. 'Well deduced. Most people don't recognise the origin of the word "Psuche". It's an ancient Greek term used to describe the soul.'

I felt light-headed. This was too much to take in.

Angelique pointed to the machine with *Athena* in it. 'So you're saying our ships are powered by souls – real, human, honest-to-gods souls?'

'In a manner of speaking, although I'd personally prefer not to use the word "soul" – it's far too emotionally loaded. I tend to think of it more like the memory of someone's energy field, their pattern of thought snagged and imprinted into the crystal. Think of it as a sort of computer backup of a person.'

Angelique shook her head. 'But that's impossible. As far I'm aware, the history books state that this planet was unpopulated until we discovered it.'

Tesla coughed. 'I'm afraid history books don't always tell the truth, Princess.'

'Just how many lies have I been told?' Angelique said.

So there had been people here before the Cloud Riders arrived. 'Where are these people now...?' My blood chilled. 'They didn't have a nuclear war or something, did they, Tesla?'

He shook his head. 'Nothing like that. We know from the records we've found buried in archaeological sites dotted around this planet that the Angelus, as they were known, were one of the most peaceful races in the known universes.'

'So what happened to them?'

'It seems the Angelus were a more advanced race than even the Cloud Riders. They evolved to the point that they no longer needed their physical bodies. Supported by their technology, they became entities of pure energy. For some unknown reason a thousand years ago, they left this planet and set out for the stars across all the dimensions.'

'They sound like something out of science fiction,' I said.

'Just so.' Tesla turned to Angelique. 'Your father found them an inspiration, too. That's why he named you after them.'

She peered at him. 'You mean Angelus as in Angelique.'

'That's right. Angelus is also the ancient word for angel.'

Angelique shook her head. 'This is too much to take in.'

'But you've got to admit it's pretty cool,' I said.

She nodded, her eyes full of wonder.

'So how come some didn't make it to the stars, but got trapped in the Psuche gems instead?' I asked.

'Trapped, or maybe volunteered to stay behind to tell us their secrets one day – which we can't be sure. But what King Alexander discovered is that within every Psuche gem is an encrypted information matrix, one that even ship-song can't access. That's why King Alexander was so keen to research a way to communicate with the Psuche gems and to learn why they left their home world in the first place. He also believed that talking directly to the Angelus within the Psuche gems would encourage peace among our people.'

'How so?' I asked.

'With the knowledge of an ancient civilisation held in every craft of our people, and with a way for them to access it, King Alexander hoped the ships' wisdom would encourage us to turn our backs on conflict, forever.'

Angelique crossed to the clock-like machine that held *Athena*'s damaged crystal within it. 'So *Athena* is, or at least once was, an actual living person?'

He pressed his fingertips together. 'Precisely, Princess.'

The thought was incredible, but now he said it, it made so much sense. The ships had always felt alive to me, not in the way a computer pretends to be alive with things like simulated speech, but in a real, living, breathing people sort of way.

Angelique bit her lip. *Storm Wind*'s and *Muse*'s songs swelled into my mind and their emotions rushed through me: happiness, love, warmth, but most of all, joy. These were real emotions, not just lines of code impersonating them. A lump filled my throat.

'I never knew...and now she's dying,' Angelique whispered.

'I promise you, Princess, I will do my best to save her.'

Angelique gazed at me, blinking back tears. 'And you've heard her, Dom, heard my *Athena* talk to you in her real voice.'

I nodded, fighting the prickling behind my own eyes. 'So all those hundreds of thousands of ships at Floating City were once people too?'

Tesla nodded. 'All the Psuche gems that power trans-dimensional ships today come from the mine here at Hells Cauldron.'

'But what about the Hades ships?' Angelique said. 'You're not telling me those twisted things were once people too?'

Tesla's mouth pinched into a scowl. 'Unfortunately, that's exactly what I'm saying. The entities within their crystals are enslaved by programmes that Cronos had specifically installed. Their purpose is to force the being within each crystal to submit to his will. Remove those coding constraints and they would become as peaceful as our own vessels.'

I thought of the sound of pain I'd heard from the Hades transporter ship. It had been the cry of a real person. Anger curled inside me. 'So, in other words, Cronos is torturing them?'

Tesla sighed. 'Effectively, yes.'

Angelique put her hands to her mouth. 'No wonder *Titan* wants you to set them free, Dom.'

'But how am I meant to do that? Smash all the crystals in the Hades ships with a big lump hammer?'

'No,' Tesla said. 'If you do that, you'll simply destroy the energy field trapped within it, although in a way that would be a release of sorts from their suffering.'

'How then?'

'I'm sorry, Dom, I have no idea. All I can tell you is that Psuche gems were formed under high pressure deep within the Earth's crust. I suspect that it was during the crystals' formation that the energy imprint of some of the Angelus became trapped inside.' He wrapped his hand around his fist again. 'And maybe in those same mines you will find a way to set them free again.' He spread his fingers and released his hand, illustrating the point.

'Great – I'm meant to help but no one can tell me how.' The responsibility felt like a huge weight I was now going to have to drag behind me.

'But maybe there is someone who can tell you,' Angelique said.

'Who?'

'You could take *Storm Wind*'s Psuche gem with you to Hells Cauldron. I know it's hit and miss being able to talk to him, but you always seem to be able to hear a ship's voice when it matters.'

'Good idea,' Tesla said.

I shrugged. 'I guess it can't hurt.'

'And I'm sure we'll find the answer down there, Dom,' Angelique said. 'Call it instinct.'

'I just hope your instinct is right.'

Tesla gestured to the floor. 'There's another matter you may be able to deal with at Hells Cauldron while you're down there.'

'What?' Angelique said.

'We need to destroy their secret weapon, the Quantum Pacifier.'

'The radio mast thing they've built?' I asked.

'Bright – very, very bright.' Tesla beamed at me. 'You're right, Dom. That does seem to be the source of the jamming signal they're broadcasting across the dimensions. However, I've no idea what's generating the signal that the mast is transmitting. Whatever it is, it's certainly beyond any computer system I know.'

'But have you found a way of stopping it yet?' Angelique asked.

Tesla sighed. 'There I have been less successful.' He gestured towards the super-sized Eye. 'I've tried all sorts of things: adaptive cryptology algorithms, fractal frequency decoders, even a counter-jamming broadcast – but nothing's worked.'

For a moment we all watched the lights in the planets wink on and off.

'But there has to be a way,' Angelique said.

'There is, but it will be very dangerous. If I were a trained soldier, rather than an old man, I would have attempted it myself by now.'

I narrowed my gaze at him. 'You need someone to blow up the mast, don't you?'

He gave me a grim look and nodded.

'Now blowing things up is something I think we can more than manage,' Angelique said.

'As long as we can rescue Jules and Stephen first,' I replied.

'Stephen – Danrick's son?' Tesla asked.

Angelique nodded. 'Yes – he was to carry out a spying mission at Hells Cauldron, but now he's gone missing.'

'Oh I see. I don't think I know this Jules you're talking about.'

'She's my friend,' I said. 'Ambra took her from my Earth as a hostage.'

'From your Earth...' A fleeting, wistful look crossed his face and was gone. He focused on me again. 'Ambra, you say...' He twirled the glass wand between his fingers. 'I was listening to some radio chatter from the aerodrome two days ago when a frigate landed. Of course I've been taking a keen interest in what our friends have been getting up to on the ground, so I took a moving pictogram recording of Duke Ambra's personal transport sent out to meet the craft. Actually, now you come to mention it, there was a young lady with him. Though I'm sure it can't be your friend.'

'Why's that?' Angelique asked.

'To answer that it will be best if I show you.' He pointed the wand upwards and a multi-lensed ball lowered from the ceiling. One of its lenses revolved until it was pointing straight down. A beam of light shone out from it and an image of Hells Cauldron palace appeared on the floor.

'I recorded this as *Proteus* came into land,' Tesla said.

He spun a dial and the view zoomed in on the summit of the volcano. I could see towers carved from polished, black stone ringing the mouth. A small airship with butterfly-like wings flew into view, heading towards the summit.

'Ambra's ship?' I asked.

Angelique glowered at the image. 'That's one of our royal yachts that was kept moored here. I learnt to fly in that very craft with Papa.'

'I'm afraid, Princess, that it's become Ambra's personal plaything, no doubt given to him by Cronos as a reward for services rendered.'

She shook her head. 'He's hasn't any right.'

I thought of Dad teaching me to fly in the ultralight. I wouldn't be too thrilled if Ambra had stolen that, either.

The craft swung in towards a raised pier jutting up from the lip of the circular battlements. Tiny specs of figures rushed forward and grabbed ropes dangling from the craft.

'It's not powered like a conventional airship,' Angelique said. 'You have to tack the sails into the wind – it takes a lot of skill to pilot it.'

The ship bucked around as the men hauled it in.

Angelique tutted. 'Call that a landing, Ambra.'

Tesla spun the dial again and the image zoomed in. 'Ah, here we go.' The view had now centred on a door opening in the gondola.

Ambra emerged from a doorway with his arm in a sling.

'I expect Jules gave him that little memento,' Angelique said.

'I certainly hope so,' I replied.

A girl emerged behind him, wearing a long, flowing, flowery dress. A hat with a lace veil covered her face. Ambra offered her his arm and she took it. My shoulders dropped. 'I see what you mean, Tesla. Whoever she is, it's clear she's not his hostage.'

Angelique gasped. 'Dom, look closer.'

Why? The girl raised her veil at the same moment Tesla spun the dial.

Jules's features filled the grainy image. She looked towards Ambra and gave him a dimpled smile. But she didn't do dresses, especially ones with flowers on. My chest clenched and I reached out a hand to the projected image. Her ghostly face played over my palm.

'But this doesn't make sense,' I said.

Angelique rested her hand on my shoulder. 'It might not be what it looks like, Dom.'

But what did it look like? Numbness surged through me. 'Jules looks like a house guest.' This couldn't be happening. What the hell had happened to her on that airship? I closed my hand into a fist, splintering her projected face. A thousand black thoughts flashed through my head.

'You may be right,' Tesla said. 'Prisoners are usually shipped straight down to the mining complex. I've seen it all from up here – little army ants playing out their games with people's lives below me.'

Angelique shook her head and made me look at her. 'But this is Jules we're talking about here, Dom.'

My thoughts stuttered. 'You don't think she's...' – I couldn't believe I was going to say this – 'betrayed us?'

'Of course not. I expect she's doing what any resourceful person would do, playing along until she has an opportunity to escape.'

My anger started to uncoil and I unclenched my fist. What was I thinking? 'You're right, Jules wouldn't join Ambra.' The fog in my head started to clear. She was alive...she was really alive – and that was the main thing. Determination flooded through me. 'We need to get down there and rescue her.'

'Now that's the Dom I know and...' She gave me a small smile.

Had she been about to say love? Really? But maybe I knew what she meant – the love of a friend. Affection for her surged through me. In the middle of all this craziness, she was the one person who kept making sense and thinking straight. Maybe I loved her too, in that same friend's way.

'Okay, what's the plan?' I said.

'My vote would be to rescue Jules and find Stephen. Then we blow the Pacifier.'

I nodded. 'Sounds good, but how do we get down without being spotted? Also, what do we use to blow up the mast?'

'I may be able to help on both counts,' Tesla said. He crossed to the locker and took out two black suits with webbed fabric between the arms and torso.

My insides clenched. 'Fly-dive suits? You expect us to make a free-fall drop from this height?'

Even Angelique frowned at me. 'Normally it requires quite a lot of training, even from a much lower altitude. Also at this height we'd surely freeze to death. Not to mention that even if we did survive, someone is bound to spot us coming in to land.'

'And I thought you knew me better than that, Princess. These suits are pressurised and heated, but more than that...' He touched a button on one suit and it vanished.

I whistled. 'They've got chameleon nets built in.'

'Indeed they have, young man,' Tesla said. 'However, to activate it takes a lot of power. I've had to save weight and the device installed will only be able to operate the chameleon system for two minutes. That means you will only have a brief period of invisibility at any given time until it recharges again.'

'In other words, leave it until we're almost about to land before activating it,' Angelique said.

'Precisely,' Tesla replied.

I remembered Angelique's first demonstration of fly-diving, when she'd almost hit the ground before opening her chute. My gut squirmed at the thought that I would have to try something that made the hardest extreme sport look tame.

Angelique's gaze narrowed on me. 'Are you up to this, Dom? It's going to be a close-run thing. One mistake and you'll be—'

'Pavement pizza, yeah I get that.'

'You don't have to go,' Angelique said.

'And I'm not going to let you do this alone, especially with Jules counting on us.'

Angelique shot me a smile. 'Thank you, Dom, and once again your bravery continues to astonish me.'

'All part of my new job description apparently. But what about blowing up the mast?'

Tesla pointed his glass wand at a large, round hatch set into the floor by the Eye. A panel slid open.

We peered down at hundreds of red boxes filling the storage compartment.

'What are those?'

'Matchbox fission reactors – the only thing powerful enough to run a chameleon net large enough to hide this ship.'

'Fission…' A memory from science class came back to me. 'You're saying these are mini nukes?'

He beamed at me. 'I'm rather proud of the design. It's taken me months to perfect.'

The room seemed to grow warmer as I imagined radiation bathing us with its invisible rays. 'That can't be safe?'

'As long as we're not shot out of the sky, they're all perfectly harmless.'

I scowled at him. 'Yeah, it's not like you're parked bang over the top of an enemy position or anything.'

Angelique leant over the chamber and peered at the boxes. 'But why so many, Tesla?'

He rubbed his hands together. 'It's my latest project, Princess. I intend to fit the new chameleon nets to the entire Cloud Rider fleet.'

Her mouth fell open. 'To make our *entire* fleet invisible?'

He nodded.

The implication sank in. 'Hades would never know what had hit them.'

'Precisely, young man.' Tesla took one of the reactors out and handed it to me. 'And for now you can use this as the impromptu explosive device that you need.'

I flinched as I held it. Handling a nuke without some sort of protective suit didn't seem right somehow. But the metal felt cool to the touch and, as far as I could tell, my fingers weren't melting – at least not yet!

'Plant this at the base of the mast and set it to overload,' Tesla said, indicating a dial on the side. 'You will have about five hours before it goes critical. The explosion will do the rest. Just make sure you're at a safe distance by then.'

'A free-fall drop from ninety thousand feet. A nuclear explosion. This day just gets better and better,' I said.

Angelique peered at me. 'Still sure you want to come?'

I forced a smile. 'No way am I going to let you have all the fun.'

She snorted and patted my back.

I took one of the fly-dive suits and began putting it on. I had no choice. This was just something I had to do. Something I had to do for Angelique, for me, for all sorts of reasons – but, most of all, for Jules.

CHAPTER Thirteen
FREE-FALL JUMP

We followed Tesla down a spiral staircase and reached the bottom. Ahead of us stood a heavy door set into a curved wall.

'This is the airlock,' Tesla said. He drummed his techy wand against the palm of his hand. 'Are you both clear on how you have to blow the mast up?'

Angelique pointed to the bag hanging from her webbing belt. 'We place the matchbox reactor at the base of the mast and set it to overload.'

'And how long will you have from that point?' Tesla asked.

'Five hours,' I said.

'Good, you've been paying attention. You will need to be well clear of Hells Cauldron once the reactor goes critical. A one kiloton explosive radius will be at least half a mile across.'

I imagined a mushroom cloud blossoming over the volcano. 'But we're going to rescue Jules and Stephen first, right?'

'Of course,' Angelique replied. 'There's no way of knowing how long it will take to find them and the last thing we need is a fission explosion going off while we are still searching.'

'That's a bit of an understatement.'

Tesla crossed his arms. 'Once you have found the others and set the charge, use the emergency lift balloon in the pack to get you all back up here. It can carry a maximum of four people.'

It didn't sound exactly like a solid plan to me, more an idea thrown together by people backed into a corner. But that's exactly what we were.

Angelique adjusted the bulky rucksack she was carrying. Tesla had already taken us through the contents: a folded silver balloon, and a pressurised tank to expand it.

I gave my own harness another tug. Probably the hundredth time I'd done so since putting the fly-dive suit on. Grandpa Alex's lightning pendant felt warm against my chest. On Tesla's advice, and he hadn't needed to spell it out, I'd placed *Storm Wind*'s crystal inside the pendant's hidden compartment alongside the Saint Christopher medal. In other words, in case I got caught.

Storm Wind's voice was only a faint, but reassuring, chant within my thoughts. I patted the Leatherman, another good-luck charm from home. I needed plenty of that where we were headed.

'Are you ready, Dom?' Angelique said.

'As much as I'll ever be.'

'Okay, let's go and pay Hells Cauldron a visit they'll never forget.'

'As long as they don't spot us,' I replied.

Tesla shook his head. 'Apart from the chameleon net, you'll also have the advantage of jumping during the twenty hours of darkness.'

'How come such a long night?' I asked.

'You've managed to time your visit during the winter on this Earth, when the sun only rises for four hours at this latitude.'

'Cool.'

Tesla spun a lever on the wall and a door rotated into view. I followed Angelique and stepped through it into a small, round chamber. I couldn't see a door on the other side of what I guessed was an airlock.

Angelique tapped the black handle dangling from the front of my harness. 'When I tell you, Dom, pull this cord to deploy your drag chute.'

A numbness filled my body. Flying was one thing, but jumping from this height was entirely another. I managed a nod.

'As soon as the mast is down, I'll try to get a lock on the rest of the fleet, starting with King Louis,' Tesla said.

Angelique gripped his arm. 'But meanwhile, you'll do everything you can for *Athena*, won't you?'

'Of course, Princess. It will be my number one priority.'

'Thank you.'

He smiled at her. 'Now let's see, what else do I need to tell you...?' He snapped his fingers. 'Oh yes, after you activate the chameleon nets, you'll hear an alarm when you have only thirty seconds of cloaking left, and then a red light will blink for the last ten.'

Two minutes invisibility didn't seem anything like long enough to me. 'But we can use them more than once right?'

Tesla nodded. 'You can, but they will take about ten minutes to recharge.'

'Got it.'

Tesla pressed a button on the airlock panel. 'Good luck to you both.' The door slid closed.

Angelique flicked a switch on her control wristband. Her voice crackled through the speakers in my helmet. 'Okay, Dom, get ready and fold your arms flat across your chest.'

I did as I was told, although I still couldn't spot the doorway to the outside. 'Hey, where's the exit—?' My throat closed up as the floor dropped away. One second we'd been standing in the safety of the airlock and the next we hurtled away from *Muse*, green aurora light filling the sky around us.

No chance to back out now. Blood roared in my ears as I looked up at the airlock door, hanging in mid-air and becoming small fast. It must've opened beneath us and we'd dropped out. The hatch swung shut and *Muse* became totally invisible again.

The whistle of the wind started to grow louder. My limbs began to cut phosphorescent trails through the magnetic storm. I felt like a fish diving down through a green ocean.

'The atmosphere's thickening,' Angelique's calm voice said through my helmet's headset.

The wind started to scream. This felt way too fast. I flapped my arms, trying to slow my descent, casting ripples through the green fog behind me. Big mistake. The fabric wings snapped taut under my arms and I began to tumble.

'Dom, stop panicking,' Angelique said. She zoomed alongside me, her arms and legs spread wide in a sky-diving pose, her body in perfect control.

Through the green haze of the aurora, a dark landscape surrounded by a glinting sea grew clearer. I fought the panic rising through my chest.

'Pull your arms close into your sides,' Angelique said.

I tried, but the air kept buffeting me. I felt like someone had got hold of both arms and was pulling hard in a tug of war. I gritted my teeth and heaved them harder.

Muscles screaming, I pulled my arms in. At once my tumbling slowed to a stop and I dropped into a head-down position. I started to accelerate away from Angelique and shot out of the bottom of the Northern Lights into the clear air beneath. Below me the dark volcanic mouth of Hells Cauldron looked up at us, a huge black open mouth in the landscape.

Angelique zoomed up alongside me again. 'Much better control.' She glanced at a dial on her wristband. 'Okay, we need to be careful we don't break the sound barrier and cause a sonic boom. That would be bound to draw attention.'

'How the hell do we slow down then?'

'Spread your arms out into the airstream, but slowly, otherwise you'll end up tumbling again.'

I pushed my arms against the friction of air. It felt harder than any weights I'd tried lifting in the school gym.

'Perfect, now do the same with your legs,' Angelique said.

My thighs burned as I pushed my feet apart. The fabric between my legs started fluttering like a flag and I began to pull out of the dive.

'And a little bit more...' Angelique said.

My muscles quivered as I pushed my limbs out further against the air. It felt like pushing against a brick wall. With a snap, the fabric tautened into wings and I levelled out. Adrenaline buzzed through me. Okay, this was cool.

Angelique appeared by my side, a bird flying in formation with me. 'It's wonderful, isn't it?'

I shot her a smile. 'Once you get the hang of it, it is. Although to be honest I could have done without the surprise start in the airlock. Talk about being dropped in at the deep end.'

She laughed. 'It's just as well you're a fast learner.'

Elation coursed through me. This was seriously great. I began to experiment with my flight, shifting the balance of my arms and legs against the air rushing past them. I discovered even the slightest changes enabled me to swoop and climb. No, this wasn't just great, this was fantastic!

I let out a long whoop. 'Now this is what I call cloud-riding.'

Angelique laughed. 'A fly-dive jump is one of the best experiences in the world. Are you ready for your advanced lesson now?'

'You bet I am.'

'Okay, let's play a game of follow the leader. Try to keep up, Dom.' Angelique pulled her arms in and hurtled downwards.

I did the same, grinning to myself, and sped after her. She jinked left and right like a fighter plane in combat, but

I kept pace with every switch in her direction. God, this felt the best thing ever – I never wanted it to end. This was the best flying of my life.

Angelique pulled level again. 'Okay, that's probably the fastest fly-dive suit lesson in history, but I think you're ready now.' Her tone had become serious, the humour gone. Angelique the soldier was back on duty and we had a mission to carry out.

I gazed down at the pinpricks of campfires and the thousands of tents arrayed around them. My exhilaration ebbed away. This wasn't a game. Suddenly, I felt exposed in the wide-open sky, dropping too fast towards an army of Hades soldiers.

'When do we turn on the chameleon nets?' I asked.

'We'll have to wait until a thousand feet as we only have those two minutes of invisibility. Then we'll deploy the drag chutes at the same time. Follow my path down and we'll land together in the crater. Whatever you do, don't take your eyes off me.'

'Okay...' I tried to ignore the gruesome image my imagination flashed into my mind – what would happen if I screwed this up.

The blue lagoons around Hells Cauldron shimmered with the reflected light of the aurora. We swept towards the black battlements at the top of the town. As we neared, the towers began to resemble black teeth around the gaping jaw of the volcano's mouth...a mouth that was about to swallow us whole.

'On my mark,' Angelique said.

My throat became dry and the snowy landscape hurtled towards us. God, we were seriously low – one mistake and, no question, it would be game over.

'Angelique?'

'Now,' Angelique shouted. She blurred to a ghost beside me.

I curled my forefinger back to press the button in the palm of my glove like Tesla had showed us. The chameleon net gave an answering hum. My body shimmered into a smudge in the air like Angelique. The rocky ground screamed towards me. Seconds left. I tugged on the ripcord and my drag chute exploded from my backpack. I slammed into my harness as the chute opened and began to slow, dropping in controlled flight towards the volcano's mouth.

For a desperate moment I thought I'd lost Angelique, but then I spotted her flitting ghost-shape ahead, shooting towards the palace. I spread my arms wider to slow down more and skimmed over the roofs of the buildings ringing the volcano. I caught a movement from the corner of my eye and glanced down.

Below us a procession of soldiers, wrapped in thick fur coats, marched up a narrow street towards the closed gates of the walled battlements at the summit. They dragged a man in chains with them. A prisoner?

I glanced back to Angelique, but couldn't see her ghost outline anywhere. Oh sweet lord. 'Where did you go, Angelique?' I said into my helmet's mic.

'I'm just ahead of you.'

Panic burst through me. 'Where?'

'Just aim—' – a pop of static interrupted her – 'volcano...'

'Angelique, you're breaking up.'

The palace towers rushed at me, pennants stretched out in a strong wind.

'Mast...interference...' Angelique's voice said.

Static crackled in my headset. Heck, the mast had to be blocking our radio signal.

'Angelique, can you hear me?'

Hisses and squeals filled my headphones.

I forced myself to think. *Don't panic, just follow the plan.*

The mouth of the volcano was only a couple of hundred yards ahead. A gust of wind buffeted me and my airspeed started to die. I knew from flying with Dad that if I got too slow, I'd stall and drop out of the sky.

Come on, come on...

I aimed for a gap between two towers and banked hard towards it. Beyond the buildings I saw a parapet encircling the black hole of the volcano's mouth. The mast rose from it, a thin metal needle, threading ground to sky.

I sped between black towers and directly over the heads of two guards talking to each other. Luckily for me they were looking out over the gate at the approaching guards and their prisoner. I shot past them and the parapet rushed towards me, but I'd hardly any height left. I pulled my legs up and skimmed over the ramparts.

I started to drop into the welcoming cover of the volcano's rim. I'd made it!

But my elation died as my chute lines snapped taut. My harness punched the air from my lungs and I jerked to a stop.

What the...?

Like a pendulum on a line, I swung backwards towards the rim. I braced myself. With a bone-jarring impact, I slammed into the rock face. I gritted my teeth, fighting the pain bursting through my sinews. What the heck had happened?

I fought to slow my fast breathing that was already misting my visor. I heard a chime inside my helmet. Only thirty seconds of invisibility left.

'I tell you I heard something,' a man's voice said from above me.

I stared upwards at a stone gargoyle's head peering down from the edge of the parapet. Around it I could see the ghostly outline of my chute draped over it. The statue must have snagged me as I'd shot past.

The fur-hooded heads of the two guards I'd flown over appeared either side of the horned gargoyle statue.

Oh god, don't let them spot me.

'See, there's nothing there,' the man on the right said. 'You're just hearing things.'

'You know what Sarge said. We have to report anything unusual now the Kraken is nearly complete. That convert they are bringing in will be taken straight down to processing.'

Convert? Kraken?

'Well, you can go and get him out of his nice, comfy bed. You're more than welcome to tell him you've been jumping at shadows. Good luck with that.'

The man on the left sighed. 'Maybe you're right.'

A second chime sounded in my helmet and a red light began blinking in my visor. Ten seconds and the chameleon net would shut down. Blood thundered in my ears.

'Now you're thinking straight,' his companion replied. 'Come on, let's get back to the guard house. It's cold enough out here to freeze the nether regions off an icewolf.'

The heads withdrew as my helmet's light turned a steady red. My heart clenched as the chute shimmered into view. I held my breath. I waited, not daring to move, not daring to think.

Footsteps started walking away and I let my breath out in a quiet sigh. That had been way too close.

Suspended in my harness, I started to take in my surroundings. I hung over a sheer drop into the black abyss of the volcano's mouth. Angelique had to be down there somewhere, but had she landed okay?

'Angelique, can you hear me?' I whispered into my mic.

Only the hiss of static answered.

What the hell was I going to do now? I couldn't see any obvious way down.

I looked up at my chute lines stretching towards the gargoyle. I'd no other choice – I had to climb.

Taking hold of the rock face, I began to haul myself up, driving my feet into unseen crevices and hanging on by my fingertips. If I slipped…

I swallowed hard. Every muscle felt like it was on fire, but I kept creeping up towards the stone demon's head leering at me from above. With sweat running down my back, I finally hooked my hands over the polished edges of the parapet and hauled myself onto the top of the wall.

I'd made it! I rolled onto my back and sucked in huge lungfuls of air. Breath thundering in my helmet, I started to scan the battlements. I relaxed a fraction when I spotted no one around on the ice-encrusted walkways. But a hundred yards along from me, light glowed from an archway of a tower. Inside, a spiral staircase led downwards.

What would Angelique be doing now? Looking for me? One minute on the ground and already our plan was going wrong.

From the direction of the basin, I heard men calling to each other.

'Corner her,' someone shouted.

Fear burst through me. *No!*

I peered back over the edge of the parapet and saw the glow of lanterns at the bottom of the basin. Near the base of the mast Angelique was surrounded by five soldiers advancing towards her. Even with her Sansodo skills, I doubted she could handle that many opponents at once. I needed to get down there and fast.

I kept close to the wall and ran along the entrance to the tower. The lamp inside my helmet still shone a steady red. No help from my chameleon net for the moment if I ran into somebody. I prayed the few Sansodo skills Angelique had taught me would give me an edge if that happened.

I began running down the polished stone steps as quietly as I could. In the confined space, the black walls pressed in on me. I felt like a mouse running through a maze.

A shout came from somewhere beneath me. I edged down the steps towards the source of the sound and reached the bottom of the staircase. With my back to the wall, I peered around the corner.

The volcanic basin stretched away and wisps of steam rose up from clumps of rock surrounding the steel mast of the Quantum Pacifier, which rose into the sky.

My heart stuttered as I spotted Angelique being dragged in my direction by two muscly guards. They'd pinned her arms behind her back. Her face was bloodied and smeared with dirt. A third man strode ahead of them, leading the group. He had a thin moustache and pointed beard. On the shoulders of his uniform I spotted three brass epaulets. A sergeant?

As the man closed, the last of my hope died as I noticed what he was carrying: Angelique's pouch with the nuclear reactor inside.

What the hell was I meant to do now? I backed into the shadows by the lift, but they were bound to see me.

'Get your hands off me!' Angelique shouted at the soldiers.

'Keep your mouth shut, spy,' the sergeant said.

The red light in my visor blinked out. The suit had recharged at last. I stabbed my index finger back into my palm and the chameleon net quietly hummed up. My suit took on the look of the black walls as they closed to less than ten feet. I could be a man of shadows again for another two minutes.

The men and their prisoner walked straight past me and entered the lift. The door rattled closed. No! With a squeal the lift started to descend into an open shaft.

No time to think this one through. I might only have this one chance.

I waited until the top of the lift drew level with the floor and stepped as lightly as I could onto it. I clung to the cable to balance myself.

The lift began to accelerate downwards. I wrapped my fingers around the pendant. No murmur answered my touch. It seemed even *Storm Wind* was holding his breath.

It was down to just me once again. But how on Earth was I going to rescue Angelique this time against a whole Hades army?

Chapter Fourteen
THE LAB

The lift dropped and kept dropping, and my stomach plummeted with it. It had got warmer too, and the hint of a rotten-egg stench had strengthened. Not nice, not nice at all. From a distant memory in science class I recalled this stench probably had something to do with the sulphur that formed around volcanoes. Whatever it was, if it didn't stop getting worse I'd soon be hurling my guts up.

I examined the top of the lift, looking for a hatch to get inside, but I couldn't see anything. So much for pulling off the classic action-movie stunt of dropping down and surprising the guards. That plan would have to remain in my imagination. I turned off the suit to conserve power till I needed the edge it would give me.

The rough-hewn walls of the shaft skimmed past, the black surfaces barely visible in the darkness. The cable securing the lift vibrated under my hand. Somewhere high above, I could hear the squeal of a wheel turning, just the right frequency to put my teeth on edge.

The lift had already been descending for five minutes. Just how deep were these mines? Floors rushed past, including large caverns with round storage tanks. For gas? Perhaps that's what the fuel transporters had been busy coming to Hells Cauldron to fill, but if so, why did Hades need so much? Maybe they were building a huge battle fleet somewhere down here. My blood iced at the thought.

From beneath my feet, I kept catching the murmur of voices from inside the lift, punctuated by Angelique's defiant tone. At least that meant she was still conscious.

I kept having to pop my ears, like I'd been dropping fast in an aeroplane. I counted another twenty floors zip past: one filled with massive turbines, the next a warehouse piled with crates all the way to the ceiling, another that was some sort of underground farm – complete with cows and pigs grazing under hundreds of arc lights in the chamber's ceiling. Whatever Hades were up to in Hells Cauldron, it looked organised and large-scale.

At last the lift started to slow and the glow of white light crept around its edges. With a gentle shudder we came to a stop and the doors slid open.

I peered through the gap between the top of the lift and the ceiling, and saw Angelique being pulled away by the guards.

So what now?

The doors began to close and with a lurch the lift started to drop again. In our world there would have been safety doors to stop someone falling down the lift shaft, but Hades obviously didn't believe in that sort of feature.

A white blazing room slid into view. As the lift's roof drew level with the floor, I pressed the chameleon net's button and stepped off the lift and out into the room.

A chime tone sounded in my headset. The suit hadn't had a chance to fully recharge – I only had thirty seconds to find cover.

I scanned the room filled with lab benches and crates, and in the middle stood a single metal chair. A large bunker-type door was at the far end.

A man with a bald head and hooked nose peered through an antique-looking microscope. He wore a long, white lab coat with numerous pockets. The guy had to be a scientist.

The red light blinked in my visor. Hell. Ten seconds and counting.

The bearded sergeant led the party towards the man, the soldiers dragging Angelique with them.

I ducked down behind a white container marked with the demon Hades logo. With a dull whine my suit powered itself down. Panic spiked through me, but no heads turned in my direction. That had been too close for comfort.

The scientist looked up from the microscope. 'Who's this, Sergeant Yanton?'

'We found her at the bottom of the basin, Duke Fellack, but she won't give us her name.'

So they definitely hadn't recognised Angelique yet, but I could understand why. With her bloodied and bruised face, I barely recognised her myself.

The sergeant offered the scientist her bag. 'She had this device with her that you may want to examine.'

Fellack took it from Yanton. 'Oh did she now?' He pulled out the red reactor cube from the bag and turned it over in his hand. 'So what were you planning, dear?'

'I'm not your *dear*,' Angelique replied.

'In your position I'd be a little bit more polite,' Fellack said.

Yanton crossed his arms and glowered at her. 'She took out two of my guards before we managed to capture her.'

Fellack grinned. 'Feisty creature, aren't you?' He peered at the reactor. 'So what's this little toy, hmm?'

Angelique glowered back at him. 'Give it to me and maybe I'll show you.'

'Answer the Duke.' The sergeant struck Angelique across the back of the head and she staggered as the guards hung on to her.

A ball of anger churned in my chest. But there were too many of them. If I tried anything I'd blow any chance of getting us out of this alive.

'We'll get you the answers soon enough, Duke Fellack,' Yanton said. 'We're taking her to the torture rooms to see if we can dig out of her what her mission was. We presume she's a spy or saboteur.'

Fellack placed the reactor in one of his oversized pockets. 'But first she should be tested.'

Tested? For what?

Yanton scowled. 'But, Duke Fellack—'

The Duke raised his hand, silencing the man. 'This is standard procedure, as you should well know, sergeant.'

'But she killed two of my men, surely an exception—'

Fellack shook his head. 'No exceptions. If she passes the test, you can console yourself that she'll face a fate far worse than a quick execution.'

'We should at least interrogate her—'

Fellack slapped the sergeant's words away with his hand like he was swatting flies. 'That's a direct order.'

The sergeant snapped a salute. 'Yes, sir.'

The scientist's expression softened. 'Anyway, if she's a candidate, she'll babble everything she knows during the conversion process.'

'Of course, sir.'

'And if she isn't, then I'll hand her over to you for interrogation. So think of this as a win-win situation.'

A smile flickered across the sergeant's face. 'Yes, sir!'

My hands felt greasy inside my gauntlets. Either way it sounded bad news for Angelique. I had to do something before it was too late.

'I'll never tell you anything,' Angelique said.

'Oh, we'll see about that,' Fellack replied. 'Prepare her for testing,' he said to Yanton.

Desperation twisted through me. What were they about to do to her?

The sergeant nodded to his two men. They forced Angelique into the chair and bound her feet and hands with steel bands. I fought the urge to rush them. I needed to pick my moment if I didn't want to blow my chance.

Fellack walked to a plinth and turned a dial. From a hatch in the floor a small marble pyramid started to rise.

'What the hell do you think you're doing to me?' Angelique shouted.

'Just a little test,' Fellack said as the pyramid drew to a stop. 'We need to see if you might be of some use to us.'

She jutted her chin out. 'If you think I'm going to help you, you're deluding yourself.'

'You'll have no option,' Fellack said. 'Now just relax and we'll run our test to see if you're a candidate for conversion.'

I slid the Leatherman out of my pocket. Hand shaking, I selected the biggest blade I could find.

'So let's find out if our house guest is a candidate,' Fellack said.

A tight expression flitted across Yanton's face. 'I just need to talk to the prison sentries. My men will assist you in my absence.' He saluted and hurried out through a door.'

The two guards raised their eyebrows at each other.

'Obviously a sensitive soul,' Fellack said to them.

The guards smirked.

I had a bad feeling about what was about to happen to Angelique. I tightened my grip on the Leatherman.

'Stand clear,' Fellack said.

The two guards stepped away and Angelique glowered at them.

Fellack flicked a switch. The pyramid split open like a geometrical flower head to reveal a ruby crystal at its heart.

A scream filled with the darkness of a Hades AI rushed through my mind.

At once I knew what I was hearing – the cry of pain of an adapted Psuche gem. Fire burned through every sinew of my body. Unable to look away, I felt stabs like pins being driven into my eyes. I gritted my teeth, trying to keep my scream locked inside my mouth.

Angelique bucked in her chair against her bonds. With a groan, her eyes rolled up into her head to leave just the whites showing. The cool, calm Princess no longer looking in control freaked me out even more than the sounds in my head.

A twisted smile filled Fellack's face. 'Well, well, well…'

I tried to move, but the pain had locked my own body down. I felt useless, a puppet with broken strings, my body no longer under my control.

Angelique…

Fellack hit a button and the pyramid slid closed. Like a switch had been thrown, the voice filled with anger and hate stopped dead in my mind. I clamped my hand over my mouth to stop myself gasping as the pain slowly ebbed away.

The scientist clutched his hands behind his back. 'Going by your reaction to the direct exposure to one of our adapted AIs, it would seem you're a Navigator.' Fellack gave Angelique a sickening smile. 'And how incredibly considerate of you to deliver yourself to us, especially when we're in need of the last few candidates to complete the Kraken.'

Kraken – that name again, the one the guards had used up on the battlements. Was it some sort of ship?

Angelique groaned and sucked in air, her eyes rolling back to normal. Sergeant Yanton reappeared in the doorway. He glanced at the closed pyramid and his face relaxed. He obviously hadn't a stomach for this sort of thing. But that didn't exactly square with how hard-nosed he was otherwise.

Fellack glanced across to Yanton. 'I'm sorry, it looks like you're not going to be able to have your fun with her – I need her in one piece for the conversion process.'

'Yes, sir.' Yanton glowered at Angelique.

With a groan Angelique looked up at the scientist through a curtain of her blonde hair. 'You'll never convert me.'

Fellack's smile thinned. 'I'm afraid, for all your bravery, this isn't something you can stop us doing.' He nodded to the sergeant.

Yanton crossed to a panel and spun a wheel. With a series of clanks the bunker door started to rise. Beyond the brightly lit room was a large domed chamber. But it was what was in the middle of it which really snagged my

attention – the base of a large mast constructed from girders, the top disappearing up through a hole in the roof.

It had to be the base of the Quantum Pacifier. But if so,
why did it run so far underground?

Around the walls I counted at least ten large corridors,
the entrance to each closed off with a portcullis. Each passageway was lined with rusting featureless doors.

The soldiers unfastened Angelique from the chair and,
with Fellack leading the way, dragged her into the chamber.

I edged along the wall of the lab until I reached the
bunker door where I could take in the rest of the chamber.

A network of cables spread out from the mast's base
to glass, ice-frosted pods, radiating around it like petals
of a flower. The pods reminded me of the sort of thing I'd
seen in sci-fi movies, where the crew on a spaceship stayed
asleep for years in cryogenic sleep chambers. But that was
the movies and this was real life.

Around the base of the Quantum Pacifier mast ran a
circular plinth with a gantry on top. One of the soldiers
patrolling along the walkway spotted the approaching
party. He pointed his crossbow at Angelique. This place
had more than a whiff of a prison about it.

Angelique stared into one of the pods as the party
dragged her past it.

'Is that a body in there?' I heard her ask.

Fellack nodded and gestured towards four empty open
ones with their lids raised. 'And when you are eventually
converted you'll be joining your fellow Navigators in here.'

So this was some sort of experiment, but for what
exactly? And why did they specifically need Navigators
for it?

The chameleon net's light stayed a steady red in my visor. Just how long till the blasted thing recharged? The thing was, I knew that if I tried anything without it enabled, the sentries would cut me down long before I even reached Angelique.

'What sort of sick thing are you up to here?' Angelique said, voicing my thought for me.

'Why don't I show you,' Fellack replied. 'We have a convert nearing completion at this very moment.'

Convert? Ice crept between my shoulder blades. That was the phrase I'd heard the guards outside talking about. I looked out over the pods.

Fellack walked towards the circular plinth, its sides ringed with steel shutters.

The sentries' eyes were still on Angelique. I grabbed my chance and, using the pods as cover, slipped unnoticed into the chamber.

Fellack strode to a control panel by the shutters. 'Time to see your destiny, Navigator.'

CHAPTER Fifteen
THE HIVE

Fellack pushed the control lever down. With a series of clunks, the shutters swivelled on their axis to reveal the glass-walled, round room that had been hidden behind.

Inside a bright interior, racks of equipment surrounded a bare-chested man strapped to an operating table. He'd been wired to some sort of monitor display that showed a steady beat on a line chart. Above him, mechanised arms swung and darted, pressing black pins into his skin. He bared his teeth and pressed his head back against the bench. The man's mouth twisted into a scream, barely audible through the thick glass. I'd seen this guy somewhere before... In a rush I placed him – the prisoner I'd seen being escorted outside the battlements.

Angelique gasped. 'What are they doing to Lord Orson—' She snapped her mouth shut, but everyone in the room was already staring at her.

Lord Orson, pilot of *Apollo*, who Hades had captured and had been used to dupe us. So this was where he'd ended up.

The sergeant grabbed her by the chin. 'How do you know that man's name?'

'I just do,' Angelique replied.

'Who are you exactly, young lady?' Fellack asked, his eyes narrowing. He grabbed her face and forced her to look at him.

'No one.' She tried to turn her head aside, but his fingers dug into her skin.

'A *no one* who turns up in the middle of a heavily armoured installation and is equipped with a very interesting toy. Let's get a better look at you.' The scientist spat on his thumb and dragged it through the blood and ash on her face.

He gasped. 'Princess Angelique?'

She sneered. 'Oh, so very slow on the uptake aren't you, Fellack.' She stood taller. 'By order of the King, I command you to let me go.'

Fellack clapped his hands together. 'Oh by the gods, how could I have missed that superior tone? But unfortunately for you, Princess, your family's royal command no longer carries the weight it once had.' He turned to Yanton. 'Inform Duke Ambra about our guest's arrival. I'm sure he'll be most appreciative to hear the news.'

'Yes, sir.' The sergeant snapped a salute.

Oh, just great. Ambra joining the party was all I needed.

The sergeant gestured to his men. 'You two, stand guard while I fetch the Duke.' They both clicked their heels together and stood to attention. The sergeant headed back towards the lab.

Through the glass walls I watched as more needles pressed into Lord Orson's body. He flinched as each and every one was pressed in. This was sick.

Fellack licked his lips. 'Oh excellent, we're getting to my favourite part.'

As if they were grass stalks being rippled by the wind, one by one the needles began to slide into his skin and their heads disappeared from view. Then, slowly at first, but gathering pace, black stains from each puncture point started spreading out over his body.

'Stop it!' Angelique shouted.

'It's too late now,' Fellack said. 'Lord Orson's body is being laced with carbon nanotubes in preparation for conversion.'

'You monster. Can't you see the pain he's in?'

The scientist shrugged. 'A necessary step, but once the carbon conduits have fused with his brain, he will be beyond feeling any physical pain.'

Angelique glared at the scientist. 'Converted into what exactly?'

'Patience, my dear, and you'll see for yourself in a moment.'

I edged closer until I was just a few glass pods behind them. The blackness spread through Lord Orson's skin like an oil slick. He thrashed his head from side to side, but the fingers of ink crept up around his neck and flowed into his face. He turned his head and his gaze locked onto Angelique's, eyes widening in recognition.

Nausea filled my throat. Hades were torturing the man.

'Stop it!' Angelique struggled to get free of her captors, but they pinned her arms tighter behind her.

Fellack's eyes slitted. 'Just a moment longer...'

The silent horror movie played out on the other side of the glass. The black ink flowed into Lord Orson's eyes, the last human-looking part of him. He froze with a silent scream twisting his face, like he'd been turned into a gro-tesque shop dummy.

'Perfect,' Fellack whispered. 'He's ready for the final part of the conversion.'

The scientist opened a door set into the glass wall. The sentries above watched the party enter the room beneath them. As the party disappeared inside, one guard offered the other a cigarette. They started walking away along the gantry.

At least that was two sets of eyes I wouldn't have to worry about for the moment.

I crept closer until there was only one line of pods between me and the room.

Fellack operated the controls on a raised plinth. A robotic arm swung over Lord Orson's head and opened his mouth with its claw.

Through the open door, I heard Angelique gasp. 'Haven't you done enough to that poor man?'

'This is the preparation for the next and final step,' Fellack replied. 'We are bringing up a modified crystal from the mine beneath us. Then things will get really interesting.'

A second arm swung round to an opening hatch in the rear wall. A shriek of pain thudded into my mind and I clutched my head, trying not to shout out in agony and alert the sentries above.

Inside the hatch, a red Psuche gem glowed, just like the one in the pyramid they'd used to test Angelique with.

Now that I knew something was alive in that crystal, even if it was just a backup of someone, fury swept through me at it being tortured.

Angelique shrieked, her face contorted. The soldiers tightened their grip on her and smirked at each other.

Fellack gestured towards Lord Orson. He remained frozen, a dark statue laid out on a slab. 'As you can see, exposure to a modified Psuche gem no longer has any effect on Orson.'

A turntable rotated the crystal out of the chamber. The robotic arm grabbed it and swung the red gem over Lord Orson's mouth.

Fellack tightened his hand on the controls. Gears whined on the claw and cracks appeared throughout the crystal. A blood-like drip, squeezed from the gem's heart, fell onto Lord Orson's stained lips. His blackened tongue darted out like a lizard's to lick the liquid. A second drop and a shimmer of ruby light passed beneath his darkened skin. A third drip, and cracks of light began to glow within his body. The gem's cry started to disappear as it bled out.

Lord Orson's body became infused with burning light.

Angelique clenched her fists. 'What's happening to him?'

'He's absorbing the essence of the Psuche gem,' Fellack replied. 'Think of it as a symbiosis between Navigator and the being inside it. This is pure scientific perfection of a Navigator, Princess Angelique.'

'You should be ashamed of yourself for coming up with something as evil as this.'

'Oh, this wasn't my idea, Princess. All credit for that must go to Emperor Cronos. That remarkable man is a genius. He came up with the whole concept of this next step for human evolution. You see, for our purposes, Hades-adapted Psuche gems have their limitations. For example, they are much less efficient than the Cloud Rider freethinking ships. Our vessels are certainly slower to react in battle.'

'My *Athena* is worth ten of yours any day,' Angelique said.

'Maybe.' Fellack smiled and swept his arms out towards the pods ringing the operating theatre. 'And you see that's why we need these hybrid Navigators to operate Kraken. In earlier experiments, our adapted AIs burned out when we tried to use them with it.'

Kraken? I gazed at all the pods around me. That was a lot of hybrid Navigators they'd converted – ready for their new fleet of deadly ships?

The light in my helmet blinked off. At last!

The Psuche gem above Lord Orson faded to darkness. The pain vanished from my body and my thoughts sharpened. I glanced up at the sentries on the gantry leaning on the rail talking to each other. From where they stood, the room beneath them had to be out of their line of sight. But I also knew it wouldn't be long till Ambra arrived, probably with more men in tow. Time to get my ass into gear.

I turned the suit's chameleon net on and crept towards the operating theatre. One of the guards glanced in my direction and I froze.

Please don't let him see me...

His gaze travelled on. Relief streamed through my body.

I moved forward again as quietly as I could on the balls of my feet and slipped into the glass-walled room. But what if one of the sentries heard something and raised the alert? Very slowly, I pulled the door closed behind me, praying that the room's soundproofing would be enough to mask the noise of whatever might be about to kick off.

I glanced at my Leatherman's blade and stared at the soldiers' broad backs. Nausea filled my stomach. Angelique might have been able to use a knife to stick someone, but there was no way I could. There had to be an alternative. Maybe if I could knock the guards out?

I spotted a large bottle of clear liquid in a rack next to me. I swapped the Leatherman to my left hand and grabbed the heavy flask. Not affected by the chameleon net, the bottle bobbed into the air like it'd been enchanted.

My neck muscles tightened. Any moment someone might spot what I was doing. I thought of my training with Angelique. Relax. I dropped into a fighting pose she'd shown me, my stance soft but instantly ready to react.

'Always take on your hardest opponent first,' Angelique had told me during one of our lessons.

I edged up behind the broader guard of the two on the left, raised the bottle and swung it down hard onto his head.

With an explosion of glass and fluid, the flask shattered onto his skull and soaked into his hair. At once wisps of smoke began to rise as his skin blistered. The guard screamed and collapsed to the floor, batting his head with his hands.

In a horrified rush I realised what the liquid was – acid!

The other guard spun round and shoved Angelique to the floor. For a moment he looked straight through me, but his gaze tightened onto where I was standing and he snarled. 'There you are, scum.' He started to move towards me and drew his sword from its scabbard.

Training… Angelique had drummed the combat moves into me, hour after hour throughout the flight, saying they might save my life.

The guard leapt towards me, sword arm raised. Before I could even think, instinct took over and I found myself spinning on my left leg. My right foot flicked out in a roundhouse movement and struck him in the chest. With the jarring blow, the man flew through the air and crashed to the floor. His sword skittered away and he didn't move.

I killed the net's power and cracked open the visor of the chameleon suit. I raised the Leatherman towards the scientist.

Fellack backed against the operating table and gawped at me.

'One word and you die – understand?' I said, trying to make the threat sound as convincing as possible.

'Just don't hurt me.' He raised his hands.

Angelique clambered back to her feet and threw her arms around me. 'Dom, you're okay.'

'More importantly, so are you.'

Her expression hardened as her eyes focused on my visor. She grabbed the knife from my hand.

I looked past her to see Fellack reaching towards a red button on the wall.

Angelique spun round and threw the Leatherman at the scientist. It blurred through the air, tumbling end over end, and buried itself into the scientist's neck. He gripped his throat, blood spurting between his fingers, and toppled to the floor.

'I saw his reflection in your visor,' Angelique said. 'He was going for the alarm.'

A chill ran through me. 'Couldn't you have given him a warning?'

Her mouth pinched. 'No time for that.'

Really? It did my head in how Angelique could switch into soldier mode in a heartbeat.

She pointed to the glass wall. 'I think Ambra is about to make an appearance.'

I turned to see a green bulb pulsing above the lift door in the lab. 'We've got to get out of here.'

'There's no time.' Angelique marched across and pulled the Leatherman from the scientist's neck. She turned to me, grim-faced. 'Dom, they don't know you're here.'

'What are you saying?'

'I can make it look like I broke free of the guards and did all this by myself. You hide until the coast is clear, find Jules and escape.'

She couldn't be serious. 'No way. We can fight them together.'

'And then we'll die together. You heard Fellack. They won't kill me as long as they need me to be one of their precious converts.'

'You don't know that – Ambra may kill you on sight.'

'That's just a chance I'll have to take.'

'But, Angelique, even if he doesn't kill you,' I gestured towards the thing on the slab that had been Lord Orson, 'do you really want to be turned into a zombie like that?'

Angelique gave me the Leatherman back and grabbed the reactor from Fellack's pocket. 'I'm sorry, Dom, we haven't got time to debate this.' She rotated the dial on the red box's side. It whirred and the dial started to click. 'Right, that's the charge set for five hours. When it blows it will bring the entire mast down onto this god forsaken place.' She pointed at the pods. 'And perhaps most important of all, it will put those poor souls out of their misery.'

Angelique knelt by the operating table that held Orson. The reactor leapt from her hand and fastened itself to the underside of the metal table.

'Magnetic attachment,' she said.

My head felt like it was going to burst. Five hours to rescue Jules. Five hours to rescue Angelique – if she hadn't been converted. Five hours to escape.

I grabbed her hands. 'Whatever it takes, I promise I'll come back.'

She hugged me. 'I managed to hide my balloon pack in the volcano basin before I was discovered. If you can't rescue me in time, take it and escape with the others.'

My insides twisted. 'I'm not leaving you.'

She pulled away and cupped my face with her hand. 'You may have to.'

'No way—'

Angelique pressed a fingertip to my mouth. 'Stop trying to be the hero all the time and let someone else take their turn.' She pointed at an open crate. 'Time for you to hide, Dom.'

'But this feels wrong, Angelique.'

'Then think of Jules. You've got to find her, and Stephen if you can. If you die by my side you won't be any good to them, will you?'

I stared at her, not able to think of anything to say. How could I just turn my back on my friend, even if it meant saving Jules? It was an impossible choice and not one I wanted to make – not now, not ever.

Angelique slipped her Tac off and handed it to me. 'You'll need this.'

I took it, my mind on autopilot, and strapped the device around my wrist.

She shoved me towards a crate. 'Now get a move on – you can hide in there until the coast is clear.'

Fog filled my thoughts as I moved towards the box.

The man I'd hit with the flask had stopped whimpering, though clumps of his hair had been burned away to the red flesh below. It made me sick just looking at him. I didn't even want to think about the pain he must have been in before he blacked out.

Angelique looked down at the two unconscious guards and sighed. She took hold of the wounded man's neck and gave it a violent twist. The man's body jerked and stilled.

Horror rushed up through me. 'What the hell are you doing? He wasn't dead.'

'But he was a witness. If either guard regains consciousness, the first thing they'll tell them about is you, and that's something I can't let happen.'

She crossed to the other guard I'd knocked out.

'Don't,' I whispered.

'I'm sorry, Dom, I have to.' She gave me a sad look, knelt down, and then twisted the other guard's neck with a loud crack.

Bile flooded my mouth. That was the difference between us. She was a trained warrior. Me...just a lad from Oklahoma who'd got caught up in a living nightmare.

A faint squeal came from behind us and we turned to see the lift doors opening.

Angelique walked up to me. 'Whatever happens, don't move, don't do anything, however much you may want to, do you understand?'

I stared at her like a dumb animal, too numb to find any words.

She gave me a small smile and gestured at the crate.

I clambered into it without arguing, and squatted down. I held her gaze as she dropped the lid into place. Darkness closed around me, just a crack of light beneath the lid. I pressed an eye to it and saw Angelique approach Lord Orson on the operating table.

She touched his face. 'I'm sorry, old friend.' She raised her hand.

'Stop her,' a muffled voice cried out. Even muted by the glass walls, I recognised Ambra's commanding tone from outside the chamber.

The warrior princess's expression hardened. She plunged the blade into Orson's chest. The red cracks of light etched over his body faded. The display on the monitor flat-lined. With a gentle sigh, his eyes fluttered closed and his look of agony was replaced with a smile.

Shouts. Running feet. Soldiers swarmed past my hiding place.

Angelique spun, kicked and struck, her blows sending opponents flying. Everything she'd taught me looked effortless as she performed the moves in her deadly dance. For a wild moment I thought she might actually beat them, but as she took out two men with blows to their necks, Ambra crept up behind her unseen and raised his pistol crossbow, ready to strike.

I wanted to shout out, to do something, but her words looped through my mind. 'Don't do anything, however much you may want to...' I jammed my teeth hard together as tears filled my eyes.

The world decelerated to slow motion as Ambra hit Angelique, my senses playing it out in awful cinematic detail: her head snapping forward with the power of the blow, spittle flying from her mouth... With a cry she sunk to the ground. One of the downed soldiers clasped his arms around her in a bear hug. The awful moment stretched out and any hope I had of her winning died.

I couldn't sit this out. I had to do something. I still had to have at least ten seconds of chameleon power left and my finger inched towards the control as Ambra strode towards Angelique.

Her words looped again. *Don't do anything...*

Ambra pulled his fist back as Angelique snarled at him. My finger hovered over the palm button.

Angelique. Jules. If I made a move now... My thoughts locked up.

Ambra's fist crashed into Angelique's face and she slumped into the soldier's arms.

Guilt swarmed through me. Even though Angelique had made sense, right here, right now, whatever she said, I'd let her down. I felt like a coward. And I hated myself for it.

Ambra gestured at one of the tunnels leading away from the chamber. 'Take her to the holding cells.'

A man hoisted Angelique over his shoulder. He carried her out of the room towards a tunnel with the number ten stencilled over it.

Ambra knelt down by Fellack and shook his head. His gaze swept past my crate to the plinth Fellack had used to operate the mechanical claws.

'So why did Fellack drag you in here, Princess Angelique?' Ambra said.

'Sir?' A young soldier said to him.

'Just thinking aloud,' Ambra said.

He crossed to the plinth and peered at a screen built into it. A slow smile spread across his face. 'Well, well, well, so you're a Navigator, Princess. No wonder you were able to evade us for so long.' He glanced at the blade in Lord Orson's chest. 'And this convert will have to be replaced in the Hive.' His smile tightened. 'Oh, that's just poetic justice after all the trouble you've caused. You'll take his place and, by sacrificing yourself, help us to create the ultimate weapon.'

Ultimate weapon? The Kraken? And what was the Hive? A beehive had thousands of bees so... I thought of all the pods and the wires linking them to the mast. Tesla had said he'd no idea how Hades had powered the jamming mast. Was that it? Were Hades using all those hybrid Navigators to create this thing they called the Hive? And if so, had they somehow found a way to power the mast with their thoughts? With a sick logic, it made a sort of sense.

A shiver passed through me as Ambra strode from the room. I stared out at Lord Orson's lifeless body. Unless I freed Angelique, it wouldn't be long before she was one of those Hades zombies in a pod, too.

Chapter Sixteen

ALIVE

Medics crammed the operating theatre. They dealt with the injured and dead soldiers Angelique had fought. The only person who hadn't been given a second glance was Lord Orson. It seemed a Cloud Rider wasn't as important as a Hades man to these doctors.

Inside the crate I'd tried to stretch out my limbs as they began to cramp. Every muscle felt tangled with knots. How much longer would they be?

The last two medics helped the final soldier, whose leg Angelique had broken, limp out. I started to raise the lid, but heard footsteps approaching. Darn it – I lowered the lid again.

Through my peephole I saw Sergeant Yanton leading an old man and a dreadlocked teenager about my age into the operating theatre. They both wore dusty, grey coveralls and had short chains linking their ankles together. On each of their wrists I noticed a demon logo with a number tattooed beneath it.

They raised Orson's body from the table and gently, like they were handling a living person, placed him on a gurney.

The moral argument cycled through my head again. Had Angelique been right to kill Lord Orson? Couldn't we have saved him and brought him back somehow?

The sergeant shoved the elderly man. 'Get a move on.'

Head bowed, legs shaking, the man took hold of one end of the gurney.

I clenched my jaw. Where did the sergeant get off being such a jerk?

'I said, get moving.' Yanton unhooked a short cane dangling from his belt and struck it across the man's bald head. He groaned but kept his balance.

The teenager's eyes flashed with the same fire I felt burning in my gut.

The sergeant narrowed his gaze on the boy. 'If you want to test your luck, go ahead.'

The old man shook his head at the teenager. A slight nod and the lad dropped his shoulders. It seemed he had a lot in common with me – a short fuse that needed to be kept in check.

Yanton sneered. 'That's right, Zack, you teach the young pup how to toe the line.' He twirled the cane through his fingers and smirked at the teenager. 'Now before I decide to use this on you, get that body down to the thermal plant for incineration.'

'Yes, sir,' the old man replied. The teenager kept mute. I could tell even a slight prod and he'd hurl a mouthful of abuse at Yanton – just like I'd have done if that had been me.

The sergeant strode out of the operating theatre and headed back towards the lift.

From my low vantage point inside the crate I could see the matchbox reactor's numerals clicking down. When that hit zero...

Zack and the teenager started to push the gurney to the door. What if they were here when the explosion went off? Hell, we were talking a nuclear explosion here. How many innocent people like these guys would get killed? I didn't want their blood on my conscience – I had to warn them.

I pulled the lid back and stood up in my crate.

They both turned and stared at me.

'Who are you?' Zack said.

I popped open my pressure suit's faceplate. 'A friend.'

He stared at me. 'But you look just like...' He glanced across at his companion, who gave him a wide-eyed look and nodded.

Zack crossed to me. 'What's your name, son?'

Huh? This wasn't the reaction I'd been expecting. 'Dom, Dom Taylor.'

'Taylor.' Zack blinked. 'And what's your father's name?'

Okay, this was getting weird. 'Shaun. He died a year ago.'

'Are you sure?'

The left-field question totally threw me. 'What do you mean?' This conversation was getting surreal real fast.

'That he's dead?'

'Of course I am. He flew into a twister and his plane was torn apart.'

Zack scratched his chin. 'It can't be a coincidence,' he said to the teenager. 'He even has the same eyes.'

'Same eyes as...' An impossible idea took root in my head. 'Are you trying to say that you've seen my dad?'

'I am.'

My mind whirled. I felt like someone who believed the world was flat had just discovered it was actually round. They had to be mistaken – it was probably someone who just looked a bit like me, or something screwy to do with parallel worlds. 'When did you see this guy?'

'I took someone called Shaun Taylor, who's the spitting image of you, some food less than an hour ago.'

Everyone had always said how much I looked like Dad, but I still didn't dare believe it. I felt a fluttering in my chest. 'Where is he?'

Zack gestured to the corridor with the number ten above it – the same one that Angelique had been dragged off down.

Alive? The information started to sink in. Could this really be true? My thoughts stopped whirling and the pattern locked into place as I thought it through. Like me, Dad had inherited the same genetic marker from Great-granddad Alex. And since *Athena* had sensed me across the dimensions, couldn't Hades have used their ships like bloodhounds to hunt Dad down to our world too? My god, it made sense. He hadn't died, he'd been abducted!

I felt like whooping, crying, I didn't know what. The enormity of this was impossible to get my head around fully. 'But why did they take him?'

'Hades have been after anyone with the Navigator gene.'

'Of course – just like at Floating City.' A chilling thought struck me. 'He's here to be converted?'

Zack's expression became drawn. 'I'm afraid time for your father has run out. He's due to be processed any moment.'

I stared at Orson's carbon-stained body on the gurney. They were going to do that to Dad? Ice spiked through my chest. One moment I'd found out that he was alive, the next I'd learnt he was effectively about to be murdered. 'But we can't let that happen – we've got to rescue him.'

'We?' the dreadlocked teenager asked, arms crossed.

'You don't understand. In just under five hours a nuke is going to go off.'

The older man stared at me. 'A fission bomb?'

'Yes, a dirty big mushroom cloud directly over Hells Cauldron.'

Zack paled. 'But all the Cloud Rider prisoners working down in the mines.'

'How many prisoners are we talking here?' I asked.

'About a thousand.'

Heck, a thousand? How could we free that many people in under five hours? Wasn't it enough that I had to rescue Jules and Angelique? Now there were all these others.

My mind started whirling once more. If this were a prisoner breakout in the movies, what would happen next? I remembered one of Dad's favourites – *The Great Escape*. The prisoners in that film had cooked up tons of genius ideas for getting out.

'Look you must have spoken to the others about escaping – you must have some sort of plan?'

The two of them exchanged glances. So that answered that.

'Go on,' I said.

The teenager shook his head at Zack. 'But it could never work. We've been over it a hundred times.'

Zack scratched his neck. 'It could if we can get access to the pumping station and shut it down.'

The teenager gazed at my pressure suit. 'Is that some sort of chameleon net you're wearing?'

'Yes it is, and...?'

'And could you sneak into the pumping station for us?'

'I might. But where is it and more importantly why?'

'Below us in the mines. As to the why, there's an underwater river that leads out of Hells Cauldron to a flooded fissure on the surface. The problem is, the entrance to it is blocked by the spinning rotors of the pumping station. Try to swim through those and you'd be cut to pieces in seconds. I was doing a reconnaissance mission on it when I was captured.'

'You were?'

He nodded. 'I was spying for my father. My cover was a Master Technician, but really I was trying to gather information to help free the Cloud Riders trapped here.'

I stared at him. Could this guy be Danrick's son? 'Your name isn't Stephen, is it?'

He stared at me. 'How on Earths do you know my name?'

Oh god, how could I tell him? I had to. 'I knew your father.'

His gaze tightened on me. 'What do you mean, *knew*?'

'He...' In the same moment I'd found out Dad was still alive, I now had to tell Stephen he'd lost his. My insides hollowed out. I forced myself to continue. I looked him straight in the eye. 'Your dad was killed by a Hades spy.'

Stephen's face crumpled and he stared at the floor. 'How?' he whispered.

'He was helping us escape Floating City. The last thing he said to us was to find you.'

His knuckles whitened as he tightened his grip around the handles of the gurney. 'First my sister, now my father? I've got no family left now.'

'I didn't know you'd lost your sister, too.'

'Lieutenant Roxanne. She was serving on an airship that was shot down during the first assault by Hades of the final battle.'

What could I say? Sorry? Like that would make a difference. Guilt edged out the joy about the news of Dad.

Zack patted Stephen's shoulder. 'Sorry, lad.'

Stephen nodded but didn't look up. I knew exactly how he was feeling – it took me straight back to the morning we found the wreckage of Dad's biplane. Ever since a shadow had fallen over my life – until now.

Zack peered at me. 'You said *us*? Is someone with you?'

'Princess Angelique, but she's been taken prisoner and they're going to convert her.'

The old man stared at me. 'She's here – and she's a Navigator?'

I nodded.

Zack's expression widened. 'Oh by the gods, you hear that, Stephen?'

He looked up and brushed away tears. The tough teenager I'd first seen had disappeared. 'What's the point and where would we run to? Doesn't it just prove that if Hades can capture someone like the Princess, none of us are safe anywhere? We may as well just accept our fate and give up.'

I glanced at the Tac ticking down. *Four hours and twenty minutes.* I knew he was hurting, but I had to get through to Stephen. There would be time for him to grieve later. I pointed at Lord Orson. 'How many of you have died already?'

'Too many.'

'And I bet plenty of innocent people have been killed by Hades as well, bystanders who got caught out in this war?'

'Yes...'

'So you've got to keep fighting them. I know it's what Angelique would say if she were here. And having met your dad, I'm also sure it's exactly what he'd do.'

Stephen took a shuddering breath.

I could tell he was drawing strength from somewhere deep inside.

'Yes – yes, he would,' he said.

Zack placed his hand on Stephen's shoulder. 'I know you've lost your father, lad, but you also know that the Cloud Riders will always be your family.'

Stephen blinked and slowly nodded. I'd just given him information that had shattered his life. But I could already tell he would get through this – just like I had.

'The Cloud Riders will always be my family...' His gaze lingered on Lord Orson.

'Just think, Stephen, we could be breathing sky air again soon,' Zack said.

Stephen gave him a fleeting smile. 'Okay, let's do this for my father, for Lord Orson, for all our people.'

The tension I'd been carrying loosened a fraction across my shoulders. 'Right, we need to put your plan into action, and fast.'

Zack nodded. 'Stephen and I will talk to the secret council and get everyone organised for the breakout.'

'And I need to rescue Angelique and...' I couldn't believe I was saying it, 'my dad.'

'I wouldn't try rescuing the Princess, or your father, just yet,' Stephen said. 'They're about to change the guards and the cells will be swarming with soldiers.'

'How long does that usually take?'

'About thirty minutes for all the guards to be relieved.'

Half an hour before the alarm would be sounded. But so little time to free Angelique – and Dad. God, I couldn't wait to see him, to see the look on his face when I opened his cell door. I found myself avoiding Stephen's gaze.

Jules's face flashed into my mind. 'There's also someone else I need to find. Duke Ambra snatched a friend of mine. He's holding her prisoner somewhere in Hells Cauldron. I don't suppose you've seen her? She's got shoulder-length dark hair and brown eyes.'

Stephen shook his head. 'No one new has joined us down in the mines recently.'

Zack gave me a questioning look. 'I think I may have seen her.'

Hope sparked inside. 'Where?'

'I had to run an errand up to the palace kitchens and I caught a glimpse of Ambra with a teenage woman. Going by your description that must be her.'

'She looked okay?'

'Yes...' Lines creased Zack's forehead.

'What?'

'She was dining with Ambra in the royal apartments.' He raised his eyebrows at Stephen.

Heat rose to my face. I knew exactly what he was think-ing and it made me want to puke. 'No way would she fall in with someone like Ambra – you don't know her.'

'I'm sure you're right,' Zack said. 'Sometimes appear-ances can be deceptive.'

I caught the lack of belief in his voice and wanted to tell him all the reasons that I was right – that nobody knew Jules as well as me. But somehow I couldn't string my thoughts together. 'Just show me where she is.'

Zack glanced up at the roof. 'I would take you, but the sentries above are expecting us to wheel Lord Orson out of here in a moment.' He grabbed a set of notes clipped to the end of the gurney. 'I'll draw you a map of where your friend is being kept.'

'Okay.'

'She'll almost certainly be guarded,' Stephen said.

'I can sneak past a few Hades soldiers.'

He gave me a brief smile. 'So I gathered.'

Zack finished his map and handed it to me. It showed me a rough sketch of the palace at the top of Hells Cauldron, with an 'X' next to one of the towers. 'That's where your friend is.'

Heck, I'd been so close to Jules when I'd run along the battlements to the stairwell. If only I'd known at the time. I could've groaned.

'Once you've found her, you shouldn't have too much trouble gaining access to the cells with your chameleon net,' Zack said.

'What about the cell doors? Aren't they locked?'

Stephen stood a little taller. He unhooked a chain with a ring hanging on it from around his neck and handed it to me.

184

'What's this?'

'As you guessed, we've been busy making plans to escape. Have a closer look at that ring.'

I studied it and noticed the circumference was filled with meshed cogs of every size. 'What does this do?'

'That's an unlocking ring in your hand. Insert it into the door mechanism and it will open any cell.'

'Like a skeleton key?'

He nodded.

'Awesome.'

'When you've freed the others, carry on to the end of cell block ten and you'll find a lift down to the mines. We'll be waiting for you at the bottom. Then we'll take you to the pumping station.'

The red light in the suit blinked off. I glanced at the Tac – four hours, fifteen minutes, and all this would be gone. 'Time to get the plan into motion.'

'May the gods walk with you,' Zack said.

'And you too.'

There was so much that could go off the rails, but I didn't even want to think about that. Somehow I'd pull this off.

I caught the determination in Stephen's eyes and realised he was thinking the same thing. He nodded to me as though he'd read my thoughts too. I was starting to admire this guy – to hear you'd lost your dad and then to pull it together enough to carry on the next moment took real guts. I wasn't sure I could've managed it if our positions had been swapped.

Zack and Stephen trundled the gurney towards the exit.

Stephen opened the glass door and peered upwards. 'Incineration,' he called out.

'You've taken your sweet time,' a man's voice said from above us. 'Get moving.'

The clank of footsteps above and the portcullis above cell-block ten began to rise.

Another minute ticked down on the Tac. The sooner I got going, the sooner I'd get back for the big reunion with Dad. Not to mention the fact that I couldn't wait to see the look on Jules's face when I strode into her room. Only an hour earlier everything had seemed lost, but now my whole world was full of hope.

I pressed the palm button in my glove and my suit's cloth shimmered to camouflage me against the background. I cast a last look towards the cells.

The sentries' attention was fixed on Zack and Stephen pushing the gurney into the tunnel. My pulse sped and I crept towards the lift.

CHAPTER Seventeen
BETRAYED

Fine snow blew across the staircase as I reached the top of the landing. The wind howled with icy fingers probing for any gaps in my fly-dive suit.

I wiped away the powder melting on my visor and studied Zack's map. According to the 'X' he'd marked, Jules was in the tower on the far side of the volcano's mouth around the walkway. Under the shimmering aurora light, the tower's arched stained-glass windows with airship designs shone out like jewels.

Would Jules really be in there? I still couldn't quite believe I was about to see her again. The anticipation was killing me.

I scanned the battlements. No sign of soldiers. Good – I could conserve the suit's power for now.

Keeping in the shadows cast from the blazing aurora, I began to circle along the wall around to the tower.

The wind moaned through the mast, draped with icicles like an over-decorated Christmas tree. It towered over me, a tall metal splinter scratching at the Northern Lights. A faint hum came from it and a soft, blue light played over its surface.

I thought of the cables in the chamber at its base that linked the mast to the glass pods of the Hive. So where were all of the Kraken ships the converted were going to pilot? Hidden in the hangars we'd seen? Maybe Jules would know. Perhaps that was why she'd decided to play nice with Ambra – gain his confidence and get him to tell her everything. Knowing Jules, that was exactly what she'd do. That had to be it and explained why she wasn't down in the mines. Although there was still a lot we needed to sort out between us, I felt a weight lift from me.

The last time I'd seen Jules she'd completely misread me. She'd convinced herself that I had chosen Angelique over her. How wrong could one woman be? Jules was my future, my everything, even if she hadn't realised it just yet. And that was a misunderstanding I intended to clear up as soon as I saw her.

A flurry of snow moaned over the battlements and the world became a swirling mass of powder. In the white-out I kept my hand to the wall. It would be far too easy to get lost and find myself plummeting over the battlements.

The blizzard started to thin as I edged forward. A pool of light appeared just ahead. In a doorway at the tower's base, I spotted two figures silhouetted against a bright interior. One of them was Ambra wrapped in a cloak. They stepped out into the snowstorm together and headed my way.

Ambra's companion, a man with long sideburns wearing a lab coat, presumably another scientist, wrung his hands together.

I'd nowhere to hide. They were going to be right on top of me any moment. My breath misted my mask as I powered up the suit, praying they wouldn't spot my concealed outline in the darkness.

As they approached I heard the scientist say, 'With two more conversions the Hive will be complete. Orson's loss is unfortunate, but not insurmountable. Thankfully, as you say, Princess Angelique will be able to take his place.'

Ambra clasped his hands behind his back and paused close to my position to gaze at the mast. I tucked myself deeper into the shadows.

'That's true, Simean, but as it seems so appropriate, I want to convert her last. After all, she'll be the final piece of the jigsaw.'

Final piece? Did that mean Dad would be converted before Angelique? Did that also mean I might be too late to save him? My stomach did a slow roll.

'What a fitting celebration for Emperor Cronos's arrival. We received his signal but an hour ago, my Duke. His flagship should be arriving any moment.'

Just what I didn't want to hear. Things kept going from bad to worse and picking up pace as they did so.

'Excellent news. I'm relying on you now, Simean, and I trust with your rapid promotion after Fellack's death that you'll be able to keep everything on track?'

Simean gave Ambra a twisted smile. 'I hope to make some improvements on my predecessor's estimates.'

'Good man. And about the progress with Kraken, I'm sure the Emperor will be keen to see a test flight.'

'We're on track for completion in a few days' time. Of course we will need to select a target to test its main weapon on.'

Its... Was it a single ship rather than a fleet? And the mention of the weapon sounded like bad news.

Ambra set off again with Simean hurrying after him. 'I know the ideal target – one that I visited recently: Earth DZL2351.'

My heart froze colder than the ice around me. My Earth. And to be precise, probably my corner of Oklahoma. Ambra had a score to settle and he wasn't the sort to let a grudge drop.

I pulled up my sleeve to examine the Tac's display. *Four hours and ten minutes.* The explosion would hopefully take the Kraken out before they could use it. And if Cronos was here, maybe we'd get lucky and he'd be killed too...

Reflected inside my visor, I caught the hardness in my eyes. I was thinking like a soldier, thinking like Angelique again. When had I crossed that line, exactly?

Ambra's and Simean's conversation faded into the distance. They reached the stairwell and disappeared down it.

Time to get my ass into gear. I set off at a run towards the entrance to the tower. My mouth dried out as I took hold of a wrought-iron handle on the door and twisted it. Here went nothing.

The red light blinked on – I had only thirty seconds of juice left. But Stephen had said there might be guards, so I couldn't take the risk of entering without it.

I prayed the hinges wouldn't squeak as I pushed the door open. I let out my breath when I saw an empty, ornate room. It looked like I was going to have a clear run after all. I killed the suit's power.

The moan of the wind died away as I closed the door behind me. I found myself standing on a deep, soft, red carpet. A glass chandelier hung from the ceiling and its crystals shone like diamonds. A polished marble staircase spiralled to an ornate golden door on the landing above. All around the curved walls hung large, faded tapestries decorated with airships against cloudscapes of sunsets, lightning storms and star-filled skies.

I found it hard to imagine a younger Angelique spending her time here on vacation. Once again it brought home just how different our lives had been. Mine, growing up in a diner, flipping burgers, and hers, born into the life of luxury within a royal family, complete with life experiences that I would've killed to have had. No contest, my life sucked big time compared to hers.

My gaze fell on a tapestry larger than the rest, featuring a big man with dark piercing eyes and a crown perched on his head. It was stitched with bright, fresh threads and hung from floor to ceiling. Compared to the others, the portrait looked gaudy and new. Something told me this had to be Emperor Cronos, partly because everything about the man in the portrait creeped me out.

I gazed up to the landing. So where were all the guards? For some reason this was making me more nervous. It was far too easy.

I crept up the stairs. Half expecting guards to leap out from their hiding places, I held my finger over the palm control ready to reactivate the suit, but nothing happened.

I reached the landing and placed my ear to the gold, carved door, but I couldn't hear a thing. Maybe Ambra was keeping Jules chained up in there, and gagged. I turned the handle and, taking a deep breath, tiptoed inside.

A crackling fireplace illuminated a room filled with paintings and more tapestries, as well as three polar-bear heads mounted on plaques. Different world, different rules. My gaze swept over the surroundings to a door on the far side. A bedroom?

I crept to the door and listened – I could hear the murmur of someone breathing. I wasn't taking a chance this time and powered up the suit. At once the ten-second warning light started to blink. Blood thumping in my ears, I pushed the inner door open, ready to duck back out if it turned out to be a soldier asleep inside.

No one grabbed me.

It took a moment for my eyes to adjust to the dark interior. I became aware of an old clock ticking in the corner. Forms started to emerge from the uniform blackness. I made out a large four-poster bed with fabric draped down from the ceiling over it like an indoor tent. My eyes adapted enough to make out a woman curled up in it, her dark, shoulder-length hair framing her head.

Relief burst through me. 'Jules!'

I rushed over and grabbed her hand.

Her eyes snapped wide. She stared at her wrist and tugged at it. She bared her teeth and got ready to scream.

Hell. I was still invisible. I clamped my hand over her mouth and turned off the chameleon net. 'Jules, it's me.'

She stared through the visor into my eyes. Shock and relief swept through her face. But in a split second that vanished and panic twisted her expression. Her hand flew to a circular pendant around her neck, a dark, black stone with an eye design at its centre.

'Thank god you're okay.' I hugged her.

She stiffened in my arms and pulled away. The smile was gone. She gave me the weirdest look, like seeing me was the worst moment in her life.

'Get away from me,' she said.

Perhaps she didn't recognise me. I flicked up my visor. 'Jules, it's Dom.'

'Please don't hurt me.'

I stared at her. Huh? 'I'm here to rescue you.'

She jumped from the bed and backed into a corner. 'Leave me alone.'

Now she was seriously spooking me. 'What's wrong, Jules?'

She dashed for the door. Running away? From me? She had to be drugged – or brainwashed.

I stepped in her way and grabbed her arm. 'Just calm down. I'm here with Angelique, but she's been captured. You won't believe this but my dad is alive too.'

Jules blinked, wonder filling her expression.

'Hades took him prisoner because of his Navigator ability. He's here in the cells.'

But fear filled her eyes again and she shook her head.

Whatever Ambra had done to Jules, I needed to get through to her. 'They're going to convert him, Jules. I've got to get him out of there.'

She clutched at her necklace.

This wasn't going the way the script in my head was written, but I pressed on. 'It wasn't a twister Dad got caught up in, it was a Hades Vortex.'

Jules gave me a desperate look. Before I could stop her, she darted to a cord hanging by the bed and yanked it.

Something felt wrong, very wrong. 'What the hell did you just do, Jules?'

She held my gaze. 'I called the guards.' Although her tone was harsh, I could see she had started to blink back tears.

I couldn't believe this was happening. 'You did what? But why?'

'So they can throw you in the prison with Princess Angelique. You always liked her more than me.'

My words came out a whisper through my tightening throat. 'What have you done, Jules?' The suit's light was still off. Suddenly I felt trapped, caged in this room with her.

Jules's fingers twined around the pendant. 'If you hurt me, Duke Ambra will have your head.'

The world spun under my feet. What had happened to my best friend, the woman I'd fallen for? Was she seriously jealous enough of Angelique to betray me?

Footsteps thundered up the stairs. Numbness spread through me – I couldn't move if I'd wanted to. My whole life had just been torn into tiny pieces.

The doors flew open. Ambra stood there with two guards either side of him, aiming their steam-powered crossbows at my chest.

'Well, well. What have we got here?' Ambra said.

'He was trying to abduct me, my Duke,' Jules said.

My Duke? A chill raced through me. I reached out towards her.

Jules flinched away. 'He said you have his dad in prison.'

A slow smile filled Ambra's face. 'His father, we have him?'

Jules stood like a statue, her eyes hard, avoiding mine. 'He says his father's a Navigator, just like him.'

Ambra laughed. 'Oh, now this just gets better and better. On the same day Princess Angelique delivers herself into my hands, irony of irony, my other prisoner's son presents himself too. And another Navigator at that.' His amused gaze fixed on me. 'I'm sure we'll find a special space for you in one of our experiments, boy.'

This couldn't be happening. I glared at Jules. 'How could you?'

Her mouth pinched. This wasn't the Jules I knew. This person was a stranger.

'She's decided where her true loyalties lie, boy,' Ambra said.

I turned to Jules and glared at her. 'I thought you were my friend?'

She crossed her arms and gave me the barest shrug.

Ambra gestured to the guards. 'Seize him.'

I started to spin round, but I was too slow. A blow slammed into my neck and I crashed to the floor.

A guard towered over me and lowered the stock of the crossbow he'd struck me with. Pain rippled through my body. The other guard pinned me down and yanked the helmet from my head. He ripped off my fly-dive suit and bound my wrists together.

I twisted my head in Jules's direction. 'Just tell me why?'

Her mouth curled down. 'Because Duke Ambra is on the winning side.'

Her words struck me like a knife in my gut, burning and tearing at my flesh.

The guards hauled me to my feet.

'Take him to join Angelique and Shaun,' Ambra said. 'Let it not be said I don't have any compassion, boy. You can say your goodbyes to your father before he's converted.'

I snarled at him. 'I'm going to make you pay for this, Ambra.'

He sneered at me. 'Only in your imagination I'm afraid.'

Jules brushed Ambra's hand with hers. 'You have a good heart, my Duke.'

Her smile for him twisted the hot knife in my stomach.

'We'll be able to put on quite a show for Emperor Cronos when he arrives,' Ambra said. 'I'm sure the completion of the Hive ahead of schedule will put him in a splendid mood.'

Anger surged up through me and I glared at Jules. 'You're dead to me.'

She flinched, but then glowered back at me. 'Goodbye, *boy*.'

In that moment the person I thought I knew was wiped away. I'd no fight left, just a big pit in my chest that her knife had cut out of me, raw and hollow.

I wasn't even aware of being taken away until the freezing wind bit into my face. We were outside on the battlements. The guards shoved me towards the stairwell. I felt like a robot, barely aware of anything around me.

Betrayed. Jules had betrayed me.

A boom filled the sky. In the distance a massive twister began to form, ringed by four smaller tornados. The funnels started to flow away, revealing a massive red and gold ship, at least the size of a large shopping mall. Red pennants flew from dozens of silver wings and the drone of its engines growled like a pack of barking dogs. Around it four ships, each at least twice the size of *Athena*, flew in tight escort formation.

I felt myself crumble inside. Cronos had arrived. Game over. Life over.

Our plans had fallen apart, all because of Jules. Everything we had fought for, lost. My vision blurred with tears. I hung my head and stared at the floor.

I had one thing left. Whatever they did to me, I wouldn't tell them about the nuke. If we slowed them down from attacking Earth for just a moment it would be worth it, even it took all our lives. And when the nuke blew, I just hoped it would take with it as much of Hells Cauldron and as many Hades to hell as possible – and Jules too.

CHAPTER Eighteen
DAD

Helped by the shoves of the guards, I traipsed towards cell-block ten like the walking dead. It was only as the cell door slid open to reveal pitch-darkness and a rank restroom odour filled my nose that I remembered who was in there.

Could it be true about Dad? My heart thudded harder. I spoke into the gloom. 'Angelique...?' I swallowed. *'Dad?'*

'Dom, is that really you?' a man's voice replied. A shape emerged from the darkness: broad-shouldered, blue-eyed, face lined and tired, a stubbled beard – but it *really* was him.

I rushed forward and threw my arms around Dad, flooded with joy so fierce it felt like I'd burn up with it.

Dad kissed the side of my head, clamped his arms around my back like he was never going to let go again. 'I thought I'd never see you again, son.'

I'd stopped fantasising about him being alive years ago, so I still couldn't get my head around this being real. A lump the size of a boulder filled my throat. 'We all thought you were dead.'

He cradled the back of my head. 'I'm so sorry.'

Angelique smiled at me from the corner of the cell she crouched in.

'This family reunion is all very touching, but I ain't got all day,' the guard said. He shoved me hard in the back and I sprawled into the cell. Angelique leapt to her feet, but Dad had already squared up to him.

The other guard raised his crossbow. 'Calm down.' He aimed his weapon at me instead. 'Or would you like us to kill your son in front of you?'

Dad raised his hands and backed into the cell.

The guard grinned and hit a button on the wall. 'That's more like it.'

The riveted metal door clattered down and utter blackness clamped over us.

I felt a hand pulling me up. 'Are you alright?' Dad's voice said in the gloom.

'I've had better days.'

He snorted. 'And I've had better years.' He pulled me into another hug.

'God, I've missed you.' I felt like crying and laughing all at once.

'And me you, Dom. Thinking of you and Sue has been the only thing that's kept me going. Since I flew away from the diner that morning, it's been one huge nightmare. And it sounds like, from what Angelique's told me, you've been going through it as well.'

'Hanging out with a Cloud Rider is a pretty wild ride at times.'

'I'll take that as a compliment,' Angelique said.

Dad laughed.

God – that was the best sound in the world. The shadow that had lurked inside me, years of hurt since he'd disappeared, was swept away in an instant by that laugh.

Despite being held in a Hades cell and the horror of what lay ahead, this was the best moment of my life – no contest.

'So what happened to you?' I asked.

'As you probably guessed, that wasn't any old twister that snared my plane, but a Vortex from a spy ship.'

'I realise that now. I just wished you'd told me about Great-granddad Alex being a Cloud Rider long ago.'

'I'm sorry I didn't, Dom. But when I discussed it with your mom, it seemed the right thing to do. We wanted to leave it till you were eighteen. I remember how I felt when my parents told me. Nothing was the same again. I wanted your life to be normal for as long as possible.'

So my parents had just being trying to protect me so I could enjoy being a regular teenager. Problem was, the universe had other ideas. 'I get it, Dad.' And I really did, after everything I'd gone through. If I'd been in his position I'd have probably done the same.

Dad's hand cupped the side of my face. 'I hope so. You can imagine how I felt when that Vortex formed on our own back porch. I'd been waiting for that moment my whole life, scanning the skies for any twister, hoping a Cloud Rider ship would emerge from it – just like my dad had before me. And then, bam, that morning there it was.'

'But it wasn't a Cloud Rider ship inside the Vortex,' Angelique said.

'That kinda took me by surprise. You see, I didn't know about Hades – Emperor Cronos and his goons hadn't been invented back in Grandpa Alex's day. The last thing I remember was flying towards the Vortex and then this awful scream filled my head.'

'A Hades AI?' I asked.

'You've got it. The next thing I knew I was aboard a Hades spy ship that had been hunting for Navigators. After that, I was held in a number of penal colonies before eventually being transferred here for their little experiment.'

I remembered the scientist's conversation with Ambra and shuddered. Dad was the next to be converted. 'We've got to get out of here. As they were bringing me down, Cronos turned up on his ship. Ambra wants to put on a bit of a show for him and get you two converted.'

'Oh gods,' Angelique said from her corner of darkness. 'So much for our plan. How come they captured you anyway? Didn't you find Jules first?'

A chasm opened inside me. For a wonderful moment I'd forgotten what had happened. 'It's Jules's fault I'm here.'

'What do you mean?'

'She—' The word stuck at the back of my throat. I swallowed and tried again. 'She betrayed us.'

'What?' Dad said. 'You're talking about Julia Eastwood, right?'

'Yeah.'

'Son, I know she'd never betray you in a million years.'

'Not sure I recognise her any more, Dad. She's changed. They got to her and turned her somehow.'

'That might be true, but still I find that hard to believe,' Angelique said. 'And she's your best friend, Dom.'

'Not any more, it seems. She's got very cosy with Duke Ambra.' An avalanche of images of them together tumbled through my imagination. Suddenly I found it hard to breathe.

'But that doesn't make any sort of sense...'

My hands felt hot and I balled them into fists. 'I know what I saw. Jules betrayed me, you – all of us. And in a while that nuke is going to blow and bring this whole place down on all our heads.' The heat rose up my arms to my chest. 'And right now all I can think is thank god it's going to take her with it.'

Dad's hand sought out my shoulder in the darkness. 'Dom, you're not thinking straight.'

I shook him off. 'I know what I saw and what happened. Which is why I'm stuck in here rather than rescuing you.'

Angelique's footsteps came towards me. 'Tell us exactly what happened, Dom. We'll figure it out together.'

Her hand closed around my arm and this time I didn't shake the contact off. Angelique had been a true friend to me. She'd had my back through every tough corner we'd gotten into. When I thought of Jules, I now thought of Jules with *him*. Bile rose up to my throat. I drove my fingernails into my palms and pushed aside the anger crowding my head.

With a deep breath I began to tell them what had happened.

...

I talked for ten minutes straight: about meeting Zack and Stephen; the plan to rendezvous with them at the underground pumping station and then escape through the underwater tunnels; the Hive mind powering the Quantum Pacifier; and the mysterious Kraken ship that was going to be first tested against the Earth that Dad and I called home.

The hurt and anger threatened to spill out again as I told them what Jules had done, but I managed to keep myself in check and continue. When I got to the bit about Cronos arriving in the giant ship, Angelique let out a hollow laugh.

'At least we might not die in vain then,' she said. 'If we manage to take out that monster when the nuke goes off, it will indirectly save a lot of people's lives.'

'That's what I was hoping,' I replied.

'Will you listen to you both?' Dad said. 'That's defeatist talk. While there's still air in our lungs, there is a chance we could find a way out of this alive and save all the Cloud Rider prisoners as well.'

Pride swelled my chest. This was what Dad always did – he never gave up, never said never. But all I could see in my mind's eye were dead ends and the timer on the bomb ticking down to death.

'But what can we do?' I asked.

'Look for any opportunity to escape, do the unexpected, grab any chance, and certainly don't give up without a fight.'

'Now that's a philosophy I can really believe in,' Angelique said.

Dad really was brilliant. 'Yeah, you can sign me up for that too.'

'Good to hear,' Dad replied. 'Now give me your hand, Dom, and I'll show you something to make my point.'

I reached out, unable to see even a vague outline of my fingers. 'I can't see a thing.'

'Don't worry about that.' Dad grasped my hand and pulled me in the direction of the cell door. He pressed my palm onto the wall by the exit.

A faint vibration tickled my palm.

'Feel it?' Dad asked.

'Yeah, but what is it?'

'Run your fingers over the surface.'

I drew my hand across the metal wall and my nails snagged on a recessed groove. I ran my finger around the edge, feeling its shape. A square with holes at each corner.

'Some sort of hatch?' I asked.

'That's what I reckon. I'm guessing those holes are for recessed screws.'

'Let me feel it,' Angelique said from close by.

I jumped. I hadn't even heard her move towards us in the darkness. Her fingers brushed mine as she probed the panel.

'I can tell you I've been over every inch of this cell, and apart from the latrine bucket in the corner, there's nothing else in here,' Dad said. 'All the walls are perfectly smooth, no other seams anywhere.'

'There's obviously some sort of mechanism running underneath it,' I replied. A thought flashed into my mind. 'Stephen gave me a special piece of gear which he said would act like a key and open any door.'

'I don't suppose you still have it?' Angelique asked.

'I wish. It was in a pocket of my fly-dive suit the guards pulled me out of, thanks to Jules.'

'What about your Leatherman?' she asked. 'We might be able to use one of its tools to release this hatch.'

'That was in there too.'

She groaned. 'Just for a moment I thought...' Her words trailed away.

I'd been swept up with Dad's determination too, believed we had a real chance, even if it had been for a fleeting second. The reality of our situation rushed back in. 'We have to be able to get past a few screws?'

Dad sighed. 'There's no way to lever it off by hand. I should know, I've tried and busted every fingernail in the process. I've even tried hitting it every day for a year with the bucket to see if I could work it loose, but I haven't managed to even dent it.'

'Shush, I think I hear someone,' Angelique said.

We all fell quiet. The footsteps of people marching in unison grew louder.

'It's a guard party — and quite few of them by the sound of things,' Dad said. 'The last time I heard that...' He fell silent.

'What?' I asked.

'When I was first dragged in, there were lots of people in all the cells. I shared this room with ten others at first. We all became good friends, but one by one the others were dragged off for conversion. They never came back. I heard someone being processed earlier.'

'Oh...' Angelique whispered.

I thought of the knife sticking out of Orson's chest, but kept quiet. As awful as it had been, perhaps Angelique had actually done the guy a favour. She'd set him free of his pain — that's what she believed at least. Me — I wasn't so sure.

The footsteps stopped outside. I felt Dad's arms clamp around me and pull me back into the darkness. A crack of light appeared and grew to a blinding rectangle as the door opened. A guard stood there with his crossbow pointed directly at us.

I squinted, my eyes burning with the light, and started to make out at least twenty more soldiers behind him. It seemed they didn't want to take any chances.

The guard peered into the gloom of the cell at Dad. 'Okay, your time has come.'

'Take me instead,' I said. It was probably going to happen sooner or later and this way at least Dad would get to live for a bit longer. And I'd do this with my head held high, show them just how brave people from my Earth could be. I started to step forward.

Dad shoved me behind him. 'I'm the one they've come for.'

The man shrugged. 'Makes no difference to me.'

I tried to twist from his grip. 'Dad, no.'

'I can't listen to them hurt you out there,' he replied. 'I've been through it too many times, but this time it will be even worse knowing it's you.'

'And you think I can listen to that happening to you instead?'

'I'm your dad – I get to make the choices here.'

I stared at him, arms crossed, mouth turned down. I realised my stance mirrored his. Father like son.

'It should be me,' Angelique said. 'That will give you both at least a little while longer together, to make up for lost time and say goodbye properly.'

The guard shook his head. 'No, Duke Ambra was very specific about you, Princess. You're the main attraction and you're up last for conversion. Right now Duke Ambra is dining with Emperor Cronos and your processing will be timed for when they've finished their dessert.'

Angelique sneered. 'Oh, how lovely for them.'

Dad held my shoulders. 'Dom, please let me do this.'

I stared into his eyes.

'Dom...'

I could see the love in his face, the earnest way he was looking at me and knew in that moment if I went first it would break him, break him for the short amount of life he had left. I had to be strong and let him do this. I slowly nodded, but it felt like my blood was flowing away.

He gave me a hard hug.

I buried my head into his shoulders.

'You'll always be my son, whatever they do to me.'

'And you'll always be my dad.'

He squeezed me and let go. Something crumbled inside me and my fingers curled like claws.

Dad walked out, head held high. The guards formed a square formation around him. He gave me one last grey-eyed look and walked away. The door hissed shut and darkness slammed down on us.

How could I have just found Dad and lost him again? The darkness felt like a chasm, a bottomless one – and I was falling into it. I thumped on the door. 'Stop!'

The footsteps grew fainter.

'Dad!' I screamed. We should have been a family again, Dad flying back with me and Angelique...the look on Mom's face when she saw him...

Angelique rubbed my back.

The moments stretched forward and the silence pressed in.

I pounded the door with both fists, felt my skin breaking, blood wetting my hands.

A distant Hades AI howl filled my mind.

The world stopped turning. I loved Dad so much. There was so much more I wanted to say to him.

'Dad,' I whispered.

A muffled scream.

My guts writhed, legs folding. Angelique hugged me as I wept. The screams made my bones hum. Thoughts splintered and I pressed my hands against my ears, but his screams still got in.

Dad...

The chill in my stomach turned to ice and I hung on to Angelique, a beacon in the darkness.

Her face was against mine. No words, just holding me, wrapping me with her warmth. She gently kissed my cheek.

I turned to her like a flower seeking out the sun. Our mouths met and I hung on to the warmth of her lips, trying to cut out the scream echoing in my mind. I kissed her until I lost all sense of myself.

CHAPTER Nineteen
A VISITOR

I didn't know when the muffled cries had died away, didn't notice when I stopped shaking in Angelique's arms, couldn't have said when the stark images of Dad turning into a carbon statue stopped flashing through my mind, but now there was only emptiness left inside me. All I'd wanted was for his pain to stop and I didn't care how. At last the silent intervals had grown longer. It had been several minutes since his last scream.

Angelique rubbed my arm, her body's warmth pressed into mine. 'Dom, I think it's over.'

I tried to respond, but I hadn't the words...they'd become lost in the total darkness along with everything else.

'Dom, look, when they come for me, I'm going to fight them. I'd rather die with a crossbow bolt through my heart than go through what's just happened to your papa.'

She was right. I knew she was right. I forced myself to claw to the surface from the whirlpool of emotions. Dad had said we had to look for any opportunity to escape, to not give up. But it was my dumb luck we were stuck in here.

'I'm sorry, Angelique. I've let everyone down.'

'No you haven't. You couldn't have known Jules was going to turn you in.'

Jules – the knot of anger tightened in my chest. 'How could she do that to us?'

Angelique's fingers reached around mine in the darkness. 'You don't know what they did to her, what she had to face. Hades have ways of breaking people's spirits – in fact they pride themselves on it.'

'She didn't exactly look like someone who'd been tortured, if that's what you're saying?'

'There's a thousand ways to break someone and not all of them leave visible scars. For all we know they may have drugged her.'

I thought of the joyful look Jules had briefly given me before an expression of fear had taken its place. What had that been about?

Footsteps approached our cell. Several people, by the sound of it.

I felt Angelique stiffen. 'Dom, let's fight them together.'

'Okay, I'm up for that. After all, we've nothing left to lose.'

I edged into the darkness. The door mechanism whirred behind the panel.

'We'll jump the first person who comes through, seize their weapon and make a run for it,' Angelique said.

'Got it.'

I breathed through my nose and backed into the corner of the cell. The door opened and a slit of light flowed across the floor.

With a hum of electricity, white light flooded the cell from bulbs high above in the arched ceiling, bright enough to burn out my vision. I was blinded like an animal emerging from a burrow into daylight. With that simple trick they immobilised us. I heard people move into the cell. Just like that we'd lost our edge.

I blinked, forcing my eyes to adjust to the stinging brilliance.

A guard had pinned Angelique down in the corner of the cell. A woman stood in the doorway with another guard by her side. The woman wore a long, green silk dress and her hair had been curled up in a fancy style. I almost hadn't recognised her. Jules.

My fury burned white-hot. I leapt towards her. The guard stepped forward and struck me aside with a chopping blow. I crashed into the wall. Before I could react, he'd stepped around me and locked my arms behind my back. Angelique struggled against the guard holding her head to the floor.

'Stop!' Jules shouted at them.

I tried to twist away, but the guard tightened his grip.

I stared at Jules. 'How could you?'

Jules flinched and she fingered the pendant around her neck. 'I've come to say goodbye to you both.'

'Shouldn't you be with your Duke?' I said.

The guard struck me. 'Hold your tongue, lad.'

Crimson spread through Jules's face. 'Duke Ambra allowed me to slip away from the banquet with Emperor Cronos. I wanted to see my friends for a last time.'

I gawped at her. 'Friends? You've got to be kidding me after what you've done. Do you realise my dad is as good as dead? Turned into one of those carbon zombies because of what you' – I shouted the last word at her – 'did!'

Her face crumbled. 'Oh god, Dom, I'm so sorry.'

Angelique pulled her head around far enough to look up at Jules. 'Just leave us. If you're looking for some sort...' – her eyes widened at Jules and she blinked – '...looking for some sort of forgiveness, you can forget it.'

My skin itched with heat. 'I just hope you can live with yourself after what you've done.'

'Dom, please don't be like this.' Jules crossed to me, the silk of her dress shimmering under the blazing lights. 'Let him go,' she said to the guard.

The guard peered at her. 'Are you sure?'

She gave him a sharp nod.

He shrugged at the other guard and released me.

I scrambled back to my feet and glowered at Jules. 'I never ever want to see you again. And you know what, I can't wait to be converted so I don't have to remember your stupid lying face.'

'Dom...' Tears filled her eyes. I caught the strange look in Angelique's expression as she watched us.

Before I could move, Jules closed the distance and wrapped her arms around me.

I tried to shove her away, but she tightened her grip. 'Get off me.'

'Miss,' the guard said, stepping forward.

'I'm so sorry,' she said. Something in her tone caught at my guts and made them twist. I shoved her away against the wall, hard.

The guard raised his hand.

'Don't,' Jules said, grabbing the man's arm.

His nostrils flared and he lowered his hand. 'Yes, miss.'

Jules gave me a broken look, tears rolling down her face. She turned and headed towards the door, followed by the guards. The door slid shut and the darkness returned.

I pressed my head against the wall, thoughts crashing around in my head. How could she?

I heard Angelique approach me in the darkness.

'Dom, check your pockets.'

'Come again?'

'I'm sure I saw Jules slip something into them.'

A last message, pleading for forgiveness? I shoved my hand into my jeans and felt something in my pocket, but not paper. I pulled out three objects and ran my fingers over the edges, mapping the shapes in my mind. 'I think...' Everything that I'd been thinking about Jules shifted. 'I think she gave me the Leatherman and the Tac.' I fumbled for the Tac's button and pressed it. The display lit up and cast a small glow across the cell. *Three hours and thirty-three minutes.* I examined the third object by its faint amber light. 'It's the unlocking ring that Stephen gave me.' I stared at the objects, trying to process the sudden change in our fortunes.

'I told you Jules was playing along,' Angelique said. 'She must have rescued them from your fly-dive suit when you were captured in her bedroom.'

'God, I've been such a fool.' For a moment I wanted to bang on the door, to shout out after Jules, to scream I was sorry I'd ever doubted her. 'But why didn't she saying anything to me when we were alone? Why alert the guards at all?'

'Because she had no choice.'

'Pardon me?'

'She was wearing a compliance.'

'A what?'

'That pendant around Jules's neck is actually a spying device. Its feed is relayed to a security monitoring station. Everything she sees, hears and says is picked up by that. If someone tries to escape, and I bet she has, the guards can give her an electric shock to immobilise or even kill her.'

My thoughts fell together. 'You mean when I went into her room—'

'Hades guards would have seen you. That's why Jules would have been playing along. She knew if she tried anything else she would have been electrocuted and you would have been captured anyway.'

The world turned the right way up again. This made sense, made *real* sense.

Angelique's hand closed around mine in the darkness. 'Hades hurt your dad, not Jules.'

She was right. I felt a stab of shame. I realised I'd given up on Jules the moment I crossed the line with Angelique. We'd kissed, really kissed. Jules had been lost to me during that moment. Angelique had been there to pick up the pieces. But now the rules had switched back again. What a mess, what a stupid bloody mess.

'Jules doesn't know about the bomb either,' Angelique said, oblivious of what was going on in my head. 'She thinks we have all the time in the world to escape.'

My guilt and the consequences would have to wait. I needed to keep focused on what was happening in the present, not think about the future.

I slipped the Tac onto my wrist. It ticked down another minute. 'In that case, we'd better get to it.'

'Okay, give me that tool of yours and I'll use its blade on the next person who comes through that door,' Angelique said.

My mind felt clear again and an idea came to me. 'I think we can do better than that.' I unfolded the flathead screwdriver in the Leatherman and crossed to the door panel. I used the Tac as a faint flashlight and pushed the tool into the hole at one of the corners. I felt it lock into position on one of the screw heads. I twisted the Leatherman.

'Oh, now that's a real plan,' Angelique said.

With her holding onto the panel, I undid one screw, two, three... The fourth clinked onto the floor and the panel came away in her hands.

'Let's try inserting that magic cog of yours,' Angelique said.

In the middle of all the spinning gears inside the panel I noticed a space.

Angelique pointed at the gap. 'Try it there.'

Careful not to trap my fingers in the turning gears, I slipped the cog ring into position and gave it a gentle push. With a click the gears around the ring's edge expanded until their teeth meshed with the neighbouring cogs. The door mechanism within the panel whined to a stop.

'Nothing's happening,' I said.

'Give the flywheel a moment to reverse.'

The door gears spun up in the opposite direction and the cell door started to slide open.

'We need to get down to the mines as quickly as possible,' Angelique said.

'You go rendezvous with Stephen and Zack.'

'You're going after Jules?' Angelique asked.

'Of course. I know I've as good as lost my dad, but I can't lose my best friend too.'

'Okay, just so we're clear, I'm not leaving here without you.'

'But you may have to. Listen, Angelique, if I don't make it, it's up to you to get your people to safety.'

Angelique stared at me, her face lit by the crescents of light coming through the doorway. She slowly nodded. 'I'll wait for you for as long as I can at the bottom of the lift.'

I knew we needed to talk about what had happened, but now wasn't the time. 'Good luck.'

Angelique leant forward and kissed me on the cheek. 'You too, Dom.' She disappeared out of the doorway and headed towards the lift shaft.

I gazed into the corridor at the other cell doors that had been emptied of their Navigator prisoners. My anger rose through me and I hung on to it. No complications, just straightforward revenge. Ambra, Hades, Cronos, the whole blasted lot of them would pay for what they'd done to Dad.

I crept towards the chamber filled with glass pods, one of which contained whatever remained of Dad.

CHAPTER Twenty
CRONOS

I stole along the corridor towards the lowered grate that blocked the exit from the cells. How the heck was I going to get past that? I glanced at my Leatherman and the giant bolts holding the lattice of steel together. No way would the multi-tool's pliers shift those.

Through the grill I saw the chamber had filled with men in lab coats. They bustled between pods, examining read-outs and scribbling down numbers on glass slates. In the middle of the activity, a group of soldiers lowered a black-stained man into one of the open pods. They closed the lid and the glass on the inside crazed with ice.

The air caught in my throat. Through the lid I saw Dad's body shot through with black carbon, his eyes completely black, like someone had turned him into a grotesque statue. I stared at him, looking for any sign that he was alive, a flicker of movement, something to indicate he was just sleeping. Nothing. My insides turned to stone.

Only two pods remained open – intended for Angelique and me. *Not today, Hades.*

But what about Dad? Should I stick him with the Leatherman's blade like Angelique had with Lord Orson? I shuddered at the thought. No way could I ever go there.

The scientist called Simean nodded to Sergeant Yanton. 'We're ready for the final conversion process. You can bring the Princess now.'

Time was up. But what about Jules? Everything had changed since Angelique had told me about her compliance pendant. If I didn't find her, she'd almost certainly be killed when the nuke went off. I glanced behind me down the tunnel to the mines, my only route of escape. I had no plan and everything seemed to be hanging by a thread.

The sergeant snapped a salute and turned to his soldiers. 'Prisoner escort duty.'

The group of guards stepped into a square formation and started marching towards the grate I was hiding behind. No chameleon net to hide me this time. I pressed myself behind one of the entrance pillars and kept still.

The grate rumbled upwards on its runners. I held my breath. *Please don't let them look sideways...*

Yanton, at the head of the guards, marched straight past my hiding place towards the cell. I let my breath out. That had been way too close. But I still wasn't in the clear. In a moment they'd discover the cell was empty. Then all hell would break loose.

I ducked around the corner and circled along the edge of the chamber, staying low, keeping the pods between me and the scientists at work.

A shout and Yanton raced back into the room. This was it. Things were about to get interesting.

'The prisoners have escaped,' the sergeant called.

At once an alarm warbled out and soldiers swarmed towards the cell.

'They must have escaped to the mines,' Yanton said as Simean reached him. 'I'll send a patrol down after them.'

Heck. Angelique hadn't got much of a head start.

The scientists had begun to gather in a huddle around Dad's tomb. A bald-headed man in a grey long coat had his hands pressed to the pod's lid.

I felt a surge of darkness swell in my mind. Pain burned my limbs. I felt broken, torn apart. But it wasn't my thoughts, it was someone else's. I let out a small gasp and pushed the feelings away. The bitter taste like Hades ship-song. But this had felt different, familiar somehow, and suddenly I realised why: Dad... Oh god, it was Dad's thoughts I could hear. The bald man had to be a Hades Navigator and he was interrogating Dad, even though he was unconscious.

The Navigator frowned. 'There's some residual memory here... I can't quite...' His frown deepened and paled. 'There's a bomb,' he whispered. Somehow, despite the noise, everyone in the chamber heard him. They stopped whatever they were doing and stared.

Of course – Dad knew all about the nuke. And through no fault of his own he was about to spill everything to Hades.

'Where?' Yanton asked.

'He doesn't seem to know.' Beads of sweat broke out on the man's bald head. 'I'm losing the memory.' He withdrew his hands from the pod lid. 'It's gone.'

I slumped against the wall. Thank god.

The sergeant grabbed an old-fashioned telephone and spun a wheel. 'Put me through to Duke Ambra at once. We have a bomb threat in an unknown location on the base.'

I was running out of time. Where was Jules? She'd mentioned something about a banquet. Maybe up in the palace? I'd have to use the lift to get up there. But everyone kept casting glances towards it – the only way to the surface.

Yanton clapped his hands together. 'Come on, people, you have jobs to do. Get back to work.'

His words seem to break the spell. Soldiers and scientists started to swarm through the chamber, shouting instructions to each other.

Simean stepped forward. 'But shouldn't we be evacuating?'

The sergeant glowered at him. 'With the Kraken nearly ready to launch, no one is going to abandon their post, do you hear me?'

The scientist nodded and shrunk away.

Keeping low, I started to make my way towards the lift. If I could just slip up there without anyone seeing me... A green light started blinking in the lab. Heck, someone was coming down. I reached a line of gurneys and crept beneath one.

The lift doors opened and Ambra strode out, followed by a man with a heavily jowled face wearing a uniform dripping with medals. His tunic was pulled tight around the buttons over a well-fed belly, and a thin band of gold was perched on his head like a slipped halo. The man from the tapestry – the monster in person – Cronos.

The two men strode into the room. My heart leapt as I spotted Jules behind them.

'What the hell has happened?' Ambra said to Yanton as they reached Dad's pod.

'The prisoners have escaped and planted a bomb,' the sergeant replied.

A brief smile flickered across Jules's face, but she quickly hid it.

How could I ever have doubted her? It wasn't Jules who betrayed me – I'd betrayed her with a kiss. But if I was honest it had been more than a kiss – I'd lost myself in Angelique.

'Very, very regrettable,' Cronos said. 'And this bomb that's been planted – do we know when it's set to explode?'

'We have no information on that, my Emperor,' Yanton said with a bow.

'In that case we'll have to assume its detonation is imminent,' Cronos said, his tone calm, like this happened every day.

He might have had a badassed reputation, but I had to admire the man's cool.

'We need to get Kraken out of the blast radius and get the ship airborne as soon as possible,' Cronos said.

Ambra's gaze travelled to the empty pod. 'But it's not fully operational yet, Your Excellency.'

'That depends.' Cronos waved Simean over. 'Can we launch if we're two short of completing the Hive mind?'

'I'm not sure the calculations allow for that,' the scientist said. 'One, but not two, otherwise there might be consequences for the stability of their collective consciousness.'

Cronos nodded. 'I see...' His eyes narrowed. 'Initiate loading the Hive onto Kraken.'

'But the shortfall?' Ambra asked.

'Let me worry about that.'

'Of course, my Emperor.'

I stared across at Dad's glass coffin. That meant him too. Was this going to be the last time I ever saw him? I studied the mask his face had been trapped behind. The warm, brave man who'd been an inspiration to me from the moment I'd been old enough to realise how awesome he really was – Dad, the hero – had been reduced to little more than a mental cog in Cronos's war machine.

I could see Jules staring at his carbon-stained face in the pod next to her. Her eyes widened. She took a half step towards him and stopped herself. She'd recognised Dad.

Ambra gazed at Simean. 'Begin loading the Hive.'

Simean nodded. He turned to Dad's pod and rotated a brass handle.

Red lights flared inside the glass lid. A billow of steam. The pod shot upwards on a piston towards a metal iris opening in the ceiling and disappeared through it with a whoosh.

Just like that, Dad, or at least what remained of him, had gone. To lose him once had been bad enough, but twice... I felt like someone had yanked my heart out of my body.

The other scientists ran to the other converted Navigators and repeated the procedure. As each was sent on their way, the room started to fill with a forest of metal pistons lapped by a sea of rising steam.

So *Kraken* was somewhere above us and Dad was probably inside it by now.

'My Emperor, what are we going to do about the missing Navigator if we are to launch?' Ambra asked. 'We may not be able to recapture the prisoners in time.'

Jules stiffened. I knew she'd be thinking that I was escaping with Angelique, not caring what happened to her. In her place I'd be rooting for the others to escape, too. The Jules I knew – had always known – would be no different.

'Let's see what we can do about our shortfall,' Cronos said.

Ambra glanced towards the Hades Navigator. 'But we only have a few left. I'm not sure we can spare—'

'I'd expect some more original thinking from you, Duke Ambra.'

Ambra gave him a puzzled look. 'I'm not sure I follow.'

'We need to find someone expendable. Not everyone has been forthcoming about their genetic gift.'

I watched Cronos sniff the air. His tongue flicked out like he was tasting something on his lips as he looked around the chamber. For a moment he seemed to peer straight at my hiding place. I stiffened, ready for the order to grab me. But instead, Cronos took a deeper breath and his gaze travelled past me to settle on Yanton.

A cold smile curled the corners of Cronos's mouth. 'Here's your volunteer.'

I caught a brief look of something in Yanton's eyes – what, fear? He quickly replaced it with a blank expression. 'Volunteer, my Emperor? For what exactly?'

'Come, come now, sergeant, why be so shy? You should be proud of your gift.'

Ambra's gaze narrowed on Yanton. 'You're a Navigator?'

I thought of how the sergeant hadn't hung around while Lord Orson had been converted. Made sense if he was a Navigator. Of course it did. He knew he'd give himself away when the Hades AI was exposed, almost like I had. No wonder the man looked so afraid now.

Yanton blinked. 'I...'

'You want to please your Emperor, don't you?' Cronos said, voice thickening like treacle you could get stuck in.

'Of course, but...' The man looked at Cronos, eyes pleading.

Ambra's eyes hardened into marbles. 'For the greater good, sergeant.'

Yanton began to back away. 'Please, my Duke, surely—'

'It will be a noble sacrifice,' Cronos said.

Jules stared at him, looking horrified, but saying nothing.

Yanton spun round and sprinted towards the lift.

'Seize him,' Ambra shouted.

Several guards rushed the sergeant before he'd even taken three strides. Yanton kicked and yelled, pleading with them as they dragged him towards the operating theatre.

Cronos sighed. 'It's such a shame I didn't get to see Princess Angelique processed. I have to say I was rather looking forward to that.'

'I promise you, Emperor, the Princess and her companion will be hunted down in the mines and executed on sight.'

'Yes, yes.' Cronos ran his tongue over his lips. 'What I don't understand is how she and the lad could have escaped?'

'I have no idea, my Emperor.'

Ambra's eyes seemed to grow darker. 'Unless they had help.' He turned to Jules.

I saw her tense and a shiver ran through me. I had an awful feeling about where this was headed.

'Emperor Cronos?' Jules said.

'If I'm not mistaken, you asked Duke Ambra for permission to say goodbye to your friends only ten minutes ago?'

Her face flamed. 'I don't understand what you mean?'

'Oh come now, don't be so coy. Tell me the truth.' Cronos ran a finger down her cheek.

Ice crawled up my spine.

'I'm not following you,' Jules said.

Cronos tapped the necklace around her neck. 'What would the memory of your compliance device show if we checked it for the moment when you visited your friends? A fight or some other distraction to disguise you handing them something that aided their escape?'

It was like he was reading her mind. Perhaps he actually could! My pulse raced.

Jules's face paled. 'You've got this wrong.'

Ambra shook his head. 'I have to say I'm disappointed, Julia.'

I knew exactly where this was headed – somewhere bad, very bad.

Ambra unhooked a pocket watch with a display like the Tac on my wrist.

Jules spread her hands. 'Please don't.'

The Duke's smile thinned. 'Oh, I think I will.' He twisted the watch's dial.

Sparks crackled from the pendant around Jules's eye necklace. With a cry, she spasmed and fell to the floor.

I clenched on to the leg of the gurney. I had to do something.

'What a shame,' Cronos said, shaking his head.

Ambra stood over Jules. 'This is how we deal with traitors, young lady.'

Jules writhed on the floor and whimpered.

The Duke sneered down at her, fingers ready to twist the watch's dial again. The hardness in his jaw told me that this time he was going to kill her.

Dad's words came to me. *Grab any chance you can.* My eyes darted around, looking for something I could use. My gaze settled on a pod next to the gurney where I was hiding. Its round handle, just within reach. It could just work. I reached over and twisted it.

With a rush of steam from around the pod, it hurtled towards the ceiling. The fog spread out in a wave to obscure Cronos, Ambra and the others.

Under the cover of the fog I clambered out from the stretcher and rushed to where Jules had fallen. Like a blind man, I felt over the ground through the thick mist. She had to be here somewhere. I spotted a vague outline curled in a foetal ball just ahead – thank god.

The necklace around Jules's neck spat blue sparks. Driven by my instinct to help, I grabbed her arm.

An electric shock jolted my body and it felt like my heart was going to explode. My teeth jammed together and I gripped the Leatherman. Muscles screaming, hand shaking, I slipped the blade under the chain of the necklace and yanked it. The blade sliced through the links and the pendant skittered away, trailing sparks into the steam. The electric shock that had coursed through my body stopped dead.

Jules gasped and her head sagged onto the floor.

'Duke Ambra, there's another Navigator here, I can smell him,' Cronos said from somewhere nearby.

I snatched a lungful of air and stood.

The fog had started to thin. Vague shapes moved within it just ten feet away. We had to get out of here and fast.

Legs quivering, I pulled Jules up. 'This way,' I whispered to her.

She stared at me, blinking back tears, and nodded.

'The lad is helping the girl escape,' came Cronos's voice.

How did he know that? A lucky guess, or perhaps he really could read minds?

I spotted Ambra's broad-shouldered outline heading in our direction.

'Come on,' I whispered. Jules and I stumbled away into the steam.

Figures loomed out of the gloom and we darted from them. Within moments I became disorientated. Which way to the cell entrance? Which way to safety?

'Find them before they escape,' Cronos said, his voice calm but filled with threat. 'I will be on the bridge of *Kraken*, preparing him for flight. Only join me if you kill them, Duke Ambra.'

Ambra's response was muffled by a long, drawn-out scream from the mist. My skin became clammy despite the heat of the steam. They'd started the process of converting Yanton. Despite what he'd done I felt sorry for the man. No one deserved to go that way, not even him.

'Lock this place down!' Ambra shouted. 'No one enters or leaves.'

'Oh hell,' Jules whispered, her fingers holding tight on to mine.

A rumble of sliding metal came from just ahead. It had to be the portcullis to the cells closing!

'This way.' I pulled Jules's hand. We sprinted towards the noise and the exit loomed out of the mist. The steel grate was dropping down.

'Halt!' someone shouted.

We dived and slid under the dropping portcullis. A bolt whizzed over our heads and the portcullis slammed down behind us like a guillotine's blade.

'They're in cell-block ten,' someone cried out.

Yells and cries came from the chamber.

We jumped to our feet and raced down the passageway as the steam started to evaporate.

'Get this bloody thing open!' Ambra shouted behind us.

Jules panted as we ran. 'Where are we going?'

I gestured at the open cage lift ahead of us, big enough to carry at least hundred people. 'The only place we can go – to the mines.'

We skidded into the lift and Jules slammed her hand against the big, green button control inside. The heavy gate started to swing shut.

Footsteps thundered towards us. I stared at the door, willing it to close faster. 'Come on, come on.'

At the head of at least twenty guards, Ambra loomed into view and pointed at us as the gate slammed shut. 'Kill them!'

Bolts whizzed through the lift's open cage walls. But with a whine of gears, the floor juddered and we began to drop fast.

'You won't get far,' Ambra bellowed at us as we hurtled away.

A couple of arrows ricocheted off the top of the lift and his howling faded into the distance.

I panted, clutched my sides and looked at Jules. 'You okay?'

She nodded and rushed into my arms.

'For a while I thought I'd lost you, Jules. I really did.'

She wrapped her arms tighter around me. 'You'll never lose me.' Her hair brushed my face.

I was glad that with her head resting on my shoulder she couldn't study my face right now. How could I tell Jules I'd betrayed her, even if it had only been for a moment?

I swallowed. 'Dad's part of the Hive now.'

Jules pulled away and pressed her hands to her mouth, eyes filling with tears. 'Oh, Dom, there was nothing I could do.'

'Me neither.' A sense of emptiness swelled in me. 'I've lost Dad.' The back of my eyes started to sting.

'We'll rescue him, find someone who knows how to reverse the process,' Jules said.

That sounded like a wild hope to me. 'How can we bring someone back from the hell that Hades have sentenced him to?'

She clutched my face. 'I don't know, but we'll find a way, Dom.' She pulled me back into a hug as we hurtled down into the stifling heat of the mines. It took all my strength not to fall apart in her arms.

CHAPTER Twenty-One
DESCENT

We sat cross-legged on the floor of the cage as it squealed and rattled its way down through the shaft hewn through the solid, black stone. In the minutes since we began our descent, I'd done my best to bring Jules up to speed with everything that had happened. She kept shaking her head, eyes ever wider, as I told her about Floating City and finding *Titan*, Tesla hidden in the Northern Lights, how we'd used fly-dive suits to get into Hells Cauldron, and the planned prison breakout. The hardest thing had been telling her what had happened to Dad. On hearing that she'd cried and hung on to me.

Of course that made the bit I skipped worse – that kiss with Angelique. How had I become that guy? I knew telling Jules might kill our relationship before it even had a chance to get going again. Could I risk that? Did I even have the courage to see the look of betrayal in her face as I spilled out my guts to her? No, I wasn't sure I had – or ever would have.

I felt grateful for the gloom in the shaft. I was sure that if Jules had clearly seen my face she would've read me in moments.

'So what about this bomb you guys planted?' she asked, oblivious to my internal dialogue.

'It's not just any bomb, it's a nuke.' I felt amazed I could bring up something so shocking so matter-of-factly. But I guessed that was how crazy my life had become.

Her mouth fell open. 'You're kidding, right?'

'I wish.' I showed her the Tac's display – *three hours and twenty-five minutes.* 'We need to find Angelique and the rest of prisoners, then hightail it out of Hells Cauldron before this thing hits zero.'

'God!' She dropped her gaze and began picking at the hem of her skirt. 'Look, Dom, about everything that I did and said before...'

She so didn't have to explain herself. Not to me. If she only knew I was the one that should've been begging her forgiveness. I held my hand up. 'You don't need to say anything, Jules. I get it.'

'But I do. You thinking badly of me cuts me up.'

'I don't.' I didn't add the *not now.* How could I tell her that for a moment I'd completely lost faith in her, enough to shatter the dream of our future together, enough to fall into the arms of another woman?

Jules gave me a quizzical look.

I had the uncomfortable feeling that, despite the gloom, she was peering into my mind. I kept my poker face as blank as I could.

She bunched her skirt in her hands. 'What Hades have been doing here is totally wrong.'

I tried to ignore the thought of Dad's carbon-stained face. 'That conversion experiment Cronos dreamed up is pure evil.'

Jules nodded. 'And you should hear Ambra on the subject – he's so darned proud of it. He even showed off to me what they were doing with the Navigators. I had to play along of course and pretend to be impressed. Although, in my defence, I did have that blasted choker around my neck which he took great delight in using when I didn't behave.'

'That man's twisted.'

'They all are.' Jules found a loose silk thread and pulled at it. 'At first I tried to escape, but Ambra kept shocking me with that pendant till I got the message.' Her voice dropped to a whisper and she stared at the ground. 'It got so bad, Dom, I wanted to die.'

I stared at her. Jules was one of strongest people I knew. And if Ambra had nearly managed to break her enough to think like that, it said everything. 'But you managed to hang in there.'

'Only because…' Her words trailed away and she gazed at her hands.

I raised her chin so she looked at me. 'Because?'

A small smile. *'Because* I knew you would come after me…that you would do everything you could to make sure I was safe. Even when it was so awful I thought I wouldn't stop screaming, it was knowing that I'd see you again that kept me going.'

My guilt twisted tighter. Dad had said the same about thinking of Mom and me – it'd helped him to hang on. For the good that had done him. And Jules…with every sentence she said to me, the hole I'd gotten myself into seemed to be growing deeper and deeper, the sides becoming too steep to climb out of.

I tried to marshal my thoughts. 'But what I don't understand is why Ambra made you his personal pet, rather than just send you down the mines?'

Jules sighed. 'In a sense I was lucky. Ambra said I reminded him of his daughter. She was killed when their planet was destroyed.'

Despite myself, I felt a pang of sorrow for the Duke. 'I guess even someone like Ambra has suffered in this war. But if he was so fond of you, why the choker?'

'He just needed to know he could trust me. And the only way he could do that was by breaking me – and he almost did. It was a living nightmare, Dom. At least until I decided to play along.'

I could tell Jules wasn't telling me a fraction of what had happened to her. These were the edited highlights to spare my feelings – in other words a secret she'd never share. Hardness grew in my chest. 'I'm going to make that creep pay.' I clenched my fists.

She prized my fingers apart. 'None of what happened matters now. The main thing is that you came for me. And when you turned up in my bedroom, all I wanted to do was fling my arms around you and escape. But I knew if I did...'

'The guards would see what was happening and we'd both be caught anyway.'

Jules gave a sharp nod. 'I thought the best way I could help you was by pretending I'd seen the light and had become a loyal Hades citizen. Of course, I was really only waiting for my chance to do something. That started the moment the guards dragged you out of my bedroom. I searched your flying suit and found the things I slipped to you in the cell. I'm guessing by the fact we're having this conversation that they helped?'

I smiled. 'We wouldn't have escaped without them.'

'That's good.' Her expression tightened, sudden tears appearing. 'I'm so sorry about your dad, Dom. I'd no idea he was still alive until you told me he was in the cells. Every plan I'd dreamed up hadn't covered that. If only I'd got down to you sooner, he might be with us now.'

'You weren't to know.' I couldn't share half of what I was feeling, otherwise I'd lose it. And we didn't have time for that. 'None of us knew until it was too late to do anything.'

'But now he's onboard *Kraken*.'

I peered at her, grateful for the change of subject. 'Do you know anything about that ship?'

'Ambra didn't say a lot about it. All I know is that they couldn't find a single Hades Navigator to pilot it without his brain being fried.'

'That's why they developed the Hive with lots of Navigators linked together.'

Jules nodded. 'Apparently they've been experimenting with it for over a year, building it up person by person.'

'By why so many? A hundred seems a lot of minds. And just how big is this ship anyway?'

'I've never seen *Kraken*. Wherever it is, it's well hidden. Ambra never took me with him when he went to inspect it. But hopefully your nuke will take care of it.'

'But Dad's on that ship.'

She bit her lip. 'Sorry, didn't think that bit through.'

But she had a point though. If *Kraken* was headed to my Earth, even if Dad was onboard, wouldn't it be better that it never took off in the first place? I felt torn in two. How was I meant to work this one out? How could anyone when they were talking about killing their own dad?

Jules peered at me. 'Don't give up hope, Dom.'

'But even if we ever make it back, I don't think I could bear to tell Mom that I found Dad and lost him again.'

She cradled my hands in hers. 'We *will* make it back and we *will* free him.'

Despite everything she'd gone through and what we were about to face, Jules's confidence hadn't been knocked. I knew a big part of that was her belief in me. If only she knew that I was just a liar putting on the big hero act. But Jules on the other hand was brilliant, a burst of sunlight when all I could see around me were shadows. She certainly deserved someone better than me.

My breathing started to feel laboured. I realised the air around us had grown stifling.

Jules flapped her hand over her face. 'God, this heat.'

I pulled at my T-shirt, stuck to my chest with sweat. 'This used to be a volcano. Knowing our luck it's probably about to erupt.'

Jules raised her eyebrows at me. 'Out of the frying pan and into the fire, huh?'

Despite everything, I actually smiled. I'd forgotten she could make me do that so easily.

We peered down through holes in the cage floor as the bottom of the shaft sped into view. The lift came to a shuddering halt and the gate swung open.

'Angelique said she'd meet us here,' I said.

'What about the patrol that Ambra already sent down after her?'

I gave her a grim look. 'I'd forgotten about them.'

We stepped out into a tunnel curving away from us. Nearby, a Hades soldier lay sprawled over a rock, neck twisted at an awkward angle. Fear sped through me.

'Looks like he may have been unlucky enough to find Angelique first,' Jules said.

I knew Angelique could look after herself, but there wouldn't have been just one soldier sent after her. I scanned along the corridor, stomach knotting, but couldn't see her body. 'She must've made it deeper into the mines.'

The gate clanged shut behind us. With a squeal the cage shot back up the shaft.

Jules mouth drew into a tight line. 'Ambra must have called the lift.'

'That's all we need. We've got to slow him down.' I scanned our surroundings, looking for a way to shut down the lift for good. I spotted a large metal box mounted on a pillar, and a wiring loom running from it into the wall. Instinct told me it was exactly what I was looking for. 'I think I've got an idea.' I slipped the blade under the wires.

'Hang on,' Jules said. She tore the bottom half of her long silk dress off. I felt a rush of affection for her. With bare legs she looked much more like my Jules again.

'Why the fashion makeover?' I asked.

She held up three fingers and began counting them off. 'One: I've been slowly roasting to death wearing this outfit, two: I can now run in this outfit, and three: wrap the cloth around the Leatherman, otherwise you might get electrocuted.'

'Okay, good point.' I shot her an apologetic smile and covered my palm with the fabric. Just as well I listened to her. As I cut the wires a shower of sparks flew out of the junction box. Somewhere high above in the lift shaft we heard the cage squeal to a stop.

Jules raised her palm, fingers spread, and grinned.

I high-fived her with a satisfying slap of skin. Once again everything seemed possible with Jules by my side. Maybe together we really did stand a chance. The old team back on the case, even if one of them felt like a rat.

Chapter Twenty-Two
THE CRYSTAL MINES

Jules and I ran through the tunnel away from the lift, rounded the corner and skidded to a stop. My mind wheeled as I tried to take in the astonishing view.

Before us, in a chasm, aqua lakes – like those back on the surface – bubbled with plumes of steam. But it was what hung from the ceiling that really took my breath away. Massive crystal stalactites, hundreds of feet long, shone with blue inner light, illuminating the chamber with their eerie glow.

Jules's eyes widened and she stared at the stalactites. 'Are those made from what I think they are?'

The air felt charged and tingled over my skin. 'Psuche gems – millions of them.' The sheer number blew my mind. 'Tesla said the magnetic field of this planet runs straight through this place.'

'Is that why the gems glow then – they're like some sort of battery?'

'According to Tesla it's weirder than that. You won't believe this, but he reckoned that some of the people who lived on this planet, the Angelus, have been backed up in those crystals.'

She stared at me. 'Are you saying those blue lights are, what, their souls or something?'

I shrugged. 'It sounded pretty wacko to me too, but that's what Tesla reckoned. Although he called them "memory imprints" rather than souls.'

Wonder filled Jules's expression. 'What an awesome thought.'

'Come on, we'd better find the others.'

We started running along a natural stone causeway, weaving its way between the aqua lagoons. I noticed wooden gantries constructed in rings around one of the larger Psuche gem stalactites. Moss-draped ladders ran between the platforms.

I breathed in a rich compost smell, like a pine forest after heavy rainfall. 'I'm guessing this must be the mining operation that Zack mentioned.'

'So where is everyone then?'

'I'm hoping it means that Zack and Stephen managed to get the evacuation started.' But if that was true, why hadn't Angelique met us at the lift? I kept my growing sense of unease to myself.

We headed towards a stalactite hanging near the causeway. A ripple of blue light started spreading down it as we approached.

But Jules's gaze wasn't held by that. Instead she halted and pointed into the water.

Then I saw them too and forgot the beauty of the chamber. Dozens of dead soldiers and prisoners floated in the lagoon, their blood staining the aqua pools.

'I think this means we're definitely on Angelique's trail,' I said.

Jules nodded and wrapped her arms around herself.

If I could have transported her straight back home right then, I would have. Jules hadn't asked for any of this – it had been forced upon her. I gently took her hand and led her away.

Once again, seeing people who'd died brought home just how high the stakes were. And when the nuke blew, how many more would be killed, even if indirectly, by my hands? But I couldn't afford to think like that. The futures of whole worlds, countless billions and billions of people, would be decided on whether we succeeded here today or not. So for now I couldn't afford to let my emotions get to me. I had to be more like Angelique. Time to act the soldier, even if I didn't believe it deep down.

We reached a fork in the path where the rail tracks joined and ran along the side of our causeway. They were part of a large network of tracks that extended to the larger crystal formations. At the far end of the chamber, bathed in misty haze, all the tracks seemed to converge.

I increased my pace to match Jules's and ran alongside her as we passed a line of stationary wagons full of Psuche gems. 'I bet wherever these rails are headed is the destination for the mined crystals.'

She nodded. Her expression sharpened. 'Hey, did you hear that?'

I tuned into the cathedral silence and caught a faint whooshing coming from the direction of the mist. 'Water?'

'Lots, by the sound of it. Maybe an underground waterfall?'

A thought struck me. 'I wonder if that's the pumping station that Zack mentioned?'

Jules shot me an excited look. 'I bet it is. I also bet that's where we'll find Angelique and the others.'

Fresh hope filled me as we sprinted along the path towards the far end of the chamber.

'How long do you think it will take Ambra and his men to repair the lift?' Jules asked.

I glanced back over my shoulder, half expecting to see him running after us with a group of guards, but there was no sign of any pursuit. 'Let's just pray that it's enough time for us to be long gone.'

I noticed the light from the stalactite we'd just passed had started to dim. 'Hey, look.'

Jules glanced round. 'Wonder what's causing that?'

'Kinda neat, whatever it is.'

We'd nearly reached the end of the chamber, but my sides had started to burn. I'd never been that great at longer track distances, but Jules, a natural athlete at school, sprinted like an Olympic runner ahead of me. Directly in our path was a last stalactite, reaching all the way to the floor. It started to glow brighter as we approached.

'They're almost like those security lights that switch on when they detect someone,' Jules said.

I pulled up next to the bottom of the stalactite and clutched my sides, lungs burning with fire. Even though the clock was running, I needed to catch my breath. 'Jules, give me a second.'

She nodded and jogged back to me. The hiss of water from the end of the chamber had grown to a roar.

I dropped my head and took a deep breath. Leg muscles shaking, I reached out to steady myself on a number of crystals jutting out from the rock formation. My fingers brushed the surface and a jolt of energy surged up through my arm. I let out a yelp as my hand clamped on to the stalactite.

But it wasn't electricity zapping through me. Instead, thousands of voices cried out in my head. *'Whisperer...'* they said together, like a stadium of people all chanting in unison.

It felt like my head would shatter. My hand locked harder into place. I groaned and dropped to my knees,

Jules stared at me. 'Dom?'

I wretched. 'Voices in my head all talking at once.'

She squatted by me and rubbed my back.

'Free them...'

I jammed my jaw together, my breath wheezing between my teeth. The mind storm started to ease.

'Free our trapped brothers and sisters,' the chorus of voices said.

The same thing *Titan* had said to me back in Floating City. I tried to focus. 'Are you talking about the Psuche gems that Hades have messed with?'

Jules's eyes widened.

'Yes... Those men have twisted our brethren's souls and we feel their pain.'

The cries of the Hades ships – souls being tortured. My resolve hardened. What Hades had done to Dad was the tip of a vast iceberg of cruel experiments. 'Tell me what to do?'

'End their suffering and let their songs weave into the world's song once more.'

World song – what did that mean? 'How exactly?'

'Follow your destiny, Whisperer.' Blast, the same cryptic answer that *Titan* had given me. The energy coursing through my body snapped off like someone had killed the power switch. My hand fell away from the crystal.

'Are you okay?' Jules asked.

I massaged my tingling palm. 'I'll live.'

She gestured towards the stalactite. 'What did they say?'

'Something about following my destiny – freeing their brothers and sisters. Same line *Titan* fed me.'

'Don't suppose that advice came with a list of instructions?'

'I wish.'

She scowled. 'Have you caught your breath yet? We need to press on.'

I realised my body felt refreshed, like I could run a marathon if I wanted to. 'Think those Psuche gems just gave me a turbo charge.'

Jules raised her eyebrows. 'Maybe you can keep up with me this time.'

'Let's find out, shall we?'

We set off at a sprint along the causeway towards the waterfall. This time my legs didn't burn, my breath as easy as if I'd been taking a stroll.

The roar became deafening ahead of us as we reached the end of the chamber. We approached the edge of a cliff bathed in mist and peered over. The sheer scale of the luminous waterfall took my breath away. It thundered, its base lost in rising spray.

'It has to be as big as Niagara Falls,' I said.

'Bigger I think,' Jules replied. 'And look at the glowing water. I read about plankton glowing in the sea and I bet something similar is causing this.'

'Whatever it is, it looks awesome.'

'Reckon there's lots of tourists who'd pay big bucks to see this.'

'Think the locals might put them off a bit,' I replied.

Jules almost smiled.

The railway tracks headed on over a viaduct and out through a tunnel in the far side of the cavern. Beneath us a path dropped away in a steep series of steps carved into the cliff face.

'That way?' I asked.

'Makes sense.'

We hung onto a rope pegged into the rock and began our descent. Within moments the drifting spray soaked our clothes and beaded our hair with water pearls. Through the veil of mist I spotted a brick building. It spanned a river running from the base of the falls. Water boiled through a large sluice gate set directly beneath.

'That must be the pumping station,' I shouted over the roar.

Jules dragged her hand through her sodden hair and nodded.

We descended another flight of stairs and the spray started to thin. Over the sound of the water, cries and screams drifted up from the bottom of the cavern.

Jules grabbed my arm. 'Look!'

I followed where she was pointing. Hundreds of people, Hades and Cloud Riders, fought each other with swords and shovels.

My stomach filled with nails. 'Angelique must be down there. We've got to help.'

We started jumping down the steps two at a time, hanging on to the rope to keep our balance on the slippery surfaces.

The shouts grew wilder as we neared the bottom. In the middle of the fighting I caught a whirl of movement. Angelique spun round and struck a Hades soldier with a neck blow, sending him flying.

Without pausing, she ran towards the pumping station. 'Forward!' she shouted.

Cloud Rider men and women, armed with pickaxes and spades, followed her with battle yells. They rushed towards a group of Hades guards who'd formed a defensive circle around the building. A stream of arrows flew out from the soldiers' ranks and several Cloud Riders dropped to the floor.

Angelique waved both arms at the Hades men. 'You missed.'

My heart gripped as the soldiers aimed their weapons at her and fired again. She stepped neatly to the side like it was a dance move and the projectiles sped past.

'Call yourself soldiers? You couldn't hit a target if it was stuck to the end of your nose!' Angelique shouted.

A fresh wave of bolts flew out towards her. She whirled away and, like she was swatting a fly, she knocked aside one arrow zooming straight towards her head. The arrow spun away and struck the ground.

Pride surged through me. 'Angelique's deliberately trying to draw their fire!'

'That girl's seriously brave,' Jules replied.

We ran down the last flight of stairs and onto the edge of the battlefield. Up close, the reality of what was happening struck me like a slap around the face. This wasn't a video game, where another death didn't matter. This was far too real.

The wounded and the dead lay sprawled everywhere, faces twisted in agony.

Jules slipped in blood pooling from a dead Hades guard. I grabbed her hand to steady her. Her face paled, mouth pinched. I didn't let go until we'd hurried past the man's body.

'To freedom!' Angelique shouted.

Her people cheered and banged their improvised weapons on the ground.

I saw her turn to face the Hades guards. With a yell she sprinted towards them, golden hair trailing behind her. Worry spiked through me as the warrior princess charged into the enemy line.

Cloud Riders swept after her in the maelstrom of battle. I lost sight of Angelique. My heart rose to my mouth. *Please, god, let her survive this.*

We ran over and joined the back of the Cloud Riders pressing forward into the melee.

I didn't know how many bodies we stumbled over, but suddenly Angelique's voice rang out over the heads of the others ahead of us.

The cries of battle died away like a mute button had been pressed.

A moment of stillness.

'Victory!' Angelique shouted.

The men around us stumbled to a stop and leant on their weapons, breathing hard. We pressed on through the throng.

At last I spotted Angelique just ahead, kneeling by a man with an arrow sticking out of his chest. She held his head in her arms and my heart clenched as I saw his face.

Zack. His lifeless eyes stared upwards at her.

My throat closed up. 'Oh god, no.'

Jules squeezed my hand.

Stephen pushed through the Cloud Riders, clutching his left arm, wrapped in a length of blood-stained cloth.

His face paled as he saw Zack. He dropped to his knees by the old man's side. 'My old friend, too brave for his own good.'

'May your soul find freedom among the clouds,' Angelique said. She looked up and noticed Jules and me. She rubbed away her tears and gave us a broken smile.

CHAPTER Twenty-Three
PUMPING STATION

Jules's hand tightened around mine, as we watched Angelique lay Zack's head gently on the ground.

Stephen reached out and closed the old man's eyes.

Emotions flitted across Angelique's face: pain, sorrow, anger – and everything in between. She took a deep breath and stood, her expression set to determined.

I knew Angelique was digging deep so she could put on an act for her people. She had to. Every face was turned towards her. She was their leader, their light in the dark, and right now she knew they needed her to be strong for them.

She gazed around at the Cloud Riders. 'Attend to the injured, my countrymen.'

The prisoners split into groups and began picking their way back through the fallen.

Angelique's eyes flitted to my hand in Jules's. I hoped I was the only one who noticed her brief grimace, quickly replaced with a smile.

She reached her arms out. 'Thank the gods you're both alright.'

Jules stepped forward and hugged her. She pulled back and peered into Angelique's eyes. 'But are you okay?'

I pressed my lips together. I hoped Jules hadn't seen what I had.

But Angelique didn't miss a beat. She gestured towards the prisoners. 'I have to be for their sakes.'

Jules nodded and Angelique's eye caught mine. She looked away.

It seemed she and I were on the same page – at least for the moment. Thankfully, it seemed that Jules wasn't.

But as I watched Angelique the leader having to juggle everything in her head, including the loss of her people, it struck me exactly what it meant to be her. To have to always hold it together, whatever she was feeling, to never let her mask slip. I felt in awe of her.

Around us the Cloud Riders gathered flasks from the belts of the dead Hades guards. They poured the contents into the mouths of dying companions and enemy alike.

'What are they doing?' I asked.

'Easing their passing by giving them some Plam,' Angelique replied.

That made sense I guessed. Plam might turn Hades soldiers' eyes red, but it was also a drug that would help take their pain away. And anything that eased the awful suffering around us had to be a good thing.

But Jules looked horrified. 'You're going to leave them here to die?'

'We haven't got time to do anything else,' Angelique said. 'There can only be three hours left till the fission reactor goes critical.'

I glanced at the Tac. 'Two hours and fifty-five minutes to be precise.'

Jules pressed her hands to her mouth. 'But surely we can't leave them?'

I took her arm. 'Angelique's right. If we delay for even a moment, everybody could lose their lives.'

She stared around at the people around us, her face clouding. 'Oh god.'

I felt bad too, but if it was like this for us, it had to been even worse for Angelique. These were her people. And the difference was, she couldn't afford to let her true feelings show in front of them. Once again, I didn't envy the princess her role.

I glanced up at the pumping station towering over us. A huge copper pipe ran from it up the cliff face and disappeared through the same tunnel that the viaduct led to.

My attention switched to the white-water river boiling below us. It rushed underground through a sluice gate, bellowing like an animal on its way. 'Is that the route out you were talking about, Stephen?'

Stephen raised his gaze from Zack to me, his eyes dazed. 'Yes – yes, it is.'

Angelique placed her hand on his shoulder. 'Can you show us how to close the sluice?'

Stephen's eyes twitched like someone waking. He focused on her. 'We'll need to get access to the hydraulic controls inside the pumping station, my Princess.'

'Can you lead us?'

He nodded. 'Follow me.' With a last lingering look at Zack, he turned away and took a deep breath. Angelique wasn't the only one having to dig deep. He set off towards the pumping station with us close behind.

Two Cloud Riders emerged from the building as we approached.

'We took care of the Hades officers inside there,' the burlier one said.

'Good men,' Angelique replied.

They snapped her a salute. I couldn't help notice the blood sprayed across their grey shirts.

We entered the building and the smell of damp filled my nostrils. Every metal surface was pitted with rust. Lichen had crept in and spread over the walls. It felt like a derelict slum – all it needed was graffiti and the effect would be complete.

'Are you sure this place is still working?' I asked.

'If it wasn't, the turbines that power Hells Cauldron would be dead,' Angelique replied.

'That's not all it powers nowadays though,' Stephen said. 'Cronos built a facility for adapting Psuche gems in the next chamber.'

Angelique's mouth pinched. 'I don't remember another chamber.'

'Cronos had us blast through to it. The water is pumped from here to the adaptation facility to keep it cool.'

I gazed at the pipes that ran from the pumping station and out through the tunnel. 'You're saying that's where the mined crystals are changed into ones they use in the Hades ships?'

'I believe so.'

My skin tingled. Maybe this was my chance to free the Angelus trapped by Hades. 'We have to destroy it.'

'Because of the mission that *Titan* gave you?' Angelique asked.

'I can't think of any other way to stop Hades torturing them, can you?'

She shook her head.

Stephen gave us both a quizzical look.

'I'll explain later,' I replied.

'I can see your thinking, Dom,' Angelique said. 'When the fission bomb explodes the whole mine complex should be caved in.'

'Should?' I asked.

'We're a long way underground – there's no guarantee the blast radius will penetrate that far through the rock.'

I guessed even a nuke had its limits. 'In that case I'd better go there in person to make sure it's destroyed.' I'd work out the *how* part of the plan when I got there.

Angelique tied her long hair back in a knot. 'I'm not going to let you go alone. But first let's get the evacuation started. Then you and I will see what mischief we can cause in that processing plant.' She extended her hand. 'Deal?'

I shook it. 'Deal.'

Stephen crossed to a barnacle-covered door and heaved it open. 'The control room is just through here.'

We followed him into a dingy room lit by a single light bulb.

Jules grimaced and pointed at two bodies on the floor by control panels. Pickaxes were buried up to their handles in their backs. She sucked her cheeks in, shoulders shaking, a faraway – *I want to go home* – look on her face.

I wrapped my arm around her and scanned the area. In contrast to the decaying surroundings of the room, the console's surface had been polished and looked brand new.

The rest of the room was empty, apart from two large levers set into the middle of the floor.

Angelique gestured at the controls. 'I'm guessing we open the sluice with those, Stephen?'

'We do, but Ambra added extra security measures.' He pointed towards two copper plates at either end of the console, with handprints stamped into them. 'The officers activate the controls by pressing their palms into those.'

Jules blinked and focused on him.

She was back with us.

'That shouldn't be a problem,' she said. 'If you operate the left one, Dom, I'll take the right.'

I gave her a small smile and let my arm fall away.

Stephen shook his head. 'The handprints are coded to the officers' palm prints only.' He unsheathed a rapier sword from one of the soldier's belts. 'Princess Angelique, could I ask you to extend that man's arm?'

I glanced at the two handprints and felt nauseous. I knew exactly what he had in mind.

Jules gasped. 'You can't.'

'He won't mind, he's dead,' Stephen replied. He took a couple of practice swipes through the air.

Angelique turned to face him, arms crossed. 'We have to show respect for the fallen, even if they are Hades.'

He scowled at her. 'With respect, Princess, Zack's dead because of men like this. These officers showed us little *respect* when they were alive.'

Angelique drew herself to her full height. 'But Cloud Riders have to be better than that, Stephen. Hades may have lost their humanity, but we haven't. If we allow ourselves to cross that line, we'll become as bad as the enemy we've been fighting.'

A glow filled my chest. This woman wasn't just a soldier, she was a born leader too – and a great one at that.

Jules shot me a quick smile, obviously thinking the same.

'Let's move these men over to each of the control panels,' I said. 'That way they get to keep their hands.'

Stephen shrugged. 'Have it your way.'

I dragged one officer on his chair to a handprint stamp, while Stephen pushed the other man over to the far panel.

'Now that's more like it,' Angelique said. She crossed to me and pressed the dead man's hand to the plate.

Stephen did the same at the opposite end of the console.

With a hum, green lights glowed up.

Stephen nodded towards the levers. 'Now we need to pull those all the way back.'

'I'm on it.' I took hold of the first one and heaved. I swung the lever backwards with a grinding noise. The rumble of water softened beneath us.

'It's working,' Jules said.

I pulled on the second lever but it didn't budge. I braced my legs, muscles straining, and gave it everything I'd got, but the lever remained stuck in place.

I shook my head. 'It's jammed solid.'

Jules walked over and wrapped her hand around mine. 'Let's try that again but together.'

I could feel her hand shaking. No wonder, with everything she'd just witnessed. But at what point had I started to be able to cope with it – like this happened every day?

It seemed more than a little of Angelique's attitude had rubbed off on me.

I pulled the lever using my whole body weight as Jules screwed up her face with the effort. With a screech the lever shot backwards and we both had to hang on to it to stop ourselves falling. The vibration died beneath our feet and the roar outside hissed to silence.

Angelique beamed at us. 'You've done it.' She let go of the officer's hand and it slid off the control panel.

'Stop,' Stephen shouted.

With a whine the panel lights darkened and the two levers sprang back forward. At once the sound of water bellowed through the pumping station again.

Stephen shook his head. 'We will have to keep their hands in place till everyone is out.'

'Hang on, doesn't that mean that two people will have to stay back to allow everyone else to escape?' I asked.

He shrugged. 'Zack and I had been planning to do that.'

I stared at him, starting to realise just how brave this guy was. God, he had guts.

Lines ridged Angelique's forehead. 'First let's get this sluice closed and our people evacuated. We'll worry about the rest later.'

Angelique placed the hand back into the recess and the panel lit up again.

'Okay, Jules,' I said.

She brushed her hair from her eyes and nodded.

We heaved the lever together again and this time it slipped easily into the shut position. We pulled the second lever over and silenced the rumble buzzing through the building.

'What now?' Stephen asked.

Jules took a deep breath and crossed to Angelique. She forced a smile. 'Do you want a *hand* with that... After all, you need to be free to help Dom deal with the crystals.'

Angelique peered at her. 'If you're sure?'

'I am.'

From the time I'd had to deal with the Hades scout, I knew just how hard this would be for Jules to touch a dead man. I'd hurled my guts when I'd been faced with the scout's corpse.

'We can always get someone else in here to do that?' I said.

'I just need to do my bit to help, you know?' Jules replied.

I more than understood. Like me, there was no way she could stand by and do nothing. No wonder I'd fallen for her in the first place. And I also knew that if it came to it, I'd do anything to make sure she got through this alive.

Jules slipped her trembling fingers under Angelique's and around the man's wrist. A look of revulsion filled her face. 'You can let go, Angelique.'

'Okay...' Angelique stepped away from the panel. This time the levers remained in place.

'Nice one,' I said to Jules.

She gave me the barest nod, looking anywhere but the dead man's hand she was holding.

Angelique crossed to the doorway. She glanced back at Jules and Stephen. 'Whatever you do, keep that sluice gate shut. In a moment there will be hundreds of people in that tunnel.'

'We understand, Princess Angelique,' Stephen said.

Jules's nostrils flared. 'And we won't mess up.'

I squeezed her shoulder, although what I really wanted to do was hold her in my arms and never let go. 'We'll be back for you, I promise.'

'You'd better,' she said with a forced smile.

I caught the shadow crossing Angelique's face. I knew immediately what she was thinking – how were we going keep the sluice shut when the others had gone? Two people were going to have to stay behind to make sure everyone else got away. There was no way I'd let Jules stay, and knowing Angelique and her loyalty to her people, she would insist Stephen got to safety instead of her.

She caught my expression and nodded to me. In that moment it was like we'd had a whole conversation and agreed our plan, all without any words. We'd stay and, whatever arguments Jules and Stephen gave us, we'd make sure they both got out – because that was how we both rolled.

I glanced at the Tac and flashed the display towards Angelique. *Two hours and fifty minutes.*

'Let's do this,' Angelique said and headed outside.

I nodded, but paused to gaze deep into Jules's eyes. I saw the fear there, but not fear for herself, fear for me.

I had to turn away to look at Stephen instead. 'You watch out for her.'

'I give you my word as a Cloud Rider.'

'Thank you.'

'And you make sure you get back here in one piece, Dom,' Jules said, her voice wavering.

This was starting to feel like goodbye. 'I'll do my best,' I said without looking at her. Before my resolve crumbled, I turned and rushed outside after Angelique.

CHAPTER Twenty-Four
PROCESSING

Outside, what had been a rushing torrent was now a dribble of water running down a slime-filled tunnel.

'Time to get the evacuation underway,' Angelique said to me. She clambered onto the top of a small boulder, clapped and waved her hands at the Cloud Riders. 'Attention, please.' All heads turned in her direction. 'We have planted a bomb in the heart of Hells Cauldron that will bring it crashing down around Hades ears.'

For a moment the cheer from the prisoners drowned out even the falls roaring all around us.

'Once the Quantum Pacifier has been destroyed, we will be able to communicate with our fleet again. And then, my countrymen, we will make Cronos and his followers pay for all they've done to us.' A second louder cheer thundered through the cavern. Angelique gestured to the closed sluice gate and the tunnel beyond. 'The time for your liberation has come.'

With a third and final cheer, the Cloud Riders surged towards rusting ladders set into the rocky embankments. In twos and threes they began to descend onto the slimy river bed. As they entered the gloom of the tunnel, some of the prisoners with miner helmet lights guided the others.

Half-walking, half-slipping, men and women started to disappear down the escape route, many helping the walking wounded to limp away.

'That was quite the motivational speech,' I said.

'I hope so,' Angelique said with a half-smile. 'Now let's see what we can do about your mission from *Titan*.'

We began to thread our way through the battlefield filled with the dead and dying who'd been left behind. Those still conscious had red-stained irises from the Plam they'd been given. But despite the seriousness of the wounds, their faces looked relaxed. Brave men and women, ready to face their deaths with dignity, and at peace with themselves.

Even though we hurried, Angelique snatched a moment here and there to stop with many of the dying — even the fallen Hades soldiers — her gentle whispers to them tugged at my heart each and every time. I began to realise that until now I'd only glimpsed a fraction of who Angelique really was. This is what she'd been born to do. A princess not just in title, but in every fibre of her being.

We finally reached the stairs and started our climb back up the cliff face. The viaduct looked intimidating up close, just the width of the rails, and walls low enough to keep me looking straight ahead, rather than down. The minutes that it took to cross felt like a lifetime, but at last we made it to the far side where the viaduct met the pipeline rising from the pumping station, and followed it into the rocky tunnel ahead of us.

At once the air started to heat up and made my tongue stick to the roof of my mouth. A strange sense of dread flooded me. Something felt wrong, very wrong.

Angelique studied my face, her own expression drawn. 'You feel it as well, Dom?'

'Yeah, like I've just woken up from a nightmare.'

'But one that's getting worse?'

My sense of foreboding strengthened and I nodded. A red glow started to build at the end of the tunnel. I pressed on, pushing through my fear, but could never have anticipated what was waiting for us.

We stepped out into a huge cave shimmering with heat. Far below the viaduct, huge glass panels had been constructed over a sea of bubbling lava, each panel refracting the image like the face of a jewel.

I stared at the black crust breaking and reforming in hypnotic patterns beneath the panels. 'Holy cow, what's that?'

Angelique frowned. 'Nothing Hades could have built. It looks like some sort of screen built to stop an eruption. No wonder Hells Cauldron has stood on a dormant volcano for so many centuries.'

I thought of what Tesla had told us. 'Do you think the Angelus built this?'

'That makes sense. Certainly, looking at the way those panels are catching the light, I wouldn't be surprised if they were made from solid diamond.'

'You're kidding, right?' But I could tell by her serious expression, she wasn't. I did a quick mental count of the massive triangular panels slotted together – there had to be thousands of them. 'But they must be worth a fortune. Where on Earth did they get them?'

'Where on Earth indeed. For an advanced race like Angelus, sourcing them wouldn't have been a problem.

They probably mined them from asteroids, or found them on one of the parallel worlds where diamonds are as common as granite.'

I whistled. 'That's incredible.'

She shrugged. 'I suppose it might be considered that in your world.'

We started forward again and ran out over another narrow viaduct towards a squat stone building sitting on a column of rock. A silver metal tube led straight from its roof to the top of the chamber.

But with each step the dread inside me grew stronger, the nightmare digging its claws in. It took all my willpower to keep myself from turning tail and running. This was a test, a test where I had to fight my deepest fears.

I caught the same haunted expression on Angelique's face. That at least made me feel a bit better – to know it wasn't just me.

'I'm guessing what we're experiencing has to do with whatever they're doing to those crystals in that building,' I said.

Angelique gave me a tight look. 'This is worse than anything I could have imagined.'

The impossible heat intensified, but we pressed forward. Through eyes running with sweat, I saw the stone structure was bathed in a fine mist sprayed from a network of pipes around it. Presumably some sort of cooling system. Sure enough, as we entered the edge of the mist, the water straight away began to chill my burning skin.

Angelique and I stood for a moment catching our breath. We looked out at the shimmering heat distorting the view around us. Next to us an empty wagon rested against buffers at the end of rails. Its contents of blue crystals had been tipped into a hopper built into the building. So this is where the mined Psuche gems ended up. But going by the nightmare in my head, what awful thing happened to them next?

Angelique gazed at me through her soaking curtain of hair. 'Ready?'

'No, but let's do this anyway.' I pressed my hand against a door set into the squat structure and it swung open. At once thousands of screams flooded my mind. It felt like someone had punched me in the head.

An impossible weight loaded down my limbs and Angelique gasped. We both sprawled into the building and the door swung shut behind us. Trapped.

I clutched my hands over my ears, trying to shut out the horror of the voices swirling through my brain.

Angelique groaned. 'I can't move.'

I tried to stand, but it felt like somebody had pinned me to the floor. 'I can't either.'

Neck muscles screaming, I managed to twist my head enough to look around the room. A large basin in the middle was filled with a heap of blue Psuche gems. With a whir of cogs, a mechanical arm picked up one of the crystals and swung it towards a stone crucible bubbling with lava. I had a hunch that we were about to witness Hades processing a crystal.

The arm jerked to a stop and released the gem into the molten rock.

A woman's shriek drowned out all the other cries in my head. I writhed, the flesh feeling like it was burning off my body. Angelique whimpered and tucked into a foetal position.

Through the awful pain, words formed in my head.

'*Help me!*' the woman's voice shouted.

God, this was sick, more than I could take. Tears spilled down my face. Her tears, my tears? I wasn't sure where the soul in the crystal began and the edges of my body stopped.

The robotic arm withdrew the crystal from the lava. It crackled with sparks. The claw swung it towards a drill connected to a glass flask filled with red liquid. The drill sped up and plunged into the crystal.

My body jolted like I'd been given a shock. With a hiss, the red liquid was injected into the heart of the crystal.

'That's Plam,' Angelique said through gritted teeth. 'I can smell it.'

The core of the Psuche gem's blue light became stained with red. The woman's scream died away – now just one of the chorus echoing through my mind.

The arm pivoted round and placed the processed crystal on a claw mount inside a glass chamber.

'I don't care if we die, but we have to stop this,' I said, my eyes blurring with tears.

Angelique sucked in lungfuls of air. 'But we can't even move.'

A speaker crackled above us. 'That's excellent news,' Ambra's voice said.

I stared up at metal spider clinging upside down to the ceiling, its camera eyes directed towards us.

'Go to hell, Ambra,' Angelique said.

He laughed. 'I think you're already there ahead of me, Princess.'

Angelique glowered up at the spider.

'So please tell me, now I have your undivided attention – what do you think of our Voice Scream weapon?' he said.

'Your what?' I replied.

'Everyone knows about Voice Shout, which ships use on each other, but we discovered that when we gathered a number of processed crystals together, it magnified the effect. The building you are in is shielded with an electromagnetic mesh woven into the walls. That stops the telepathic screams leaking out. Before we had that fitted, we found that any of our Navigators within a hundred mile radius of your current location were unable to move. It's that effect that we developed into the Voice Scream weapon, an early version of which we used to cripple *Apollo*. We even managed to knock out your father's ship, *Olympus*, Princess. But he somehow still managed to escape.'

'You'll never capture the King with your sick weapons,' Angelique replied.

'Yet, we've managed to capture his beloved daughter with exactly that.'

'You haven't caught us yet. Any moment this place will come crashing down,' I replied.

Ambra chuckled. 'Oh, you must be referring to your precious little bomb.'

Something about his confident tone gave me the chills. Angelique shot me a worried look. I glanced at the Tac. *Two hours and forty minutes.*

'If I were you I'd be more worried that Hells Cauldron will soon be a big smouldering hole in the ground,' I said.

'Oh, I wouldn't be so sure about that. You see, I'm afraid we discovered your little toy in the operating theatre. Right now my scientists are busy deactivating it. Which,

I might add, they're confident they will do long before it reaches zero.'

Angelique gave me a desperate look. Once again Ambra had turned the tables on us. Was that it – would our fight end here?

'Now be good little prisoners and behave yourselves until we can get round to dealing with you. Then I'm personally going to teach you both the true meaning of pain.'

Who the hell did this guy think he was? Dad had said never to give up. I would never throw in the towel to someone like Ambra. I'd never give him the satisfaction.

Leg shuddering, I pulled myself to a kneeling position. With every ounce of strength I had left, I staggered to my feet, reached up and grasped the spider.

Angelique stared up at me. 'You can do it, Dom.'

My bones felt like they would snap any moment. But I gritted my teeth and ignored the spider's pincers snipping at my fingers. I lobbed it towards the crucible of lava. It splashed into the molten rock and melted in sparks. My legs buckled and I collapsed back to the floor.

'Thank you,' Angelique said. 'Ambra's annoying voice was starting to get to me.'

'Anytime.' I tried to move again, but I'd nothing left.

'We've lost, haven't we?'

'Don't talk like that,' I replied.

'But we have. You heard what Ambra said. Any moment they'll deactivate the fission reactor.'

'There has to be a way.' The howling in my mind started to soften and a familiar tingle swept through me. Ship-song?

'*Whisperer, hold me,*' *Storm Wind*'s voice said.

My eyes widened. I'd forgotten I even had his Psuche gem hidden in my pendant. I slid my hand to it, flicked the catch open and the crystal tumbled into my hand. Coolness swept through my body and the shrieking in my mind stopped dead. At once I felt like I'd lost a hundred stone in weight. Energy surged through me and I clambered back to my feet.

Angelique stared up at me. 'How?'

'I'll show you.' I headed over to the basin, grabbed a blue shining Psuche gem and rushed back to her. 'Here, take this.' I pressed the crystal into her hand.

Her shoulder blades relaxed the moment she gripped it. She rolled over, her face clearing of pain.

I helped her up. '*Storm Wind* told me what to do. The Psuche gems must be protecting us somehow.'

'Thank the gods for your whispering ability. But what now?'

'After seeing what Hades are doing here, we have to make sure we total this place.'

'Absolutely. In which case, we need to get back up to the lab, find the bomb and make sure it detonates. Now we have an edge – Ambra won't be expecting us to be able to move.'

I remembered what I'd done back at the lift shaft and groaned. 'I disabled the elevator after we got down here. Do you know another way to get back to the surface?'

She pressed her hands to her mouth. 'No I don't.'

'Oh rats.' I stared at the red processed crystal glowing in the claw. I hated what was being done in this room with every ounce of my being. We couldn't let Hades win and continue this torture.

I tried to order my thoughts and my gaze wandered around the room. I noticed a tube set into the roof. We'd seen that pipe outside rising from this building and into the roof of the chamber. What was that for? A smoke vent?

I examined the base of the pipe. It was connected to the glass chamber the processed gem had been placed in. Inside, the red crystal glowed in its claw mount on a turntable. So why did that whole set-up seem familiar?

A flash of memory and I knew exactly where I'd seen something similar before. 'Angelique, do you remember in the operating theatre how the Hades AI crystal appeared in that hatch thing?'

'Yes, what about it?'

'You don't suppose it was transported directly from here – up through this tube – do you?'

Her eyes widened. 'Do you think it could be some sort of service elevator?'

'That makes sense.'

'In that case, let's see if we can work out how to operate it.'

We examined the glass cylinder. At the back I spotted the outline of a hatch. I felt a glimmer of hope and pointed it out. 'I do believe we've just found our way back up.'

Angelique gave me an excited look. 'But how do we open it? I don't see anything in the way of controls.'

'This has to be all automated, right?' I ran my fingers around the edge of the turntable. 'So thinking this through – when a gem is processed it's moved towards the back to be loaded into the service lift.' I spun the turntable. The crystal rotated towards the back and the hatch in the metal tube slid open.

Angelique clasped her hands. 'You're a genius, Dom.'

I grinned. 'I guess I have my moments.' I peered through the hatch. 'Okay, it's a tiny space in there. I'm not sure we can both fit in.'

'You don't have to. I'm going up there by myself.'

I stared at her. 'Come again?'

'Look, we know they're up there defusing the bomb. Ambra is going to have a lot of men with him, so just remind me which of us is the more highly trained fighter?'

'You are, but—'

She swatted my words away with a chopping gesture. 'No buts – it has to be me. We both know that I can handle whoever's up there. And to be blunt, I stand a better chance than you of making it back down here in one piece.'

I wanted to tell her the million reasons it should be me, but I couldn't find even one. 'I'm sure if I tried I could fit in there—'

She took my shoulders in her hands. 'Dom, it has to be me.'

I stared at her, but I also knew she was right. 'Okay, but this better not be goodbye. I'll be so pissed at you if you get yourself hurt.'

'What did your dad say? While there's still breath in our bodies...'

'We still have a chance.' My eyes stung. 'Just make sure you get your butt back down here, or I'll give you hell.'

She pulled me into a tight hug. 'Whatever happens next, just know that I consider myself lucky to know you.'

'Me too.' Whatever was going on between us, at some point she'd become a great friend. It cut me up thinking this might be the last time I'd see her.

Tears pooled in the corner of her eyes and she kissed my cheek. This was starting to feel like another goodbye.

Angelique folded herself into the chamber and pulled her knees up tight to her chin. 'Here goes nothing.'

'Sock it to them,' I said.

'Oh, I intend to.'

I rotated the turntable until the closing hatch shut away Angelique's smile. A whooshing sound came from the tube.

I glanced to the ceiling. 'Safe voyage, Angelique.'

A pulse of light came from *Storm Wind*'s crystal still clasped in my fingers. *'Whisperer, someone is coming for you.'*

My stomach tensed. I raised the gem to eye level. 'Who?'

Light danced within it. *'Duke Ambra and his men.'*

Panic gripped me. I'd assumed Ambra was still up in the operating theatre with the scientists deactivating the bomb. But of course Ambra was way more sneaky than that. *I'll get around to you eventually.* Yeah right. Just a ploy to keep us distracted as he closed in on our position.

I rushed to the door and looked out along the causeway. Sure enough, at the far end, a group of men sprinted towards me along the viaduct. Even at this distance I could see the flowing, white hair of Ambra. My brain raced. This had to mean they had passed the pumping station where… Jules and Stephen! My heart clenched. If she was dead…

The Tac chimed and I looked at it to see the numbers spin down from over two hours to only thirty seconds. Despite the heat, my blood iced. How could that have happened?

I took the Leatherman out of my pocket and opened the blade. I'd die fighting rather than let them take me. I heard a hiss come from the service lift.

Oh thank god, Angelique had come back. We'd fight Ambra together. That would even the odds a bit.

The hatch slid open. My heart rose to my mouth. No Angelique, just the red reactor cube inside.

My attention locked on to its timer clicking down.

Twenty seconds...

I grabbed the cube, mind numb.

Nineteen...

The nuke was about to blow and take me with it. What the hell could I do in the few seconds left?

CHAPTER Twenty-Five

ERUPTION

Fifteen seconds...

What had happened to Angelique?

Twelve...

Storm Wind's voice filled my mind. *'Whisperer, throw the bomb into the lava field.'*

'What?'

'Hurry.'

The timer ticked down to single digits.

Nine...

Ambra charged along the viaduct towards me, his group of men right behind.

Steam belched from the soldiers' crossbows. I threw myself flat and bolts whistled over my head. I scrambled back up and rushed to the edge.

Storm Wind's Psuche crystal pulsed in my hand.

'Throw the bomb.'

Without stopping to think I pulled my right arm back, like I was going for a baseball throw, and flung the metal box far out in an arced lob. It tumbled away through the air and struck the diamond panels. It skittered away across them – the panels were way too strong to be even cracked by the projectile.

Another barrage of arrows hissed over my head as Ambra and his men crossed the last span of viaduct.

I squeezed my eyes shut and continued the countdown in my head. *Five, four, three, two...*

A blaze of light glowed through my eyelids and a hurricane of air smashed into me. I clung on to the rock as the wind tore past. Heat blazed over my skin.

'*Whisperer, you must get back into the building and escape while you can.*'

The ground shuddered beneath me. I opened my eyes to see panels spinning away from a mushroom cloud billowing upwards towards the roof of the chamber.

The wind died away with a moan. I hauled myself to the edge and peered over. Lava flooded up through a hole blasted through the diamond screen, like blood pouring from a wound in skin.

I clambered back to my feet as the molten rock started to lap around the legs of the viaduct. With a crack of splintering rock, it began to buckle.

'Retreat!' Ambra shouted. He sprinted back with his men the way they'd come. The bridge groaned and fell span by span behind them, like a giant set of dominoes toppling over.

I watched, unable to tear my eyes away from the horror show, as two, four, six men tumbled into the lava, each screaming as they fell. Only Ambra and one of his men reached the safety of the tunnel on the far side.

The Duke turned towards me. For a moment we stared across the flame-filled chasm at each other. Even at that range I could see the hatred burning in his eyes. I met it with my own fierce gaze. If I could have leapt across the fiery gulf and grappled him, I would've, there and then.

Another quake roared through the chamber and threw me to the floor. The air boiled with heat as lava flooded the cavern. It sped up the column of rock towards the processing plant and me.

With a final stare, Ambra turned and ran. I prayed he wouldn't get very far.

My skin started to blister with the furnace air. I stumbled back into the cool of the building, clutching the Psuche gem.

Inside, light blazed from the mound of blue crystals. In the middle of all the chaos and destruction, their joy-filled songs overpowered the screams of the processed gems in my mind. It was almost like they wanted this to happen.

I rushed towards the service elevator, my only hope of escape. The space inside looked even smaller than when Angelique had clambered into it. I grazed my knuckles on the hatch as I jammed my body into the lift, having to fold my legs hard against my chest to fit. I shuffled the turntable platform round beneath me and the hatch slid closed. Wrapped in darkness, the walls banged and shook around me.

Please, god, let this work... A hiss of air, a kick of acceleration in my butt, and the service lift shot upwards like a rocket. But with a howl the tube started to unravel beneath me, like someone had begun to open a zipper along the length of it. Through the opening slit I spotted lava flood over the dome of the processing plant. My mind filling with noise, the building disappeared beneath the molten surface. Red streamers of light shot away from it. The processed souls being freed? I hoped with all my being that was so, because, even if I didn't make it, it would be one comforting thought to cling on to.

The volcanic scene, framed by the circle of the elevator tube, hurtled away into the distance. *Storm Wind*'s crystal blazed brighter to illuminate the shaft walls skimming past.

Another quake rattled me in the lift like a stone in a can. My heart raced and a nightmare image crowded my skull. Jules and Stephen! I pictured lava pouring through the door of the pumping station where they were waiting for us.

No! Suddenly I couldn't breathe.

Jules… She hadn't asked to be brought here. First Dad, now her. Something broke inside me, the pain inside worse than the blisters on my hands. I pounded my fists on my knees.

No, no, no!

I was dimly aware of the service elevator beginning to slow.

What was the point in fighting? I'd lost my girlfriend, Dad… Who knew what had happened to Angelique. Now I was all alone. What difference could I make? I was just one teenager against a ruthless army. An army, like Angelique said, that had lost its humanity a long time ago.

With a juddering lurch the lift came to halt. The door rotated open and a klaxon pounded into my eardrums.

For a moment I thought I was seeing things.

Angelique staggered to her feet. But this was real and actually happening. She was alive and kicking ass.

Around her scientists and soldiers lay injured. My joy swept away as I saw a giant of a Hades soldier gather himself to rush her from behind. Before I could cry out a warning, he leapt forward and brought her crashing down with him.

I unfolded myself from the lift and scrabbled towards them.

The soldier pinned her to the ground and unhooked a knife from his belt.

Anger burned hotter than the lava I'd just escaped. No way would I lose another friend today.

I lunged at the solider and clamped my arm around his neck.

Released, Angelique gasped and struck his knife away.

The soldier stood up with me hanging on like I weighed nothing. My muscles screamed as he clawed at my arms, but somehow I managed to keep my hold as he shook me. With a yell, the soldier threw himself backwards and crushed me against a wall.

I sagged to the floor and stared up at him. I felt calm, no longer afraid, my mind too numb to think any more. I just wanted this roller-coaster ride to be over.

The man towered over me with a fierce grin and raised his sledgehammer fists. I braced, waiting for a blow that I knew would kill me.

Instead, his arms slumped to his side and his grin twisted. Eyes wide, he toppled over and landed next to me with a thud.

I saw the knife he'd been brandishing only a moment before, stuck in his own back. Angelique lowered the hand she'd just thrown it with. She stood up, gasping for air.

A quake rippled through the lab. I staggered over to her, the ground buzzing like a drum skin through the balls of my feet.

'We've got to get out of here,' I said. 'The shield holding the lava back has been destroyed.'

'The bomb?'

I nodded. '*Storm Wind* told me what to do with it when you posted it down to me.'

'I'm so sorry, Dom. This place was crawling with guards protecting the scientists. I just managed to get hold of it when their reinforcements arrived. There was nothing else I could do. I reset the countdown to be sure they couldn't deactivate it. You see I had to be sure they couldn't get their hands on it again...' She hung her head.

But I understood. 'So you did the only thing you could and shoved it into the lift.'

'I thought I'd killed you.'

I grasped her shoulders. 'I'd have done the same in your place. At least now the processing plant has been flooded with lava.'

Angelique's gaze widened. 'Flooded with lava, but that means Jules and Stephen...'

Jules's dimpled smile rushed into my mind. The ache inside me spasmed. I spread my hands, words flowing away. Nothing I could say would bring her back.

Angelique wrapped me tight in her arms. 'Oh gods, oh gods, if I hadn't sent that reactor down to you...'

Jules had gone. Something went white-hot inside me. This was Ambra's fault. I'd make him, Cronos and every

277

one of their Hades soldiers pay for what had happened to Jules, Dad and all the others.

A roar came from the ground beneath the operating theatre.

I grabbed Angelique's hand. 'We have to get to the surface while we still can.'

She nodded, eyes hardening. We rushed out into the round chamber where the pods had been. The stone floor started to flex like it was made of rubber and we hung onto each other as everything shook around us. With a bang, a fissure crackled across the polished floor, heading straight towards a scientist working at one remaining pod. Too late, the man turned as the crack reached him. With a cry, he plummeted into it.

Angelique pulled on my hand and pointed towards the elevator on the far side of the widening ravine. 'We're going to have to make a leap for it, Dom.'

I gave a sharp nod and tightened my grip on her. Do or die. Together we sprinted towards the fissure and leapt. I glanced down and saw lava rushing up through the crack from hundreds of feet below – the eruption didn't seem to be running out of steam. We landed on the far ledge and, without breaking stride, ran towards the lift.

Wild-eyed, a soldier repeatedly shoved the elevator button. He spotted us and started to raise his crossbow.

Angelique closed the distance in two strides. 'I don't think so.' She slammed her fist into his throat. With a whimper the soldier collapsed to the floor.

Molten magma sprayed from the fissure. The lights flickered and gloom swept over us, the only illumination from the lava starting to flow around the operating theatre.

This place was beginning to have more than a passing resemblance to every idea I'd ever had about hell.

I battled my panic and stabbed the lift button. 'Will you come on!'

A whine, and the cable streaming past started to slow. I peered up the shaft and saw the bottom of the elevator rushing towards us. I yanked my head back to avoid being decapitated. The lift ground to halt in front of us and the doors opened.

'Thank the gods,' Angelique said.

We rushed inside. I turned to see the lava surge towards the operating theatre's glass wall. It detonated with a bang. Molten rock flowed into the room and around the legs of the operating table Lord Orson had been strapped to. As the doors closed, with grim satisfaction I saw the table capsize and melt, like a boat sinking into a lava sea.

With a lurch the elevator began to ascend. The mountain groaned around us, emitting bass notes so deep, I felt them in my body rather than heard them. Another quake hit and slammed us against the walls.

My body tensed, waiting for the rush of the cable as it snapped. Angelique, head bowed, mouthed a silent prayer. But the vibration died away and we kept shooting upwards.

Angelique blew her cheeks out. 'We may just make it.'

'I don't much fancy our chances of outrunning an erupting volcano.'

'You're forgetting that our balloon pack is in the basin where I hid it.'

I felt a flicker of hope. Maybe Angelique was right and we could make it out of this alive. I looked back down at the shaft beneath us. 'At least Ambra's down there with the rest of them. It's just what he deserves.'

'He is?'

'Turned up with his men to pay me a house visit in the processing plant. It was a pretty close call.'

'In that case I hope he's burned to a cinder by now.'

Along with Jules...

My stomach twisted. So many dead and it all came down to one man and his crazy ambition: Cronos.

'Even if Ambra had been killed, Cronos will still have escaped,' I said.

'The moment the Quantum Pacifier goes offline, we'll be able to make contact with the King. Once we've done that, this or any other universe won't be a big enough place for Cronos to hide.'

We sped past one of the large, open caverns that had been filled with crates, but was now empty. Had the stores been loaded onto their secret ship?

'So what about *Kraken*?' I asked.

'With the Cloud Rider fleet fully functional again, any Hades ship won't stand a chance.'

I wasn't so sure Angelique's confidence was justified. After all, hadn't the Hades Voice Scream weapon knocked out *Apollo* and almost *Olympus*? And the Hive...what edge would that give Cronos in battle?

My attention snapped back as the elevator sped into a bank of steam whistling from a fractured pipe. We shuddered to a stop. The doors whined and managed to open halfway before jamming solid. Through the gap I saw the basin of the volcano – we'd made it.

I squeezed through after Angelique.

Outside, the volcano groaned and bellowed around us, as ash plumes vented into the sky. Rocks and pebbles showered down in deadly, black rain. Above us the solid stone towers of the palace rocked back and forth, the mast humming like a tuning fork. But over the thunder of destruction I heard a squeal of metal. I turned to see the lift doors shutting again. No way could anyone make it out alive now.

We staggered into the basin as the whole world shook around us. The stairs to the battlements had already disappeared under a landslide. No escape that way.

A rumble came from deep beneath the ground, like the lava express train from hell was on its way to the surface.

'I think this thing's going to blow any moment,' I said.

Angelique nodded and pointed to the far side of the basin. 'I left the pack in a crevasse over there. Let's get a move on.'

Half running, half stumbling, we sped across the basin as lightning arced outwards from the mast and played across the top of the battlements. A huge strike blasted one of the towers to rubble.

'Watch out,' Angelique shouted. She pulled me to the ground as the masonry showered down on us.

Stones slammed into my body and we clutched on to each other. For a moment the world was obscured by dust, but gradually it started to clear.

Coughing, we stood together to see a heap of rubble at the base of the cliff directly in front of us.

Angelique put her hands over her mouth. 'Oh gods, that's where I left the balloon lifter pack.'

I scanned the pile of boulders, most the size of large refrigerators. No way could we clear those in time. The volcano's mouth had sheer sides we couldn't climb. No wonder Angelique had been trapped in the basin by the guards before. This was it – we'd nowhere to run to.

Fear knotted in my chest as the earth groaned beneath us and solid rock started to splinter like breaking wood.

With a yelp Angelique clasped her leg and collapsed. Her foot had got wedged into one of the cracks. She pulled at her leg. 'Oh heck!'

I hooked my hands under her shoulders and pulled.

She grimaced and shook her head. 'It's no good, I'm stuck, Dom. Get yourself to safety.'

'I'm not leaving you, and besides, where's there to run to?'

'You're so stubborn.'

'And so are you.'

In the middle of all the madness Angelique actually smiled at me.

And just like that my fear evaporated and I found myself smiling back at her. I gestured around us. 'I don't think Hades are going to forget our visit anytime soon.'

'Oh they'll probably be singing songs about us in Floating City taverns for years to come.

I shook my head at her. If I had to die, she was certainly one of the coolest people I could have shared this moment with.

With a whoosh, ash billowed from the lift shaft.

Angelique struggled into a sitting position and pointed.

Through the rolling smoke the elevator rose into view.

Angelique's hand tensed around my arm. 'Somebody's coming up in it!'

'Might as well go down fighting.' I stuck my hand into my pocket. The Leatherman had gone. I must have lost it somewhere back down in the mines

'Just use your hands, Dom. Remember your Sansodo training.'

Obscured by the thickening smoke, I heard the doors squeal open.

I stood up, balancing my weight on the balls of my feet and kept my hands relaxed by my side, just like Angelique had drummed into me.

'Remember to feel what your opponent is doing and try to trust in your body's instincts.'

I nodded. 'I'll do my best, coach.'

A shape loomed from the smoke. A man with a blistered face appeared, his uniform half-burned away. He trailed a curved sword over the ground and stalked towards us. My heart started to thunder in my chest.

Duke Ambra stared at us, eyes stained bright red with Plam. He coughed up some blood and stood straighter. 'Like two rats caught in a barrack's brandy barrel.' He advanced towards me and raised his blade.

Chapter Twenty-Six
AMBRA

Ambra swung the blade towards my neck. A tingle shot through my nerves where the blow was headed. My Sansodo training kicked in, muscle memory taking over from fear.

I tilted away, but kept the balance on my feet, like somebody spinning a hula hoop around their stomach. The blade hissed past my head.

I straightened up, took a deep breath and forced my muscles to relax.

Ambra gave me a slow clap. 'Oh very good. I see Princess Angelique has been giving you lessons.' His lips curled. 'That's going to make killing you all the more satisfying. And when I've finished with you, I'll deal with the Princess.' He raised his sword, balancing its weight in his burned left hand, and stalked towards me.

'You can do this, Dom,' Angelique said, yanking at her trapped foot.

Could I? Could I really take on a highly trained soldier like Ambra and win?

A whisper filled my thoughts. *'Yes,' Storm Wind* said. His confidence wove through my worried thoughts, easing their hold on me. Perhaps I did stand a chance if I believed in myself.

Ambra lunged and, despite his speed, it felt like his thrust happened in slow motion. I watched the sword tip plunge towards me. I began to pivot away from the blade. But he grinned and swerved the hilt of the sword and struck the side of my skull.

The blow rattled my head and I sprawled into the black dirt.

The Duke laughed and brought his sword level again. Who was I kidding that I could win this? Ambra was just toying with me.

'Don't watch the sword, Dom,' Angelique said.

'That's right, remember your training, young pup.' Ambra gave his sword a couple of practice swipes.

I stood and glowered at him.

Ambra advanced towards me, swirling his sword in a figure of eight. 'I'm getting bored – time to finish this.'

Don't watch the sword. Trust myself. Trust my instinct.

Ambra stabbed the blade towards my chest, but I didn't feel a tingle around my body, no tightening of muscles where I would have expected the blow to land. The sword swerved away.

'That's it, that's it, you're reading him now,' Angelique said.

Ambra's sword continued to swoop, a flash of silver in a hypnotic dance. I ignored it and tuned into my body instead. My chest started to tingle. Sure enough, Ambra shifted his attack from a sideswipe to a lunge for my heart.

Without even thinking, I let my body flow around the strike and I spun around Ambra. My fingers became an open fist, my arm an extension of my whole body. With my full weight behind it, I drove my hand upwards into his chin.

The power of the blow lifted Ambra up. He sprawled to the ground and his sword clattered away. He didn't get up.

I'd done it, I'd really done it!

Angelique whooped. 'Now that's what I call an impressive demonstration.'

I raised my eyebrows at her. 'I had a great teacher.'

'Maybe I should give up being a princess and go into training.'

'I'd sign up in a flash, although you're a great princess too.'

'Thank you for the compliment, kind sir.' Her smile froze as the earth screeched and the whole basin shook around us. The crack beneath Angelique shuddered. She grimaced as her foot came free.

With a belch of cinders, lava began to flood up through the cracks, making the whole basin look like weird crazy paving with molten rock as the mortar.

I helped Angelique to her feet. 'Hells Cauldron is getting ready to erupt.'

'And we're trapped!'

There had to be a way out of this nightmare. I scanned the basin as the heat began to build fast. My gaze caught on the mast. It was the only option we had.

I grabbed Angelique's hand. 'Come on.'

We rushed to the mast. Together we started to clamber up it, using the struts as ladder runs. Deep hums ran through the metal structure.

I knew that no matter how strong the mast was, it couldn't hold out much longer.

Hand over hand, we climbed up towards the circle of the night framed by the rim of the volcano above us.

I glanced back down to see the lava begin to flood the basin. My gaze shot to where Ambra had fallen.

He wasn't there. Huh?

I scanned the area and caught movement right beneath us. Clothes on fire, Ambra was clambering up the mast after us.

I pointed at the Duke. 'Doesn't this guy ever give up?'

Angelique stared down at Ambra and shook her head. 'It must be the Plam keeping him going.'

A bang came from below. A boulder the size of a car shot up past us. It trailed smoke and arced out and away over the landscape.

'I'm so sorry I pulled you into all this,' Angelique said as we climbed.

'I'm the one who thought I wanted a life of adventure. Reckon I might have got more than I bargained for though.'

'As they say, be careful what you wish for.'

But that was just it. Had I really wished for this? Wasn't it more a case of being thrown into this madness, whether I'd wanted it or not? Life had been so much simpler back home. And if I was honest with myself, happier too. Funny how it took a parallel world and being in the middle of an eruption to make that clear to me.

We climbed faster, but despite the flames burning Ambra's flesh away, he kept pace with us. Plam or not, his pain had to be unbearable.

The struts began to heat under my hands. The lava boiled and hissed below us like one of Mom's tomato soups on the stove, only with a lot more attitude and heat. If I slipped I didn't much fancy the idea of becoming human barbecue.

We climbed and the top of the battlements drew closer, but I couldn't see anyone on them. Another rock projectile whistled past us into the sky, spitting fire as it went. The remaining towers around the rim began to vibrate.

'Looks like the palace is about to collapse,' Angelique said.

Steam started bellowing from round vents dotted around the rim.

I gestured towards the steam geysers. 'What's that all about?'

'No idea,' Angelique said.

Laughter drifted up from beneath us.

'And so it begins,' Ambra shouted.

Angelique stopped and stared down at him. 'What begins?'

Ambra's laugh became a cackle. 'Oh, you'll see in a moment, Princess.'

There was something strange about the movement running through the towers on the battlements. At first I thought it was the earthquake fooling my eyes, but as I watched more closely, I realised the towers were all steadily moving in one direction – up.

We gawped as the whole palace rose around us up into the sky.

Angelique shouted down to Ambra. 'You converted the palace into a ship?'

Ambra gestured around us. 'You're witnessing the maiden voyage of *Kraken*, Princess. And not just any ship at that, but a capital ship.'

'Oh by the gods,' Angelique said.

'What does he mean, "capital ship"?'

'There have been blueprints for the design of something like this for years, but it wasn't thought practical. The flight demands were considered too complex for an AI to control.'

In that moment I knew exactly why Cronos had begun his sick conversion experiments. 'But not for a Hive mind powered by lots of Navigators!'

'Oh by the gods, you're right.'

'Very well deduced, boy,' Ambra called up. 'And with the armaments of *Kraken* operated by their collective consciousness, we don't need a battle fleet any more. *Kraken* is a battle fleet in one vast ship.'

With a boom, a huge ring of linked balloons burst from the rock. The palace began to rise faster in a shower of stone.

'The Cloud Riders will stop you,' Angelique shouted at him.

Ambra laughed. 'There is no ship in your fleet that will stand a chance against the Voice Scream of the Hive mind.'

'We'll ram it if we have to and bring it down,' Angelique replied.

'That would do little good against *Kraken*'s main weapon.'

'We'll find a way to beat your Voice Scream.'

'That's not what I'm referring to.'

'What then?' I called back.

'The one that in due course, and with thanks to the Cloud Riders, will be tested out against your home world, boy.'

I stared down at him. 'What do you mean?'

He grinned at us through a mask of burned flesh. 'It was the Cloud Riders who showed us the potential of the Vortex as the ultimate weapon. At the heart of *Kraken* is a Vortex drive powerful enough to rip a planet apart – as the Cloud Riders so effectively demonstrated when they destroyed our planet. We call it Fury. A rather apt title, I've always thought.'

Cronos wasn't going to attack my home, or even the whole of Oklahoma. That wasn't a big enough target for him. No, instead he was going destroy our whole planet!

My resolve powered my tiring limbs. I'd climb into the sky if I'd had to – escape and stop Cronos.

'You murdering scum!' Angelique shouted at him.

Ambra laughed. 'For all of your noble causes you believe you're fighting for, Princess, just ask yourself who's got the most blood on their hands today?'

She growled at him and shook her head.

He was twisting everything and I hated him for it. 'That was an accident – no one knew it was going to happen. And who is it that has just launched a dirty great ship with the ultimate weapon to destroy worlds? Yeah, you're obviously the good guys!'

'It's a matter of perspective, boy. We will bring order to all the Earths that submit to the rule of Emperor Cronos.'

'And those who don't want to be part of your circus?'

'They'll be destroyed of course.'

So there it was. The logic of a madman. Hot anger surged through me. 'The lot of you are nothing but cold-blooded killers.'

'Oh, you've seen nothing yet of our skills for destruction and chaos, boy.'

The beat of wind swept over us from vast rotors beneath the palace. They slid past, driving the floating mountain higher into the sky.

A deep growl filled my mind and a wave of fear washed over me. I wanted to let go, do anything to get away from *Kraken*.

Angelique gasped. 'The mind storm in my head.'

Nausea rose up my throat and screams echoed through my skull. Voice Scream. We needed to shut it out like we had before. I thrust my hand into my jean's pocket and clamped my fingers around *Storm Wind*'s Psuche gem. Thank god, I hadn't lost him like my Leatherman.

A cooling pulse ran up through my arm and at once the noise in my mind died to a whisper.

'Angelique, use your Psuche gem like we did before.'

Gritting her teeth, she nodded and withdrew her crystal. She held it and her expression relaxed, as ash swirled around us.

'That was the Hive mind on the ship, wasn't it?' she said.

'It has to be.' I thought of Dad locked into his pod, his mind filled with shadows. 'Maybe I can use my Whisperer ability to reach him?'

'Try quickly before they jump,' she replied.

The ship began to accelerate into the sky. The volcano belched smoke that clamped in around us, dimming the view and choking the air.

I closed my eyes and the shrieks of the Hive sharpened. I concentrated and began to pick out the slight differences in the voices. The tones seemed to be made up from a dark harmony of many people. In the maelstrom of noise and pain, *Storm Wind*'s crystal felt like a lighthouse, his voice a beacon to stop me being lost in the mind storm. And through that storm I searched for Dad's thoughts, a murmur in a hurricane.

A faint cry snagged my attention. It had a familiar feel to it. I clutched the Psuche gem tighter and focused onto the sound.

Dad, can you hear me? I said in my mind.

The voice faltered among the others.

'*Storm Wind*'s crystal is burning really brightly now,' Angelique said.

Dad?

A sound started to form, a single syllable, a scratch across the noise. I screwed my eyes up. The heat of the eruption disappeared from my skin and the thunder of it became muted in my ears.

The word focused. '*Dom?*'

My throat tightened. *Dad, it's me.*

'*Where…where am I? It's so dark, I can't see anything,*' he replied.

A crackling roar filled the world around us.

'They're beginning their jump,' Angelique said.

Dad, you're on a Hades ship and they're using your mind to help control it.

'*I don't understand.*'

The shriek of a twister howl grew around us.

They're taking you away, but I'll rescue you, I promise.

'*Dom…*' Dad's voice started to fade.

Fight them, Dad.

I opened my eyes to see the tornado had swept the smoke into a spinning column and was clearing the air around us. Above, the palace towers of *Kraken* crackled with Vortex light. With a rush of wind the ship started to disappear.

'*I will…*' Dad's voice said.

With a boom, *Kraken* vanished. The walls of the twister rushed in around us and the world dropped back into a swirl of black shapes.

Angelique shook her head. 'Military textbook strategy – get your leader to safety at all costs. And when this volcano erupts, there's not going to be a lot left of anything else around here.'

'I spoke to my dad.'

'And he heard you?' Angelique asked.

I nodded.

'That means there's hope we can save him.'

Before I could answer, Ambra's disfigured shape loomed from the smoke and he clamped his hand around Angelique's ankle.

'I'd worry about rescuing yourself first,' he said.

She tried to shake him free, but he just laughed.

'Time for you to die, Princess.'

Ambra heaved on her leg and with a cry she dropped a couple of rungs before managing to grab hold again.

I clambered down and locked my hand around hers. 'Hang on, Angelique.'

With a screech, the mast shuddered and started shaking us like leaves on a storm-swept tree.

The Quantum Pacifier tilted. Ambra tumbled off the antenna, but dangled by his one hand still clamped around Angelique's foot.

Her face contorted in pain as she took his weight.

'Just let go, Princess Angelique,' Ambra whispered with a thin-lipped smile.

'You first,' she replied.

I caught a glimpse through a gap in the smoke of lava slurping towards the mast's base. With a screech we began to tilt further. Ambra swung out and Angelique's hands ripped free of the mast.

She started to plummet away with him, but in that split second I reached down and locked my fingers around her outstretched hand. My arm felt like it would explode as I took their combined weight. I hung on with every ounce of strength I had left.

'Okay, now you've got me really angry, Ambra,' Angelique said. She bared her teeth and stamped down on his hand with her free leg. 'That's for Mother.'

Ambra clawed at her, trying to catch her other foot.

She stamped on his fingers again.

'And that's for what you did to Dom's father, and all the other Navigators.'

The Duke's face twisted, eyes burning hatred.

Spittle flew from her mouth as she raised her left leg. 'And this is for what you did to Jules.' She slammed her foot down into his face.

With a crunch of bone Ambra's hands broke free. He screamed and tumbled away, trailing flames like a human meteor, until he plunged into the lava with a splash of fire.

I stared down at the ripples of molten rock closing over his body.

Angelique swung her legs out and rocked her body like a pendulum. My arm felt as though it was going to be torn from its socket. But just when I thought I couldn't take any more, she swung back, let go of my hand and grabbed hold of the mast.

As her weight released, I opened and closed my fist, trying to get some feeling back into it. 'He's really gone?'

She nodded, breathing hard.

'What a way to die.'

'He deserved everything he got.'

The mast started to shriek. I glanced at its base to see the struts growing white-hot. The sense of calmness that was starting to become familiar washed over me. There was no fear, just a deep sense of peace – like I'd seen on the faces of the dying men and women by the pumping station. They'd given their best too. And at the end of the day that's all anyone could be asked to do. We'd fought and almost won. That had to be worth something.

'If we're going to die, we might as well see what the view is like from the top,' Angelique said.

I nodded, my mind clearing of the shadows. 'Why not – let's do this in style.'

We set off towards the tip of the mast just above us.

Despite knowing it'd be the last thing I'd do, and maybe because of it, I was determined to get to the top whatever it took.

A shower of white sparks cascaded from the steel struts below. I could feel the shudder building through my hands. It wouldn't be long now. We both accelerated our ascent.

Angelique reached the top ahead of me and clambered onto a small platform. She leant over and hauled me up to join her.

I stood at the top of the world. We'd nowhere left to go, nowhere left to run. The two *rats* had climbed the mast of the sinking ship. But I didn't care because I'd never felt so alive in my life.

Angelique clutched onto me, eyes shining. I'd never seen her looking so beautiful.

'Dom, thank you. Thank you for everything. We made a difference, didn't we?'

I rubbed her back. 'We really kicked ass together.'

Angelique pulled back to look into my eyes. She nodded and smiled.

The mast rocked and began to drop. We clung tighter to each other. This was it, our ship was sinking.

It looked like I wasn't going to be able to keep my promise after all – I was going to let my dad down…

A whirring noise started to build over the roar of the eruption.

'Do you hear that?' I shouted.

Angelique nodded. 'What is——?'

A drone of propellers drowned out her words.

Cronos's vast flagship emerged from the ash cloud and sped towards us.

'Oh, come on!' I shouted at it. 'How many ways do you want to kill us today?'

The cockpit at the nose of the ship closed fast and I saw figures within it. Someone was waving. *Waving?*

I stared harder and for a moment I thought I was hallucinating. Jules was gesturing at us from the cockpit. She bounced up and down on her feet, grinning like a mad thing. I spotted Stephen by her side, holding the ship's wheel. He snapped Angelique a salute.

'This is really happening, right…this isn't a dream?' I asked.

Angelique laughed. 'Looks like today isn't the day we're going to die, Dom.' She grasped my hand.

A doorway opened in the side of the cockpit. The ship pivoted around its nose until the doorway was square onto us, but still ten feet of empty air away.

Angelique gripped my hand harder. 'We've leapt over worse today.'

I sighed. 'I reckon a stuntman's job is safer than a Cloud Rider's.'

'No doubt, but I'm sure it's only half the fun.'

'We'll argue about that point later.'

With a groan, the tower started to topple.

Not pausing to think, I jumped with Angelique. Legs windmilling through the air, I caught a brief view of the mast sliding into the lava. We landed together in the doorway.

Hands of Cloud Riders I recognised from the pumping station locked on to us and hauled us in.

The floor of the cabin sloped as the ship's engines roared and we began to climb.

Jules rushed over and threw her arms around me. 'You're alive, you're really alive!'

Her whole body shook as she held on to me. Angelique's gaze caught mine. A gentle smile filled her face and she nodded as if to say, *Everything's as it should be again.* She turned away and joined Stephen at the controls.

We broke free of the building ash cloud and soared into the night sky. Over Jules's shoulder I watched Angelique the soldier, Angelique the princess, but, most of all, Angelique my friend.

CHAPTER Twenty-Seven
HOPE

Jules and I sat in an antechamber deep inside Cronos's former flagship. A grey-haired female Cloud Rider had used a Chi healing stone which had worked its magic on my hand's blisters. Already my skin had started to visibly heal, and much to my relief, the stinging pain had disappeared.

So far there'd been too much emotion for any words between Jules and me. We just kept staring at each other and smiling. Even now I couldn't quite believe that she was alive, that this was real.

Through a doorway into a briefing room we could see Angelique. She'd postponed her own treatment to be briefed by a group of Cloud Riders. They kept pointing at charts on the walls of multiple Earths covered with numbers and symbols, as they muttered and shook their heads.

I gazed at Jules and tried to organise everything tumbling around my head. Finally, I spoke to her. 'I thought you'd been burned to death when I set off that eruption with the bomb.'

Her eyes widened. 'You caused that?'

'I didn't have much of a choice.'

'You could've been killed.'

I shrugged. 'It was pretty close, but we obviously made it. But the thing I want to know is, how the hell did you guys escape?'

'We waited for you as long as we could, but when the first quake struck, everything started to collapse around us. Stephen said we had to get out through the underground river before it was too late.'

Thank god for Stephen's common sense. I had a strong suspicion that left to her own devices Jules would have waited until the lava had flooded the pumping station and her.

'But what about those handprint switches that kept the sluice closed?'

A smile filled her face. 'Think you'll be proud of me, Dom. I realised all we had to do was keep the pressure on those switches and came up with a plan. We lashed a few shovels together and wedged the hands of the dead officers against the panels.'

'Okay – simple but genius.'

'That's what Stephen said.'

'Did he now.' I raised my eyebrows.

She gave me a dimpled smile and gently nudged my shoulder with hers. 'You really haven't got anything to worry about there. Just like me with you and Angelique – even if that took me a while to figure out.'

My stomach did a slow flip. 'Exactly.' I decided right there and then that I'd never tell Jules about that kiss with Angelique. It was history, a moment in time that would never be repeated. And what Jules didn't know wouldn't hurt her.

I ran my finger over the blotches on my skin where the burns had been. 'It must have been a close-run thing getting out of there in one piece.'

'It was. All hell was breaking loose as we left the pumping station. Then we saw Ambra running from the tunnel you'd gone through. He was heading back to the lift in a real hurry. Of course I imagined the worst and wanted to go after you, but Stephen said there wasn't time.'

'Seems I owe Stephen and his common sense a lot. You'd have been caught by the lava if you'd tried.'

'I know that now. As it was we only just made it out alive. We had to go through the underground river as the roof caved in. I've never been so scared in my life, Dom. But we ran and ran. Then when we saw the light at the end of that tunnel, it was the biggest relief of my life – at least until I saw you alive just now.'

If we'd been out of sight of the others, I would have leant over and kissed her right there and then. Instead, I made do with cradling her hand in mine. 'So how the heck did you manage to capture this ship?'

'That was all Stephen's doing. The other prisoners were waiting for us when we came out of the tunnel. They didn't know what to do when the eruption kicked off. And of course I was a complete mess about leaving you behind.'

'You weren't the only one. I wasn't sure you'd made it out…kept imagining all sorts.'

'If it hadn't been for Stephen I would still be sitting at the bottom of that volcano sobbing my eyes out. But he made me pull myself together and he rallied everyone else. It was Stephen's idea that we had to capture an airship to escape.'

'You're not telling me you all waltzed onto Cronos's flagship without someone trying to stop you?'

Her expression tensed. 'No, Dom, it was awful – really awful. The soldiers guarding his ship, *Eros*, were the only ones not running for their lives. They put up a fierce fight.' Her nostrils flared. 'Stephen led the attack. There was a lot of killing on both sides.' She hung her head.

For the millionth time I wished she hadn't been exposed to all of this. I wrapped my arm around her shoulder and squeezed. 'Stephen did what he had to. He's a trained soldier just like Angelique.'

'I'll never get used to it though,' Jules replied. 'Some of the things I saw will haunt me forever.'

Images of all the death I'd witnessed flicked through my mind. I knew exactly what she meant. 'The main thing is you're alive. That's what's important to me.'

Jules lifted her head. 'You too – and that's all that matters to me.'

A murmur of voices came from the meeting. The Cloud Riders snapped a salute to Angelique and hurried away.

Angelique beckoned through the doorway for us to join her.

'What's happening?' I asked as we entered the briefing room.

'We've been trying to analyse these maps we found onboard.'

Jules peered at one. 'Why, what are they?'

'They are Hades battle plans, with strategic information about the Earths they plan to attack.' She sighed and tapped her finger on one laid out in the middle of the table. It was filled with a greater number of lines and calculations than the others. 'Dom, Jules, I'm afraid that's your home world, Earth DZL2351. It seems like Ambra was telling the truth and it's their number one target to test their Fury weapon on.'

Jules cupped her hands over her mouth. 'No!'

Coldness rippled down my spine. 'You think Cronos is on his way there now?'

'Fortunately, not yet. Going by the schematics we've been able to decode from the records on this ship, although *Kraken* is flight operational, Fury hasn't been completed yet. They'll rendezvous with one of their military ship-yards and finish that first before they risk launching any attack.'

'What are we waiting for then? We need to get the Cloud Rider fleet together and arrange a reception committee.'

'Exactly. I've told the others about Tesla. They're radio-ing him now. Hopefully, by now the Quantum Pacifier is offline and he's been able to make contact with the King and the rest of the fleet.'

I saw the flash of excitement in her eyes and thought of Dad. The familiar ache filled my gut.

'What's wrong?' Jules asked, reading my expression.

'Just before *Kraken* jumped, I spoke to Dad.'

She grabbed my arm. 'He's okay?'

'I managed to reach him in the Hive mind, but he didn't know where he was.'

Angelique frowned. 'But it has to be a positive sign that part of him hasn't been affected by the conversion pro-cess.' Her expression brightened. 'And if part of his mind is still aware, there may be a way to reverse the process – and if anyone can think of a way to do that, it's Tesla.'

Both my friends beamed at me. I started to soak in their enthusiasm, their hope. Maybe we really could save Dad. 'But how do we even begin to get him off *Kraken*?'

'We'll work that part out together,' Jules replied.

Angelique nodded. 'All I know is, if we can destroy their main citadel, Hells Cauldron, we can do anything.'

I smiled. 'There you may have a point.'

A man with wiry hair rushed into the briefing room. 'Princess Angelique, you are going to want to see what's happening outside.' He looked round at Jules and me. 'You all are.'

'What is it?' Angelique asked.

The man spread his hands. 'I honestly haven't got the words to describe it, Princess. You just need to witness this for yourself on the bridge.'

Angelique exchanged a puzzled look with me. We followed her out and into the decorated corridors of Cronos's flagship.

The interior had been kitted out like a millionaire's luxury yacht. The walls had been draped with ornate, red velvet hangings. Reflected in the highly polished marble floors, large crystal candelabras lit the corridors. I lost count of the number of portraits and statues we passed on our way to the bridge. Seemed like Cronos had a very high opinion of himself.

Angelique froze as she finally reached the flight cockpit ahead of us. 'By the gods, what's happening out there?'

We entered the room behind her. Through the windshield I saw an aurora flowing down from the sky into the mouth of the volcano in a vast funnel of green light. A sense of awe filled me up.

'It's like the sky's kissing the land,' Jules whispered.

'But what's causing this?' Angelique asked.

'Maybe it's something to do with what Tesla told us – the magnetic pole being funnelled through Hells Cauldron?' I replied.

Angelique pointed towards the volcano. 'Oh my goodness, look!'

The scene below us was like something straight out of a disaster movie. The landscape glowed like a ruby. Ribbons of lava ran down the sides of the volcano and boiled out across the landscape and a single hangar floated away on a stream of molten rock. The ordered lines of tents had already been burned away. I found myself wondering how many had already died in this eruption.

A flash drew my gaze back to the volcano.

Streamers of red and aqua light curled up from the volcano. They flowed into the aurora funnel, dissolving as they merged with it.

'What are those lights?' Jules asked.

A chorus of song flooded my mind, filled with joy so strong that I wanted to laugh out loud.

Angelique gave me a wide-eyed look and beamed. 'Oh my gods, that's so wonderful.'

Jules looked between us. 'What?'

A lump filled my throat. 'I'm pretty sure those lights are the Angelus and Hades ship souls that were trapped in the Psuche gems being freed.'

Angelique gave a sharp nod. 'And it looks like they are being absorbed back into the planet's magnetic field.'

Jules pressed her fingertips to her lips. 'Whatever it is, I don't think I've seen anything so beautiful in all my life.'

Instinctively, I put my hand into my pocket and took out *Storm Wind*'s Psuche gem. Angelique had already done the same with the one she picked up at the mine. Both stones glowed fiercely, echoing the song of happiness radiating from the aurora.

I closed my eyes to concentrate. *Storm Wind*'s words formed in my mind. *'Thank you, Whisperer. You have set my brothers and sisters free.'*

My eyes stung. *But what about you? What about the souls in the other ships? Don't you all want to be set free like the others?*

'One day we may return to the World Soul, but not yet.'

And what about the ones still trapped on the Hades ships?

'In the final battle the moment will come when you can set them all free.'

A final battle? You mean with Cronos?

'Indeed, Whisperer. The future of the Cloud Riders, Hades and ourselves are entwined. And you are the one who can unravel the plans of the shadows.'

What plan? Who do you mean?

'You will discover that when your moment of destiny arrives.'

Not again. I'd already had more than enough of these cryptic clues to last me a lifetime.

'However, there is one of our brothers who you can set free right now.'

Brother...a Hades AI? I opened my eyes and gazed at the closed, jewel-encrusted, gold Eye in the cockpit. I realised I wasn't picking up any howling pain from inside the dome. But how come?

'Stephen, why can't I hear *Eros*'s AI?'

'The first thing we did was shut it down. I've been flying this ship manually.'

Angelique scowled. 'That could be a serious problem. We won't be able to jump with this ship without an AI running.'

'It's certainly too dangerous to turn back on,' Stephen said. 'I'm sure if we did, it would probably try to crash us straight into the ground.'

I held out the glowing blue Psuche gem flat in my palm. '*Storm Wind* said I need to release the AI on this ship.'

Stephen's eyes widened. 'You've been talking to that Psuche gem?'

I nodded.

'But how?'

Jules patted his arm. 'It's a long story. For now let's just say Dom is the *chosen one*.' She grinned at me.

'Thanks for the vote of confidence, but how are we going to free the Hades AI?' I gazed out at the volcano spewing molten rock. If the lava had destroyed the crystals holding the Angelus, maybe… 'How close can you get us over the spout, Stephen?'

He narrowed his eyes. 'It was pretty risky going in for you last time. If the ash cloud blocks the engine ports…' With his hand he mimicked the airship diving into the ground.

Angelique raised her eyebrows. 'I'm sure your piloting skills are up to it.'

Stephen grimaced. 'Of course, Princess.' He spun the ship's wheel until *Eros* sped towards the volcano and the plume of green light.

'What are you planning, Dom?' Jules asked.

'To set another soul free.' I placed my hands on the lids of the Eye. I tried to pull them apart, but the mechanism was locked up tight. Within a moment, Jules, Angelique and all the other Cloud Riders on the bridge had their hands on the Eye and heaved with me. With a grinding of gears the dome flew open.

A single jewel, gripped in a claw mount, glowed a dull red. I pocketed *Storm Wind*'s Psuche gem and reached out towards the Hades crystal. The air tingled on my fingertips. Even though it had been shut down, a faint sense of pain still radiated from it and coiled through my mind. I clutched the Hades crystal and pulled it from its mount. An audible sigh whispered through the cockpit. Everyone looked at me. In my hand I held the heart of the ship – a person's tortured soul.

'Not long now,' I whispered to the Psuche gem.

The feeling of pain started to ebb from the crystal and a note of hope crept into the ship's song.

Angelique crossed to the door and swung it open. The hot air of the volcano swept into the bridge and the taste of cinders filled my mouth. The ship swept into the aurora and, with a hum, every surface in the cockpit started to shine with phosphorescent light. We watched as little knots of energy formed into spheres and swarmed around the red crystal in my hands like fireflies.

'Are those…souls?' Jules whispered.

'Seems as good a word as any to describe them,' I replied.

'Just don't let Tesla hear you call them that,' Angelique said. 'Far too unscientific.'

'But "soul" is less of a mouthful than "memory imprint",' I said.

She let out a gentle laugh. 'You may have a point there.'

I held the *Eros* gem out through the open door. The globes of lights clustered around it like moths around a candle. I released the crystal and it tumbled away.

'*Freedom,*' *Eros* whispered in my mind.

The light globes tracked the gem down until I lost sight of them. With a thunderclap, a ribbon of red light burst from the volcano and sped upwards, the orbs tracking it back into the sky.

I watched with a lump in my throat as the red light raced past the ship and turned blue. Just for a moment I swore I could hear laughter on the wind. At that moment, the funnel of green light broke away from the land and spiralled back up into the Northern Lights. The sky's kiss had withdrawn from the land.

The souls' songs faded from my mind. I imagined their patterns of energy streaming out around the Earth's magnetic field. My eyes filled with tears.

Angelique swung the door closed. Not a person spoke. Many were crying. Seemed we'd all been caught by the spell of what we'd just witnessed.

Jules rested her head on my shoulder, her arm around me. In silence, together we watched the curtains of light slowly shimmering against a backdrop of burning stars.

...

The airship climbed into the sky, the vibrations of a hundred engines little more than a muted whisper through the heavily armoured shell of the former flagship.

Stephen patted the wheel. 'I just wish we could take this vessel with us. There would be a certain poetic justice in using it against Cronos.'

I gazed across at the Psuche gem glowing between Angelique's fingers. 'Couldn't we use one of our Psuche gems and install it on this ship?'

'It's not quite as easy as that,' she replied. 'To start with, it would need a Navigator to be twinned with the ship, like I am with *Athena*.'

'I guess I could volunteer to do that,' I said. 'After all, I have got the gene.'

'I wouldn't be so quick to offer your services,' Angelique said. 'It's a lifetime bond. Think of it as a sort of marriage.'

A ship of my own, this ship? But *Eros* was huge and built more like an ocean liner. When I'd imagined myself flying an airship I'd always pictured something more along the lines of *Athena*.

Jules peered at me. 'Sounds like a decision not to rush into.'

If I didn't know better I could have sworn there was a jealous edge to her tone. Not this again. And of a ship?

Stephen crossed his arms. 'But imagine what we could do if this ship was fully operational. We're going to need as much firepower as possible against *Kraken*.'

'I can't make this decision for you, Dom,' Angelique said. 'It has to be your choice.'

'Actually, there is another Navigator on-board,' Stephen replied.

Angelique gave him a horrified look. 'But I can't do it. I'm linked to *Athena*.'

'I wasn't talking about you.' He raised his sleeve to show his Hades demon symbol stamped there.

'Why are you showing me your Hades tattoo?' Angelique said. 'All the prisoners have those.'

'Only the *normal* ones,' Stephen replied. 'I did this one myself with a sharpened stone and some ink from a stolen pen.'

Jules stared at him. 'But why?'

'I was one of the last prisoners to be processed. When we realised what was happening to the others, Zack insisted I did this to protect myself. When we arrived in the mine the guards were lazy enough not to double-check my serial number and never bothered to have me tested.'

'Tested?' I said. 'You mean tested to see if you were a Navigator?'

'Exactly,' Stephen replied. 'And luckily for me, my gift was never found out.'

Lines spidered from Angelique's eyes. 'And would you be prepared to be bonded to this ship, Stephen?'

'You mean be the one responsible for converting Cronos's personal flagship into a Cloud Rider vessel?' He dragged his hand through his dreadlocks. 'Now how could I resist an offer like that?' A huge smile filled his face.

'That's settled then,' Angelique replied. 'And I think this calls for a battlefield commission.'

Stephen's smile threatened to reach his ears. 'That would be the greatest honour for me, Princess.'

She smiled and flicked a button on a control panel. A speaker crackled above us. 'Then kneel, Private Stephen Telphid.'

I heard her words echoing along the corridors. Seemed she intended the whole ship to listen into this moment.

The other Cloud Riders stopped what they were doing in the cockpit. They gathered around us in a circle, nodding and smiling to each other, like this was a marriage ceremony. Which in a sense I guessed it was – with us, the witnesses.

Stephen locked the ship's wheel into position and dropped to one knee before Angelique.

She placed her hand on his forehead. 'By the power of the royal household vested in me, I promote you, Stephen Telphid, to the rank of captain. From this moment you will be the symbiotic Navigator for this ship...' She paused and looked around at us. 'We need a new name for *Eros*.'

'What about *Hope*?' Jules said.

'Sounds good to me,' I replied.

Angelique nodded. 'Very fitting – *Hope* for a new beginning, *Hope* for a new destiny.' She smiled at Stephen. 'I hereby bond you to this ship, *Hope*. May your skies always be clear, may your battles be short and victorious.' She placed the glowing Psuche gem into Stephen's outstretched hand.

He rose and crossed to the ship's Eye. The Cloud Riders exchanged glances as he leant down and placed the gem into the claw mount. The crystal glowed like a sapphire sun and cast blue light throughout the cabin.

My mind flooded with soaring ship-song.

Angelique beamed at me. '*Hope* is reborn.'

The Cloud Riders clapped and cheers echoed along the corridors. People stepped forward to congratulate Stephen, all smiles and shrugs.

I felt a surge of envy. That could've been me. I pushed the thought away and held out my hand to Stephen. 'Well done, Captain.'

He grinned at me. 'Thanks, Dom.' His gaze tightened on my eyes. 'One day it will be your turn.'

'I hope so.' And I did, more than almost anything.

Jules walked up to Stephen and wrapped him in a tight hug.

I found myself drifting away from the knot of people to join Angelique gazing out through the cockpit window.

'Where's Tesla got to?' she said to me.

'I'd forgotten he was even up there.'

'I haven't. I've just prayed that he managed to fix *Athena*.'

How could I have forgotten that? Throughout the celebration she'd been putting on a brave face, even though she must've been worried sick about her ship. I started to reach out to pat her arm, but stopped myself. I wasn't sure where the boundaries for our friendship were any more. And maybe she wasn't either.

'I'm sure she's fine,' I said.

Angelique wrapped her arms around herself.

I'd found Jules. Stephen had his own ship. But I didn't need to be a mind reader to know that in this precise moment, without *Athena* to sing to her, Angelique felt completely alone.

The spectral Northern Lights started to fade as dawn's golds washed through the sky.

'The beginning of spring is here,' Angelique said. 'This will be the first dawn in several months after the winter darkness.'

'A new day and, like you said, a new beginning,' I replied.

'I pray so. I pray that soon I'll hear my beloved *Athena*'s song again. And even more than that, I hope that I will be able to talk to my father again if Tesla's been successful.'

'How long has it been since you last saw the King?'

Angelique sighed. 'Two years – two long years.'

People gasped behind us. We turned as red light blazed from multiple glass orbs in the Eye.

An attack? A weight filled my gut. Not now after everything we'd been through.

'What's happening?' I asked.

Stephen looked up from the Eye and beamed at us. 'Oh, now that's just perfect.'

'What is?'

'As this *was* a Hades ship, she still has their cyphers installed. By rebooting the AI we now have access to all of their communication codes.'

I thought of the way the captured *Apollo* had been able to fool us when it had used the Cloud Riders' cyphers. And if they could do it, so could we. 'You mean we can see exactly where Cronos's fleet is the whole time?'

'Precisely,' Angelique replied.

Stephen rubbed his hands together. 'This will make a huge difference in any battle against Hades.'

His excitement was contagious. This was good news. No…it was fantastic news. The room erupted with excited chatter. Cloud Riders who'd been exhausted suddenly looked fresh and alert, fatigue forgotten for a moment.

Jules pointed out of the window, eyes wide. 'Something's out there.'

The air rippled in front of *Hope* like a heat haze and two ships started to appear. My heart leapt as *Athena* and *Muse* materialised in front of us.

Hope welcomed them both with song. Joy filled me as *Athena*'s song soared to answer her.

Angelique clasped her hands over her mouth and tears splashed down her face. 'Tesla has healed her!'

Through the cockpit window of the saucer gondola, Tesla waved at us.

Jules turned to stare at me. 'How did he just do that?'

'Oh, that's another thing I need to tell you about. He's quite a guy, this Tesla.'

'Obviously.' She shook her head. 'We've got a lot to catch up on, you and me.' She smiled and hooked her arm around mine.

In that moment everything seemed possible. We might not yet have won the war with Hades, but today we'd made a real difference. And somehow, whatever it took, we'd save my dad.

Angelique joined us and took my other arm. She smiled at me through her tears. The two ships drew up alongside and *Muse*'s umbilical dock began to extend towards our cockpit.

CHAPTER Twenty-Eight
SHIP-SONG

We stood around *Hope*'s Eye. The initial pulse of excitement that had sped through the cockpit died away as the Cloud Rider fleet globes remained unlit.

Angelique stared at Tesla. 'What do you mean you haven't been able to make contact with any of our ships?'

Tesla wrung his hands together. 'I don't understand, Princess. The moment the mast toppled, the jamming signal of the Quantum Pacifier should have stopped broadcasting.'

I clasped *Storm Wind*'s Psuche gem in my pocket and felt the cool tickle of the energy within it. Why hadn't the Pacifier gone offline like planned?

Angelique sunk into a seat. 'But without the rest of the fleet we won't stand a chance if we're going to stop Cronos destroying...' She gazed at Jules and me.

Jules wrapped her arms around herself. 'Our Earth won't stand a chance against *Kraken*, will it?'

Angelique gave a brief shake of her head.

'But nothing could have survived in Hells Cauldron when that eruption went off,' I said. 'Any equipment must be molten slag by now.'

'Exactly,' Tesla replied. 'None of this makes any sense.'

'But we have *Hope* on our side now,' Stephen said. 'Surely she can make a difference?'

'You saw the size of *Kraken*,' Angelique replied. 'I'm certain we could bloody Cronos's nose, but without the backup of our fleet, we wouldn't last long in a one-to-one fight with a capital ship.'

I turned the gem over between my fingers. What were we missing? I could feel something staring me in the face but I couldn't quite see it.

'I've studied their jamming broadcast and the way it shifts frequency,' Tesla said. 'The complexity of the algorithms they are using is astonishing. I certainly thought they were far beyond the capacity of any AI to process.'

Any AI to process... The crystal tingled in my hand. My thoughts rushed together. That had to be it. 'Of course, you don't know about the Hive, Tesla. That's what's creating the jamming signal.'

Tesla peered over the top of his glasses at me. 'The what?'

Angelique slowly nodded. 'You're right, Dom. And that's why the jamming hasn't stopped, because the Hive is onboard *Kraken*.'

'Can someone please explain to me what you are talking about?' Tesla said.

'It's what they've been doing in the lab – carrying out sick experiments to combine Navigators with AIs,' I replied.

He stared at me. 'How on Earths have they managed that?'

'Something to do with filling a Navigator's body with carbon. It's what they did to Dad—' My voice caught.

Jules wrapped her hand around mine. But nothing could ever take away the sting of what had happened.

'Dom's father is onboard *Kraken* now,' Angelique said. 'He's one of a hundred processed Navigators, each one fused with a Hades-adapted AI crystal. Apparently Cronos had the Hive developed to control a capital ship.'

Tesla wrung his fingers together. 'Oh my, oh my. A collective consciousness, you say?'

I nodded. 'So what you've been calling the Quantum Pacifier is actually powered by a group of people, including my dad now.'

'But that means we have no way of stopping it, no way of contacting the other ships while *Kraken* still flies,' Tesla replied.

'There's got to be a way,' Jules said. 'We can't just let Cronos invade our world.'

I realised *Storm Wind*'s gem had started to cool in my pocket. I withdrew the crystal as it numbed my fingers and started to pulse. A tingle spread up my arm and into my head.

'*Whisperer, you must reach out with your mind,*' *Storm Wind* said.

I stared at the crystal. 'What?'

The gem's light brightened. '*Weave your song with mine and with the ships around you. Together we can break through the roar filling the heavens.*'

His song, soft and gentle, began. It was a choral song without words, but full of hope, full of longing. At once I recognised another ship's human voice joining in, her song soaring with *Storm Wind*'s.

'I can hear...' Angelique stared at me. 'Is that *Athena*'s real voice?'

I nodded, smiling at her.

'All these years and I never knew it, never knew who she really was.' She blinked.

Another female voice joined the growing song.

Tesla stared out at his ship. '*Muse?*'

'Yes...' I replied.

A final female ship voice chimed in with the others.

'And that's *Hope?*' Stephen asked.

'It has to be,' I said.

'*Sing with us, Whisperer, and reach out across the dimensions,*' *Storm Wind* said.

I looked at the others. I could feel my face flame as I began to sing along with the tune. But at once the ships' songs echoed mine and I raised my own voice in response. *Storm Wind*'s Psuche gem blazed with the brilliance of a small sun. The combined emotions of their joy became overwhelming.

With a wide smile, Angelique began to sing too.

Tesla looked between us and slowly nodded. 'This is what *Titan* meant about your ability, Dom. Your mind acts like a filter, allowing you to hear their true voices.' His gaze brightened. 'And by doing that...' He clapped his hands together. 'You can strengthen ship-song to the point where we can break through the jamming effects of the Hive mind.'

I stared at the Eye and all the unlit globes within it. Could this really work?

'I may not be able to hear what you guys can, but I make a great backing singer,' Jules said. She started humming along with us. And she was good too, her voice pure and strong, helping to blow my self-consciousness away.

'Excellent,' Tesla said, and he began to sing with a deep baritone voice.

I caught Jules biting back a grin.

Our voices climbed together, Stephen's too. I shut my eyes and felt the collective harmony grow in power and strength. The faintest echoes of individual voices started to appear in my mind, as though they were singing to us from a great distance.

'Oh my god, look,' Jules said.

I opened my eyes. Each and every one of the glass globes, which a moment before had been unlit, now blazed with green light.

Tesla slapped me on the back. 'You've done it, lad. You've broken through the interference.'

I nodded, but kept singing as the chorus of ships' voices, near and far, grew louder in my mind.

Angelique chewed her lip. 'Is the King's ship there?'

Tesla headed over to a control panel and rotated a few knobs. The glass planets began to spin until one larger than the rest sat in the middle, shining with green light. He beamed at her. 'We have a confirmed lock on *Olympus*.'

Angelique pressed her fingers to her mouth, breathing fast.

Tesla pressed a button and something whirred. A note-card dropped into a slot.

Stephen walked over and examined it. '*Apollo* is on Earth XAD1021. He's on the ground hiding beneath a sandstorm.'

'XAD1021?' Angelique stared at him. 'Oh by the gods.' She turned and stared at me.

A world of sandstorms? It couldn't be a coincidence. 'You don't mean the planet we travelled through?'

Angelique nodded. 'That close to Papa and I never knew.'

A memory tumbled from my mind. 'Hang on. Remember I said I thought I heard something?'

'A voice on the wind... Oh my gods, you must have heard *Olympus* just for a moment!'

I slowly nodded. 'It was just a murmur and I thought I was hearing things.'

Angelique rushed towards me.

I grabbed her and spun her round. I caught the question mark in Jules's eyes and quickly put Angelique down again. Although it had been entirely innocent, what else had Jules seen? The last thing I wanted to do was hurt her.

I gave her my best smile and her expression relaxed. I felt a twist of guilt deep inside.

'We need to make contact with the King,' Tesla said.

'I have the royal cypher codes back on *Athena*,' Angelique said.

'What are we waiting for?' Stephen replied.

I gazed at Jules. I knew she was my future. But everything felt on the line and with one wrong step I'd lose her.

. . .

We clustered around the radio onboard *Muse*. Tesla handed the brass microphone over to Angelique. 'I've calibrated the Valve Voice using the coordinates we have for *Apollo*.

Angelique gave me a brief, nervous smile. She took a deep breath and pressed a button on the side of the mic. 'This is *Muse* calling, *Apollo*, do you hear me? Over.'

A swirl of crackle came through a speaker in the cabin ceiling.

'*Apollo*, are you receiving? Over.'

More static.

'This radio is transmitting, isn't it?' I asked Tesla.

He gazed at a small display on the console and nodded. 'The quantum entanglement cyphers are locked in.'

Jules rolled her eyes. 'Oh, here we go again. What does that mean in English?'

'They are receiving us.'

She sighed. 'You could have just said that in the first place.'

Angelique pressed the button again and chewed her lip. 'Papa, are you there? Over.'

The static popped and hissed. 'Angelique...' a man's voice said, a roar of static filled the speaker again.

Angelique choked back a sob. 'It's him!'

Jules wrapped her arm around her.

'Just give me a moment to allow for dimensional distortion.' Tesla spun a dial and the static hissed to silence. 'Try it now.'

'Papa, is that really you? Over.'

'Yes,' the voice said, now clear and free of distortion.

She clenched the mic. 'Oh, Papa...' Tears began tumbling down Angelique's cheeks.

Jules rubbed Angelique's back. 'Hey, smiles, not tears.'

Angelique nodded and dabbed at her eyes.

NICK COOK

'Come on,' I said to the others. 'Let's give her a moment alone.'

Tesla nodded and headed for the door. Jules squeezed Angelique's shoulder and followed him out.

I hung back for a moment as *Athena*'s song swelled through my mind. Angelique gave me a smile so full of happiness and sadness at the same time that I just wanted to go over and hold her.

'Angelique?' her dad's voice said again.

Through her tears, she gave me a smile that pierced me right to the heart – the look of someone about to be reunited with their dad.

'Where do I even begin?' she asked me.

'Just tell him everything and don't stop,' I said.

She nodded and took a shuddering breath. 'Papa, so much has happened...'

I turned away before Angelique spotted the tears threatening my own eyes and headed out of the door.

...

The three ships flew together in close formation down the Vortex wormhole. From *Athena*'s cockpit I looked out at the two other crafts' cabin windows, golden points of light in the darkness.

The coordinates for *Apollo* had been safely punched into the Eye. On my insistence, I'd gotten Angelique to navigate the jump. Seemed only right as we were on our way to rendezvous with her dad.

Since breaking through the jamming, I'd been able to keep a link open by making sure I carried *Storm Wind*'s

322

Psuche gem in the lightning pendant around my neck. Whenever I tuned in, I heard the words of all the ship-song around us, a human choir that sent constant shivers down my spine. Most of the time they seemed to lapse into long, rambling poems, which didn't make much sense to me.

Steam drifted up from the kettle on the galley stove. Jules was using it to make coffee for Angelique and me. I needed to keep sharp a while longer. But when we'd found *Apollo*, the first thing I intended to do was some serious catching up on my sleep.

A chime came from the cockpit. Beneath us, the bottom of the Vortex started to fill with an orange glow, the light of a world where Angelique would finally be reunited with her dad.

She looked across at me and I saw the joy burning in her eyes.

'I'm really happy for you, Angelique,' I said. And I meant it. One day I just prayed it would be my turn.

She nodded with a deep smile. 'I know you are, and this day wouldn't be happening if it wasn't for you.'

Jules glanced between us. 'Look, will you two just hug already.'

So Jules didn't suspect anything. And maybe that was fine, because there really wasn't anything to suspect.

Angelique held out her arms to me with a radiant smile. She walked over and pulled me close. I felt the stiffness let go across my shoulders and relaxed into her arms. What Jules didn't know couldn't hurt her.

Angelique beckoned to Jules and she joined us for a group hug. I held the two people who meant everything to me. Over their shoulders I noticed the Void beyond the cloud walls was beginning to be replaced by an orange sky.

'I think we're nearly there,' I said.

Angelique broke away from us and took hold of *Athena*'s wheel.

I couldn't help notice that as she stood framed against the windshield the growing light made her hair glow like a halo. Angelique, named after the Angelus. Angelique the warrior princess. Angelique the angel.

Jules wrapped her arms around me and rested her head on my shoulder.

My fingers travelled to my lightning pendant where Dad's Saint Christopher medal nestled. One day, if it was the last thing I ever did, I'd give the medal back to him in person.

Warm light flooded the cabin as the twister evaporated. The songs of *Muse*, *Hope* and *Athena* strengthened around us.

Angelique pushed the wheel forward and we began to descend towards a billowing sandstorm.

In the distance I heard another ship singing out to us. *Olympus* welcomed us to a world where a king waited to be reunited with his daughter.

— To be continued in *Eye of the Storm* —

ACKNOWLEDGEMENTS

Of all my books, *Breaking Storm* is the one that arrived most fully formed in my imagination and begged me to be written. It was one of those lucky alignments of the creative planets where everything falls into place.

However, even when inspiration lightning has struck, an author has to nurture that flickering flame like a candle in a hurricane. Luckily I wasn't alone in this and many people helped me grow that original idea into the book that you hold in your hand today.

First and foremost I have to single out Yasmin Standen, my publisher at Three Hares, for her unwavering vision, her passion, her drive, her zeal, and above all for fighting the good fight in the publishing industry. I thank the day that you came into my life, Yasmin.

A special mention for my editor, Catherine Coe. Yours is the calm hand on the wheel of the Cloud Riders airship, your experience shining through with every edit you made. It has been a real pleasure working with you and I hope we do so again in the future.

If you look at the front of *Breaking Storm*, you will see the wonderful cover art created by the wonderful Jennie Rawlings. You have an inspiring approach to design,

Jennie. You have come up with yet another fantastic piece of work that catches the eye and draws a reader in. You are a star.

Once again I must mention my partner, Karen Errington. She is the person who has tirelessly ploughed through draft after draft with me, spotting those mistakes that I became blind to. But more importantly she is the one that has supported me on every step of my journey as an author. Karen, thank you for everything, I really don't have sufficient words for how grateful I am that you are part of my life and bring such joy to me every single day.

On a similar note I must thank my son, Josh. His belief in me has been constant, as has mine in him. To be inspired by one's son is a most wonderful gift, and I hope, Josh, that I continued to make you proud too.

To everyone else that I haven't mentioned by name, I hope you know that you're in my heart too.

And a final special thanks to you, dear reader. Without you my stories wouldn't have a life of their own. I will always be indebted for your support and allowing my words into your life to create worlds in your imagination. That is the most special gift that anyone could give me.

www.therealnickcook.blogspot.co.uk

www.threeharespublishing.com

www.threeharespublishing/bookclub.com